Praise for Anthony J Quinn

'Quinn's is a highly original take on a much-traversed topic. He writes with melancholic elegance'
– *Times* **Books of the Year**

'Atmospheric, elegant…It is a police procedural of the highest quality and has remained in my mind since I encountered it five months ago… a crime novel to be savoured'
– *Daily Mail* **Books of the Year**

'Quinn's pacy prose walks a fine line between a James Lee Burke-like melancholy and the sort of muscularity found in Michael Connelly's works… a tense and unpredictable ride'
– *Sunday Herald*

'Finely honed plotting… Quinn's greatest skill is the evocation of the landscape' – *Financial Times*

'Beautifully written… the experience of reading the book is irresistible' –*Independent*

'A powerful tale stained with the darkest of noir'
– *Irish Times*

'The truth gradually becomes clear in this beautifully written novel' – *Literary Review*

'An absolute winner – a crime novel that doesn't waste a single word in delivering its lean and muscular narrative'
– *Good Book Guide*

Also by Anthony J Quinn

The Blood-Dimmed Tide
Blind Arrows

The Inspector Celcius Daly Series

Disappeared
Border Angels
Silence
Trespass
Undertow

The Listeners

TURNCOAT

ANTHONY J QUINN

NO EXIT PRESS

First published in 2020 by No Exit Press,
an imprint of Oldcastle Books Ltd,
Harpenden,
Herts, UK

noexit.co.uk
@noexitpress

ISBN
978-1-84344-721-4 (Print)
978-1-84344-722-1 (Epub)

2 4 6 8 10 9 7 5 3 1

Typeset in 12 on 14pt Ehrhardt MT Std
by Avocet Typeset, Bideford, Devon, EX39 2BP
Printed and bound in Great Britain by Clays Ltd, Elcograf S.p.A.

For my fellow Belfast pilgrims,
Phelim Cavlan, Manuel Haas,
Timothy Lawlor, Colmog McCluskey
and Maura Toomey.

TURNCOAT

TURNCOAT

Irish Border, 1994

When the car carrying him and his police colleagues turned into the lane shortly after ten o'clock, the driver killed the headlights and let the vehicle roll along the track. Moments later, the bulk of the derelict farmhouse and its outbuildings swung into view, a collection of grey fragments tucked away amid the gloom of blackthorn and elder thickets. There was just enough moonlight for him to make out the smooth shapes of two white horses, their heads bowed together, standing eerily calm amid the thorns, as though they belonged to a dream or a different dimension.

He told the other detectives to remain in the car and stepped outside. He stared at the horses, which were hardly trembling at all in his presence, and then at the windows of the house, the broken panes covering sheets of blackness, the front door hanging slightly ajar, everything about the place receding into shadow or floating against the dishevelled pattern of silhouettes. He felt a flicker of fear in his stomach. He glanced back at the car and saw the face of Special Branch Detective Ian Robinson watching him closely, his eyes gleaming with anticipation. The insolent pleasure in the detective's gaze made his skin prickle, but it also had the effect of galvanising him.

For the past month, he had grown used to Robinson being his tail, asking probing questions about his investigations, following him wherever he went with his set stare, lingering where he stayed. He dreaded to think what his mistakes and failures might look like through the eyes of this cold and attentive shadow, a detective who had advanced his career by patiently watching and waiting for Catholic officers like him to step over invisible lines of loyalty and political allegiance.

He shifted his weight from the gravel-strewn yard and stepped on to a patch of grass. He moved as quietly as he could, but his sneaking advance disturbed the two horses, which, in the low light, were the double of each other. They bolted with a minimum of effort, leaping a broken-down fence and galloping away in a long flowing movement. His chest tightened, and, for a moment, like a coward, he wanted to abandon his duties and flee the farmhouse. His eyes followed the pale shadows of the horses dipping and rising across the moonlit fields. Their synchronised flight and the way they hurried soundlessly into the night added to the air of unreality around the farm.

He surveyed the scene and his chest tightened again. It was the lack of human life, the broken silhouettes, the complicating shadows confronting him, which belonged more to the world of informers and betrayal than that of justice and order, and the sense of guilt he felt lurking in his heart, this strange feeling that he was slinking behind his own back, a sure sign that bad things were at hand. Was avoiding this feeling not a form of cowardice in itself?

He still had time to call off the operation. All he had to do was walk back to the car, order the driver to return to the city, and then, later, tidy up and file away the details of tonight's journey as a wild goose chase into border country. It would be fitting if his career, which had been a sad trajectory through the purgatories of his accursed country, ended at this farmhouse hunched amid thorn trees. Tomorrow he would speak to his commanders, tell them he wished to give up the game of hide-and-seek with spies and suspects, the endless hours chasing down leads and examining bodies in derelict farms and border ditches. One corpse was like another, the much too long investigations blurring into each other, along with the dreamless nights and the mornings spent shakily riding the latest hangover.

However, he was almost upon the farmhouse. It would only take a few more moments to scoot around the rear and check that the place was clear. Everything was quiet apart from the whispering of the wind in the nearby trees, but somehow the air felt charged with the static of danger. The wind picked up, agitating the branches, multiplying the patterns that fell across the cracked walls of the farmhouse. He peered into the canopy of shadows trying to see what was being concealed amid the fan-like movements. He crept forwards, and then a movement made him look across.

Huddled behind a derelict tractor were three men in balaclavas with sub-machine guns. Before he could raise the alarm, they stood up, turning their weapons on him and the police car, and then they opened fire. The yard filled with the flaring of bullets and the sounds of metal rending. He felt the bullets whiz past him and bite the ground, stinging his face with bits of gravel. It was no longer a bad dream but a nightmare, moving too quickly for him to comprehend, the bullets flying everywhere, darting and unstoppable. The yard stretched interminably ahead, making it impossible for him to find cover. He knelt down and waited for the impact of the bullets, but felt nothing, a silence enveloping his body like a shield. At that instant, everything slowed down with the clarity of approaching death. He watched the shells of the bullets erupt from the jolting mouths of the guns and travel through the air in long trails and clusters, the eyes of the gunmen bulging as their bodies buckled against the recoil of their weapons.

Behind him, the police driver panicked, the gears of the car grinding horribly as he tried to reverse, and then the vehicle lurched to a stop. He looked back and saw the bewildered shapes of Robinson and his colleagues lunge for escape and then shudder under the hail of fire. Was it the whine of the bullets or their pitiful cries that he could hear, garbled and broken with echoes from the empty outbuildings?

Someone called his name. Looking up, he saw one of the gunmen take out a revolver and stand over him. The gunman raised his balaclava with one thumb to reveal a grinning face and a thick moustache that he vaguely recognised, before taking aim at close range and firing. First, he was blinded, and then he felt bathed in a searing light. He slipped forward, his mind leaving behind the dark pit of the farmyard, and the shadows of his past, all the piled-up murders of the Troubles and his entire secret history. He rose upwards, feeling so pure and free that he smiled with relief, willing himself higher towards the tranquillity of the floating stars, but then the feeling faded, and the light leaked back into darkness and the murk of the farmyard. He felt himself dragged down into the gunfire by the stubborn beating of his heart and its lonely black mass of guilt. He lay for several long moments staring at the unfathomable night sky, hearing further gun blasts and the sounds of running feet.

He raised himself to a sitting position and realised that he was uninjured and the gunmen gone. Mesmerised by his survival, he sank back to the ground, panting heavily. A while later, he hauled himself to his feet and stumbled over to the bullet-ridden car.

The interior of the vehicle was torn to pieces. Blood seeped from the opened doors, forming thick pools on the yard. The three men inside were not moving. He stared at their dying bodies with his estranged detective's eye. They were fresh-faced, but already grey lines were deepening around their features. Should he attempt resuscitation, pump their ribcages, try to breathe life back into their mouths and lungs? He could tell it was too late. Robinson's eyes gazed at him, impudent and full of suspicion, but they were open only to death now, turning glassy and cold. No longer would the Special Branch officer prowl around the edges of his investigations, or hover at his door like a gleeful messenger about to break bad news.

He was used to cold-blooded murder, and attacks like these were part of his weekly routine. However, some meaning in the crime scene eluded him. He was the lead detective, the one who had organised the operation. He should have died here, the way police heroes were supposed to die, but somehow he was still alive. What did it all mean? He had done nothing wrong. It was not his fault that the gunmen had mounted an ambush and killed his colleagues. Then why this feeling of fear and guilt? He felt the menace in Robinson's dead eyes, the suspicions that would gather at the implausibility of his survival. These officers had come to the farmhouse because of him and now they were dead. No amount of protestations would change that fact. His career as a detective would never be the same again. He did a double take of the scene and saw how it suggested the darkest form of betrayal, a ghostly farmhouse with no eyewitnesses, a carload of executed police officers, the killers mysteriously vanishing into the night and the sole survivor standing at a safe distance, completely unscathed.

He left the car and the dead bodies, and ran into the night as if seeking refuge from a gathering storm. He made long zigzagging sweeps in the shadows, running in the direction the horses had taken. He had no guide or track to follow. His journey was just beginning. Before the night was over, he would have to fashion a story for himself, otherwise no one would believe him. He would have to concoct an explanation for his unlikely escape, a reason why the gunmen had missed him in their relentless fire. The detectives in the car and the driver, they were the ones who deserved a story to themselves, not him, but already they were beginning to lose their reality, their cold faces taking on the shining edges of fallen martyrs.

He felt hollow inside, unsure of anything, least of all his own thoughts and feelings, stumbling over his shadow, the ghost of a lonely detective who had somehow escaped his own execution.

ONE

Morning-time and a sodden darkness had settled over Belfast, rain falling on to the dirty lumps of buses and army Land Rovers, the roar of their diesel engines sounding reckless and barely civilised amid the gushing flow of water. Everything was dripping wet, the gutter pipes and shop canopies, the bedraggled pigeons, the trembling shapes of the buildings and the office workers organising themselves like gangs at the bus-stops, their faces peeking from beneath soaking hats and umbrellas, even the smoke and fumes were dripping wet.

Like a prisoner breaking parole, I dashed down Great Victoria Street, avoiding the drainpipes and spraying traffic, and slipped into a café opposite the Europa Hotel.

I ignored the breakfast menu, ordered a cup of tea, and grabbed the newspapers, which were filled with headlines of the IRA ambush. I slumped into a seat at the back and scanned the reports, a lonely dread descending upon me that had nothing to do with the weather. The waitress brought me a cup of boiling hot tea and smiled, as if to reassure me, but I was far from feeling reassured.

I put away the papers and stared through the window, feeling the dripping water penetrate to the toes of my feet, wishing that the rain would wash away the newspaper headlines. I should have resigned from the force weeks ago on the day Special Branch assigned Robinson to my team. However, to do so now would only arouse more suspicions. Might I approach a doctor and ask for a medical certificate, instead? A simple enough solution, surely, especially after the shock of the ambush. I knew of detectives who had made their escape thanks to a sympathetic doctor, and they had managed the transition to civilian life well enough.

By any other measure, in any other career, I was nowhere near past it, but the fact that I had survived and walked away Lazarus-like from the bullet-strewn farmyard had left me with an unnerving exhilaration that would not settle. I checked my reflection in the nearby mirror, and caught the sight of blood staining my shirt collar. Fragments of flying gravel had nicked my neck, and the drops of blood were enough to bring out the sweat on my forehead and turn the café floor into a vertiginous tunnel.

My informer, an IRA man code-named Ruby, had supplied the tip-off for the operation that ended in the deaths of my colleagues.

The consequences of this were serious for me. Fingers would be pointed and judgement passed, casting me down into my informer's secretive and lowly world. I glanced back in the mirror at my face. In my youth, I had written off the habit as a form of narcissism, but this morning I saw it as a darker problem, a need to anchor myself in the world as a solid object, a real person not made up of rumours and half-truths.

I gulped down my tea and measured myself against my reflection. I scrutinised my eyes but saw nothing there, apart from the weariness of a detective trapped in the land of the dead, a detective with dozens of unsolved murders on his books, a detective who felt he could show his true face only in this crowded café, waiting for the look of guilt to surface in his features like that of a fox peeking from its den.

I should not be hiding here.

I should be at the station, reviewing the entire operation with a team of officers, examining where it might have gone wrong, searching for any degree of complacency or negligence in its planning. I tried to put it behind me. My hands began to feel less clammy, and I composed myself. My conscience understood and accepted the fact that the others were dead, and there was no possibility of them ever resuming their mortal lives and pursuing me with their unanswered questions.

All I could do now was try to forget their faces, bury them in the sights and sounds of the café, and afterwards a bottle of vodka and sleep. In a few days, I would return to normality. My conscience would sort itself out and become rock solid, fully secure in my role as a detective in spite of the interference of Special Branch, a trusted handler of spies and informers. Then, I remembered my last conversation with Ruby and once more, the notion of my guilt broke through. I reached for the hip flask in my jacket pocket, spilled a large measure of vodka into the dregs of my cup, and knocked it back.

'Who were you talking to?' asked a voice in the passing stream of customers.

'No one. It was a stranger,' a young woman answered. 'He thought he knew me.'

'Right, but why did he hug you?'

'I've no idea. Like I said, he thought he knew me.' Her heels tapped on the floor as she waited. Then the queue shuffled onwards and the conversation blurred into an indistinguishable murmur.

I stared at the customers, the rainy light glistening upon their wet jackets and carrier bags. Steam billowed and hissed from the appliances behind the counter. I listened into other conversations, the brief, garbled sentences preventing me from listening to my own thoughts. I tried to stay afloat in their world, without my own feelings opening up and pulling me back down to that lower plane of existence. The more people who crowded around me, the calmer I felt. The city carried on in its sodden way, unmoved by the sense of doom that hung over me and the jabbing fingers of blame I could picture in my mind's eye. A sense of peace filled me in spite of the sickness in my stomach.

I ordered a fresh cup of tea and poured myself another generous measure of vodka.

Slowly, everything grew blurred. The voices and faces ceased to cohere, like the milk and sugar dissolving in the swirls of hot tea. A moment of balance arrived, the first I had experienced since the ambush.

Perhaps I had nothing to fear after all.

In this café full of innocents, I allowed my thoughts to drift back to the events of the previous evening. I tried not to alter or distort the sequence of decisions that had led to the deaths of the three police officers, wary that my mind might filter the painful details or skim over some vital clue to my culpability.

I racked my brain, going over the details of my recent encounters with Ruby, but I could recall only fragments of what had been said, and had written down almost nothing afterwards. In fact, there existed practically no record of what we had discussed together, no traces left of the fleeting plans we had hatched, the doubts and fears that troubled us, the spoken words that might have been misunderstood or distorted as insults, or the promises I might have made and forgotten, the indiscreet remarks that might have slipped from my tongue, but had been pounced upon by Ruby to forge my downfall.

For years, I had been erasing men like Ruby and their roles from my mind because I had secretly judged our relationships to be degrading and unpleasant. I had hidden them not only from my colleagues and commanders, but from myself, too.

So little existed about Ruby's identity, and what little there remained was never mentioned or talked about to anyone. I never passed on the details that I knew, and those details were but a tiny fraction of the whole. Special Branch had preached that recruiting informers from the ranks of the IRA was the best way of obtaining information, and I had been doing my detective duty by pushing Ruby, raising the stakes with him, encouraging him to tell me more.

But what were the feelings that ran through me? What did I think when I heard his voice grow more haggard from one late-night telephone conversation to the next? I had always thought ahead, concentrating on the next task, but deep down I had known that our destinies were yoked together; Ruby, the informer, one of the doomed and lowly, and me, his handler, one of the saved and exalted, and that our relationship would end only with the death of one of us.

TWO

I was still staring at my reflection in the mirror when a man with a heavy beard came thrusting through the café doors.

Even in the reflection, I recognised the sarcastic curl to his lips. It was the journalist McCabe, but what was he doing here this morning? And who was he staring at as though he were sizing them up for the drop?

I craned my neck to follow his movements, and, with a start, realised he was making a beeline for me.

McCabe had a photographer in tow, an overweight man, holding a camera in both hands, who kneeled in front of me, aimed and started taking photographs. The bulb flashed and I felt the shock of exposure, the sense that all my years of undercover work as a detective were ending at last.

I raised myself to a half-standing position and ordered him to stop.

In all the time that I had known McCabe, I had never seen him with a photographer before. Now the reporter was staring at me as if I were an interesting object of study. What had singled me out, made me the journalistic prize of the day? Only the names of the officers who had died in the ambush had been released to the news stations, and mine had been kept secret, I presumed for operational reasons. Besides, I had always made myself accessible to the press, made it my raison d'être to be forthcoming with comments, even off the record, and always agreed to interviews. Why then did McCabe feel the need to jump upon me in public? I fell back into my seat, when I should have been moving, pushing through the crowd and exiting the scene as quickly as possible.

McCabe spoke to the photographer. 'Get a shot of him with the mirror in the background. This will be the scoop of the year.'

'What are you doing?' I said.

'Hunting down the biggest story of my career.' McCabe breathed heavily. There was something sinister but courtly in the way he leaned towards me. 'My contacts tell me the intelligence services have been searching for an IRA spy, a traitor operating at the heart of the security services. The latest word is they have you in the frame, Desmond Maguire. They're gathering evidence that you compromised yourself, your dead colleagues and the public in return for large sums of money.'

I could not get my breath. McCabe spoke in his usual bantering tone, but the firmness of his gaze and the presence of the photographer indicated the seriousness of his intent.

'I never thought someone like you would send their colleagues to their deaths in such a callous way.'

I was dazzled by the flashing camera, and the intensity of McCabe's expression. His face glowed like that of an avenging angel clearing the path of truth through a field of lies and cover-ups. I crouched in my seat, willing the hustle and bustle of the café to return so that I might slip away and hide on the streets, among people who were not tied together by secrets, and who were free to come and go as they pleased.

'Sorry for the abrupt manner in breaking the news to you.' McCabe watched me carefully. 'I had no choice, believe me. Very soon every reporter in the city will be looking for you.'

'I can't comment on such a ludicrous lie.'

'I didn't ask you for a comment.'

'Then what do you want?'

I could no longer see my own reflection, only theirs. For several moments, I lost myself, or at least the image of myself I presented to the world.

'I'm not asking you for your opinion of the reports. I want more than that.'

'But aren't you interested in hearing what I think of this outrageous claim?' I held on to the hope that McCabe's lead might be an accident, some sort of hoax or intelligence operation perpetrated on the wrong person.

'Afraid not.'

'What do you want, then?'

'I want your story. Your true story, not the false one.'

I knew one story only. The story I had been memorising for months and going over in my head all night since the ambush, the unchanging story that had allowed me to survive, the story I had been reciting to myself every day to guide my destiny as a detective.

'My story is all I have. It belongs to me and no one else, not you, or your editor or your readers.'

'Wrong, Maguire. Your story belongs to me, now. Remember that, you and Ruby belong to me.'

'Who's Ruby? I don't know anyone of that name.'

'I know you're lying. You can't fool me.'

McCabe was armed with knowledge and he was not shy of showing it. He said the botched operation had begun as a raid on an abandoned farmyard suspected of previously being the centre of a fuel-smuggling racket. The intention had been to search the premises for documents and equipment that would link the fraud back to the IRA. McCabe also knew that one of the smugglers, a man called Brian Fee, had been found dead in a fume-filled car in an Antrim forest a week before. Fee had been due to meet Special Branch detective Ian Robinson to discuss offering information about the role of the IRA's leadership in various criminal activities and their links to a corrupt police officer. The tip-off about the farm's location had been supplied after Fee's death by an informer named Ruby, and I was his handler. McCabe knew that I had been involved at every stage of the raid's planning. He even had the times of the meetings and the names of those in attendance. Special Branch had wanted to abort the raid, sensing there was something suspicious about the set-up at the farm. It seemed too good to be true, they had counselled, but somehow I had convinced them to go ahead.

'Who have you been talking to?' I asked. I would have to hunt down Robinson and find out how the information had been leaked, but then I remembered that Robinson was dead.

'It's understandable you have questions to ask, but I'm the one directing this conversation and I'm only in the mood to ask questions not answer them.'

McCabe clearly felt he had the upper hand, that he had acquired the right to dictate the interview. Or was it just a performance, a game of make-believe based on the unfounded suspicions of Special Branch and a few threats added for the occasion?

'Look, Maguire, you haven't much time to come up with some answers. I've asked the Ministry of Defence to deny or confirm that they are hunting a mole within the RUC. The department is due to release a press statement this afternoon.'

I blinked and said nothing. Now that I looked carefully in the mirror, I could see bits of myself, components of my body and facial features that had somehow been disassembled by McCabe's accusation. Perhaps when the journalist left I might pick up the pieces and put flesh back on the mask.

'Why did you ask Detective Ian Robinson to join in the operation?' asked McCabe.

Robinson had expertise in cracking smuggling cases, and I

knew he could handle himself in a tricky situation, but I was not going to tell McCabe that.

The reporter kept pushing, a smirk forming on his face. 'Nothing to do with the fact that Robinson had reported you for being drunk on duty?'

'I'm not answering your questions.'

'Listen, two detectives and a constable out of Crumlin Road Police Station are lying in the morgue, and you were the senior ranking officer. There was just one police car, no backup, and no proper surveillance on the farm. The IRA riddled your vehicle with bullets, but somehow you walked away, miraculously unscathed. It's not just me who'll be asking you these questions.'

'I suggest you ring the press office and stop harassing me.'

'Absolutely, that's the correct protocol, but you never followed it in the past. You know, I always thought you were too willing to talk to reporters. Too quick to make a comment. Too present when we attended police briefings. I always suspected you had to be hiding something. The way you searched out answers to our questions. But now I've got the inside track, you're not so confident or forthcoming anymore.'

McCabe's insistence that he had secret knowledge, mingled with my own uncertainty, was enough to make me almost believe the dangerous claim. The notion of my guilt had haunted me all night, the hopeless feeling that for months I had been pushing a wheel of grim fatality without hearing or seeing or knowing what exactly was going on, that I had been so obsessed with the repetitive nature of my detective's existence and the nightly relief in alcohol that I had never considered where it might take me. McCabe was right. I was in serious trouble if my survival under a hail of gunfire had not been an outright miracle.

McCabe pushed his card on to the table. 'Here's my number. When you feel like talking give it a ring.'

Then he swept out of the café with his photographer in tow. I could see the confident swagger that had taken hold of him, emboldened by his foreknowledge of my downfall. Yet, when he crossed the street, his walk changed. I watched him dodge his way through the crowd, his head down, his hands rammed in his coat pockets, as though he had just won the first round against a dangerous enemy.

THREE

During the worst days of the Troubles, Belfast kept its traitors out of sight, like the homeless drunks who froze to death in back alleyways, or the suicides who threw themselves off bridges into the dank Lagan waters. The bodies of spies and informers were usually transported to the border and left in ditches or covered in bin bags where they no longer posed a risk to anyone, and their deaths might not seem so terrible or pitiable. Was it because traitors were so closely connected with shame and death, their disappearances amounting to a collective act of repression? But what was being concealed from public view? What would happen if the city did not tidy away its informers and spies?

The ambush had the effect of completely obliterating my ordinary life as a detective. All those unsolved murders to investigate and meetings to attend in smoke-filled incident rooms seemed superfluous now. I lay low for the rest of the day and that night, sleeping in my car and avoiding contact with everyone, working my way through a bottle of vodka. The following morning I read the newspapers and tuned in to the radio to hear news about McCabe's claims. The picture of me in the café was splashed across the front page of the *Belfast Telegraph* with the caption: 'One of the police force's most highly commended Catholic detectives, Desmond Maguire, who miraculously survived the IRA gunfire that killed his colleagues.'

There was not a single mention about a police informer in the bulletins, but the questions the photograph and the reports raised seemed clear enough. 'By some extraordinary chance' were the words McCabe used to describe my escape. 'When questioned, Detective Maguire said he had no explanation for the events,' he had added. Betrayal or coincidence? Was I a traitor or the beneficiary of a miracle? Somehow, I was alive. In that bloodstained farmyard, I had run from the slumped bodies of my colleagues and into the night. I was still breathing and they were not. My mind had struggled with the shock of their deaths and my survival, and now it had to fight against the mounting fear that the ambush had implicated me. Was it because of something I had said? Did they die because of that? And if I was responsible, what punishment lay ahead for me?

I did not know the answers to these questions. Other people might. It was possible that McCabe knew nothing as well. If he had more evidence, he would have printed it in the newspapers. However, he had been unable to prove his claims, in spite of his bluster in the café. Perhaps he did not have any secrets. The only person who possibly did was Ruby, and I could not contact him, even though I kept imagining his voice whispering at me as I walked the streets. Was it my imagination, or did the pedestrians face me more squarely? As though they had overheard the rumours about my betrayals, and taken to the streets to confront me. I detected a collective swagger of well-being in the way they marched towards me. Even the pigeons swooping close by seemed tempted to alight and take a peck at my eyes.

However, in spite of the publicity around the ambush, the city seemed content to leave me alone and in full view. As if no longer bothered to remove its traitors from the public eye. It seemed unthinkable, but I was able to walk about, order tea in the cafés and sit on park benches, drinking vodka as though it was water, a drunken detective for all to see and pity.

In the evening, I made my way to the Lagan towpath, fortified by a half-bottle of spirits. I walked under skeletal branches that were just beginning to sprout tender little leaves, the new life uncurling and crawling onwards in its march against death and darkness. In spite of the embryonic signs of spring, it had grown cold. I had bundled myself up in an overcoat, a woollen hat and a scarf for extra protection against the biting air and any curious onlookers. My mental habits had changed. I had grown alert to coincidences, wary of what lurked beneath the surface of things, hunting for any clues of the destiny that lay in store for me.

For instance, I worried about the solitary man walking his dog towards me. I wanted to ask him to identify himself and explain his presence at the river because, for a moment, he had given me a nasty turn. I thought I had seen a ghost because he had the same long head and curly hair as Robinson. He even had a similar build and gait. I could not take my eyes off him, until I reminded myself that Robinson had never been a dog-lover and was definitely dead.

I was pondering the similarity when I saw the figure of Chief Inspector Alan Pearson, the head of my outfit at Crumlin Road Police Station, emerge from his parked car. I waved over and he looked around before walking slowly in my direction.

'Desmond, is it really you?' he asked, watching me as if I were a cornered animal, unsure of what I was going to do next. 'You don't look well. What the hell happened to you?'

'Don't even think about going back to the car, Alan. I want you to take a walk with me.'

'Are you sure?'

'Yes, the fresh air will do us both good.'

He seemed reluctant. 'Why the great secrecy? Why send me

a cryptic telephone message and ask to meet here alone? Why can't we go back to the station and talk there?'

'Start walking.'

He stepped alongside me, cold-eyed. 'I don't think you realise the trouble you're in.' He stared straight ahead, a regimental gesture, as though he were inspecting me on parade. 'You've compromised yourself by running away from the ambush and not making contact with anyone. Even your closest colleagues are viewing you with the deepest suspicion. They say they'll never work with you again.'

Hearing him mention the other officers, and the way he glanced to one side, made me think he was referring to Robinson, Clarke, and Elliott, the men killed in the ambush, who had somehow cast their judgements on me from beyond the grave. Then I realised he was talking about the surviving members of the team at the station.

He swung his arms vehemently. 'And now you're compromising me by dragging me here in secret. Special Branch has ordered me to relieve you of your police duties and ask for your gun. They want to talk to you about the ambush. Their questions will be aimed at your informer and the nature of your relationship with him.'

I moved ahead of him, walking briskly, expecting him to catch up. 'Don't worry; I know I'm in deep trouble. There's a lot I don't understand myself, but I'm determined to clear any suspicion hanging over me.'

He was at my shoulder. 'First you have to tell me what happened at the farmhouse. Were you injured or knocked unconscious? For God's sake, have you even seen a doctor?'

'I've felt better, but I'll be all right. When the IRA opened fire, I was trapped and couldn't move but somehow I managed to avoid their bullets.'

'What happened?' He watched me intently. 'Did you return

fire or radio for help? Did you check your colleagues to see if they could be saved?'

'I don't remember what I did. I knew we had come under attack and that everyone else in the car was dead or dying. I felt I had to keep running.'

Up ahead lay a bend in the river where the swirling ripples vanished into darkness. The path narrowed and swathes of nettles and brambles encroached from the hedgerow. Pearson tensed and slowed down as though reluctant to enter the murk. He stopped in his tracks and faced me. 'It's wrong, isn't it? This rumour that you helped set up the ambush?'

'Of course.'

'Utterly untenable. A pure fiction.'

'Yes.'

His tone grew quiet, careful. 'But then why did you run? Why hide from everyone?'

'I was afraid.'

'Of who? You'd survived the IRA ambush.' He kept staring at me, and I could guess the thought running through his head: I was either a traitor or a pure coward.

'I've no idea why I ran. I wasn't thinking straight. My life was under threat and I didn't know who to trust.'

'But why didn't you get in touch with us? Your colleagues and your friends. We thought you'd been kidnapped and locked up in some god-forsaken shed in South Armagh. And then we saw your photograph in the paper. Sitting in a café sipping tea as if nothing had happened.'

'I told you I don't know.'

'Desmond, you must talk to Special Branch. Make yourself available to them. They have questions to ask. Important questions.'

'I can't. I have to work this out myself first.'

'But how can you?

'I have to go on a little trip to get things straight in my head. You've got to trust me on this.'

I held his gaze for a moment, and thought I recognised the strange look in his eyes, an expression of sickening worry, torn between concern and suspicion.

'Of course, I trust you, but you're not making sense. I'm trying my best to understand why you're refusing to cooperate. This will go badly against you.'

'I'm not refusing. I'm just withdrawing my cooperation for a few days, that's all. Until I track down Ruby and find some answers.'

'Then come back to the station and let us help you find your informer. You're not the guilty one; you're not to blame for the murder of your colleagues or the fact that you survived.'

'Blame, I don't like hearing that word. Who's talking about blame?'

Pearson was silent for several moments. 'No one. Apart from a few journalists. Why would anyone else blame you for what happened? Why would anyone think you helped orchestrate the ambush?'

'I can't speak for Special Branch as a whole but I know some of its officers don't like my name. Especially people like Robinson.'

'Your name?'

'It's too Catholic for them. I'm not talking about the usual sectarian banter or the odd bit of offensive graffiti daubed on my locker. My life has been threatened in the past.'

'Your colleagues respect you for the risks you've taken, your courage to make a stand for law and order. I've defended you in the past, even when you turned up drunk for duty. I've always supported you when others didn't.' Pearson turned to stare at the river toiling below. The spring sunlight was dissolving away now, replaced by something else, the sharp empty feel of a winter twilight. 'But now I'm worried, Desmond. Your behaviour has raised alarming questions in the minds of our commanders. With all the publicity this ambush and your escape have received, I can't guarantee your safety, especially if you're intent on tracking down Ruby on your own.' Pearson turned round to face me, his eyes looking a little too straight into mine. 'However, if you come back with me to the station, I'm more than happy to vouch for you to Special Branch. As long as you cooperate with them.'

'I can't. Not right now. Like I said, I've a journey to make.'

'You've no idea of the danger you're in.'

We were walking again, our footsteps hurrying along the path.

'Have you considered McCabe's role in all this?' said Pearson. 'He was never a fan of yours. What if he's in league with the IRA, or being used by them to undermine trust in the police force?' His voice grew more animated, as though I was not just blind to my fate, but deaf and stupid, too. 'What if Ruby has been turned by his comrades in the IRA, and together they're conspiring to destroy your reputation? They might even have been working on this plan for some time, laying down a false trail of evidence to incriminate you.' His voice, though low, grew in intensity.

My mind groped about in the darkness, reaching for an answer. It seemed plausible that I had been manipulated by unseen forces in the same way that I had manipulated Ruby. Pearson was suggesting I was the victim of a counter-intelligence move, but would that be sufficient to explain why none of the bullets had struck me in the farmyard? When I came up against this puzzle, I could no longer think. I was a prisoner to the darkness.

He yanked at my sleeve. 'I don't like seeing you in this strange mood.' Then he placed a firm hand on my shoulder. 'It's time you pulled yourself together.'

I felt insulted by the chief's touch. Instead of reassuring me, it made me feel passive and vulnerable.

Pearson took a sniff of my breath and his frown deepened. 'I really think it's time you came off the booze, Desmond. You should see a doctor or a specialist.'

'Not right now. I'll come off it when this is over.'

'Spoken like a true alcoholic. But you'll go on drinking anyway.'

'I should have stayed away from Ruby, not alcohol, and never got involved in intelligence gathering.'

'What are you saying?'

'I'm thinking about how I ended up in this bloody predicament.'

The river darkened in the dusk light. Pearson's moist eyes cast me a perplexed look. For a moment, it felt as though he were giving me up as doomed, a lost detective trapped in a net of betrayal, beyond the help of his colleagues and friends.

'I've been inattentive,' he said. 'I haven't been following your relationship with Ruby. I don't doubt his worth as an informer, but it's time you gave me more details. Who the hell is he?'

'I can't tell you that. I've been sworn to secrecy.'

'He's no longer your exclusive property. Special Branch will want to interrogate him, dig into his background and motives.'

'I can't betray him. Not after the risks he's taken. I got him into this game and I have to stand by him.' It was to Ruby that I felt I now owed the greater consideration because, in wanting to tell my story, I would have to tell his story, too. We belonged to the one side now.

'But the whole thing is played out, Maguire. There's nothing useful to be gained by keeping his identity a secret. Ruby belongs to the past not the present.'

'Since when?'

'Since the moment you stepped into that farmyard.'

The water at the bend was smooth and full of fathomless gloom. Calm yet treacherously deep. Pearson refused to walk any further. The river had a dizzying effect on me, leading my eye down to where my reflection disintegrated and cohered again, trembling above the shadows.

'Why show loyalty to Ruby now? If you cling on to him, he'll only drag you down deeper into the murk.'

'I can't cling on to anything anymore. That's my problem. I don't know who or what to believe. Sometimes, I think there's a bit of Ruby in all of us, you know. That we're all capable of betraying our own.'

Was it my imagination, or did Pearson give a shudder? We pressed on around the bend, saying nothing. The feeling of shade winning the battle against light and life plunged us deeper into thought. We stopped walking and watched the river falling over a weir. Pearson tilted his head towards the water as though he were hoping the sound of it churning would help settle his mind, and make him patient with all the dangerous thoughts planted by my words. He lifted his head a little to the sky and breathed deeply, while my mind darted among all the conversations I'd had with Ruby, testing all the informer's words and actions, touching tentatively the dark patches of my memory, afraid of what might be revealed.

A pair of waterweeds drifted by on the surface of the river, their roots trailing deep below. I thought of the two white horses at the farmyard, almost the double of each other, taking off and running soundlessly into the night. Yes, I had recruited Ruby and protected his cover for years, but hadn't Ruby also recruited me? My desire to advance my police career and Ruby's love of intrigue had brought us together. Both of us were solitary players in the intelligence game, but responsible for each other.

'Tell Special Branch the truth about Ruby,' urged Pearson.

'Reveal his true identity. Expose him. At best, the information he gave you was botched; at worst, he set you up.'

The truth was I knew almost nothing about Ruby. I was a police detective, and Ruby was an IRA informer, running in darkness with violent men and criminals. According to the official record, we only ever met at isolated lay-bys, hotel car parks, and the empty corners of roads. Always amid shadows in strange places, stirring our fantasies of intrigue, our lust for secrets. There had been a dream-like quality to our encounters, two strangers bound together by fear and secrecy. To be honest, I had preferred Ruby to all the other informers I knew because he remained the most obscure, the least known.

'What if all this is a ruse from the IRA to get me to do just that,' I said. 'Expose the spy in their midst or at least undermine him. They made sure I survived so that the finger of blame would be pointed at me and my informer.'

I also knew that, if I revealed Ruby's identity, Special Branch would examine every aspect of our relationship and shine a light into all the nooks and crannies of the maze we inhabited. They would sniff out any mistakes that might have led to the murder of my colleagues and my miraculous survival.

'This story that you survived the ambush by some miracle isn't washing with our counterparts in Special Branch,' said Pearson. 'They say surviving three times is too many miracles for one detective. Even one as charmed as you.'

'What do you mean surviving three times?'

Pearson said that Special Branch was investigating other incidents during my career when I had been saved by good fortune from the hands of the IRA. However, he did not know the exact details. This was the first time I had heard anyone suggest I had benefited from other instances of good luck. I had no idea what he meant. Part of me would have preferred not to know what he was referring to and remain in ignorance, but now that he had made the insinuation, it was impossible to ignore it.

'Maybe they were just coincidences, not miracles,' said Pearson.

Was he referring to mistakes or lapses I had made, something I had done or had not done that had somehow resulted in my life being saved? Why was Special Branch reviewing my entire career? Were they intent on using my freakish good luck to undermine my record of service because they distrusted me as a Catholic?

'Where are you now with Ruby?'

I shrugged. 'I don't know. He hasn't been in touch since he gave me the tip-off about the farmhouse, and that was a fortnight ago.'

'Did you arrange to meet again?'

'No. I never forced him, you see. I was concerned he would disappear. I always waited for him to make the calls and come up with the information.'

'Have you spoken to anyone else?'

'No one but McCabe, and I denied everything.'

'What about family and relatives?'

'No one.'

'Where are you staying? Special Branch has been watching your house.'

'I've been moving around in my car. You're asking too many questions. All I need is a few days to hunt down Ruby. In the meantime, I can take care of myself.'

'Let me consider this, first.'

We walked in silence for several yards, Pearson deep in concentration. He had said he trusted me, but did he really?

'OK, I'll have to respect your judgement on this,' said Pearson eventually. 'Mostly, because I have little choice right now. You have my permission to go and track down Ruby. But, remember, at some point you will have to hand him over to Special Branch. Only then will they be in full possession of all the relevant facts. You understand that, don't you?'

'So unless I hand over Ruby, I won't be believed. Is that what you're saying?'

'No, not at all. Look, I'm not the one conducting the investigation. All I know is that Special Branch is reviewing all the operations out of Crumlin Road for the past year or so. They're looking into the records of other officers, too. This is just the preliminary stage, but they need more evidence to clear away the suspicion hanging over you.'

'What if we can't find any evidence? What if it *was* some sort of miracle that can never be explained?'

'Then you will have to pray for more miracles,' he said grimly.

I thought of the bog lake in Donegal and the holy island where I was going to start my search for Ruby. I'd had no contact with my informer since the tip-off, but I had good reason to believe an intermediary might be waiting there for me. If the chief was correct, I was heading to the right place.

'Remember, you're on your own now, Desmond. Hunt down Ruby and interrogate him and whoever else you can find. And don't worry about consulting me first.' His eyes bored into mine. 'In fact, I insist you not contact me at all.'

'Yes, that would suit,' I replied, thinking of my ordeal ahead. 'I'll maintain a discreet silence.'

'Excellent.' Pearson smiled tightly. 'Don't waste any more time, and drop the booze. We don't want the big fish getting to Ruby first.'

'I don't think he's under any suspicion from his comrades.'

'I don't mean the bloody IRA. Although they're bound to start sniffing around when they hear the speculation about you.'

Pearson did not understand my desire to stay in ignorance,

to keep drinking and avoid the damaging truth. This ignorance was the cure I was seeking for the mistakes I may have made, my impotence at the hands of more quick-witted and powerful forces, my frustrated attempts at forging a successful career as a Catholic in the police service. I looked back along the path we had taken. Dusk crept through the trees, its obliterating shadows drawing closer.

'Listen, Desmond, this country is on the cusp of a ceasefire, and a lot of secrets are being tidied away in the background. The Troubles will leave behind a bloody legacy of betrayal. Everyone knows that all sorts of information passed between the paramilitary organisations and the security services and vice versa. Now, do you know who I'm talking about when I say the big fish?'

I nodded. Pearson was talking about the British intelligence services.

'Just concentrate on finding Ruby and take care of yourself,' he said, with a grimace. 'I'll look after Special Branch and keep them from breathing down your neck.' His voice grew more formal, businesslike. 'Goodbye, Desmond. I wish you the best of luck with finding your informer.'

I shook his hand. It felt cold and lifeless, like the hand of Judas. He turned away and began walking back down the path.

'Just don't let me down,' was his final warning.

FOUR

Like a child cheating in a game of hide-and-seek, Pearson stood motionless in the shadow of a tree and watched Maguire make his way towards a bend in the path. The detective's hunched-over shoulders and stiff walk suggested something more than a police officer determined to clear his name. It was the behaviour of someone inhabiting a dream that was slowly going from bad to worse. Recognising that walk heightened Pearson's misgivings. From bitter experience, he knew that men like Maguire had a talent for dragging others into their personal nightmares.

He stood with his back to the tree and leaned forward slightly as the detective disappeared around the bend. He desperately wanted Maguire to turn around at the last moment, give him an apologetic wave, and call an end to the game. He wanted the detective to promise him there would be no more scary surprises or jumping out of dark corners, but Maguire slipped out of view without once looking back. Pearson lingered for a while on the path, wondering about the informer Ruby, if he was hunkering somewhere in a secret hole in border country, waiting to scare them both to death. He thought Maguire might also have reached the point where he wanted the game of hide-and-seek to end, if only Ruby would give it up, too.

Pearson watched the dusk advance along the riverbanks, the shadows contending with dying sunlight in every corner. He thought with a shudder that Maguire might have been a ghost, an apparition rising from the black river. He had expected a ready-made story from the detective, Maguire placing all his cards on the table in the apparent hope of fair play, not this tangle of confusing thoughts and fears. He should have fled Maguire's troubled face, rather than plead and press him with more questions. He felt irritated at the role he had been forced to play, and more than irritated, alarmed. Maguire had been one of his best detectives, and Ruby's secrets had played an important part in advancing Pearson's own career, allowing him to lead a team of detectives in one of the busiest stations in Belfast, while all the time disdaining to look too closely at his officers' operations or learn anything about their informers beyond a strict need-to-know basis.

Reluctantly, he made his way to a phone box and stepped inside. He lifted the receiver and hesitated. He felt genuinely sad at the thought of what lay ahead for Maguire. For a while, he stared at the window in an unfocused way, dimly aware of the lights of passing cars, the streetlights glittering along the river embankment. There were no such things as coincidences. Everything was part of a plan, some more subtle and underhand than others. If he believed in coincidences, he would not have agreed to meet Maguire and tip off Special Branch at the same time. He told himself there were things about Maguire and his career that could not be written off as good luck or serendipity. He gathered himself together, disciplined his thoughts, and pressed the numbers with a cold firmness. After a few rings, the voice of Special Branch Commander Tom Bates spoke in a flat tone at the other end.

'How did it go?' asked Pearson.

'Good job. We recorded the entire conversation.'

Pearson wasn't surprised when the inspector failed to address him by his proper rank.

'A pair of eyes is following him as we speak,' said Bates.

'Are you going to arrest him?'

'Not yet. We're more interested in finding Ruby. Especially since we can't find any trace of him in Maguire's files. He wrote up nothing about him. Nothing at all. Why do you think that was?'

'Maybe his notes were lost or destroyed.'

'Or eaten by worms. I thought you were a stickler for paperwork.'

'I never checked because it was need-to-know.'

'How often did he file his notes?'

'I don't know. I didn't go through all his records. Your officers should know as much about his routine as I do. They've been watching him for weeks.' Pearson had never explored the boundaries of Maguire's world of informers and touts, but this evening, with the detective's confused outpourings still ringing in his ears, he could feel the unsettling presence of shadows hemming him in, handlers and spies, heroes and traitors, the heroes in danger of becoming traitors themselves.

'He claims all the bullets missed him,' said Pearson.

'Do you believe him?'

'Possibly.'

'But that's madness. Forensics traced over five hundred rounds in the farmyard; the spent cartridges were scattered like confetti at a wedding. The car was riddled with bullets and the victims had multiple wounds. The IRA clearly had intelligence about the operation. It was a deadly trap and somehow Maguire escaped without a scratch.'

'But his confusion is so strong it's almost a guarantee of his honesty. If he did betray his colleagues, don't you think he would have covered his tracks a little better?' Pearson squinted through the window of the phone box to see who might be watching. The headlights of passing cars shone mercilessly upon him, filling the phone box with troubling shadows and reflected haloes of light. He thought of haunted companions like Maguire and his informer, coming and going in pairs. A police Land Rover with wire-meshed windows slid past darkly.

'Are you suggesting he's innocent?' asked Bates.

'I'm not suggesting he's innocent. Nor am I suggesting he's guilty. We shouldn't be too hasty in branding him a traitor.'

'If he's not a traitor, then what is he?'

'A detective who wants to clear his name.'

'You're not claiming Maguire is without suspicion, are you?'

'No, of course not.'

'All right, if he's not without suspicion then what is the source of your suspicion?'

'I have no firm opinion because I'm not sure exactly where my suspicion comes from. Do you?'

'Well,' said the Special Branch inspector, 'we don't for one moment believe he survived because of a miracle.'

'No, me neither.'

'Then why did he run and why won't he tell us who Ruby is?'

'Maguire always kept Ruby's identity secret. He was paranoid about his informer's safety. He wanted to shield Ruby from any danger.'

'Did it never occur to you to dig a little deeper?'

'The information Ruby supplied was first class. There never was a problem before. As long as Maguire took reasonable security precautions, I had no concerns.'

'So you stayed aloof. Never made a fuss. While Maguire made the breakthroughs and the entire team earned the plaudits.'

Pearson did not like the Special Branch commander's insinuation. He felt a surge of tension. He was being included in Special Branch's interest and curiosity, gathered into the net of suspicion surrounding Maguire and his informer.

'Don't be alarmed, Pearson,' said Bates. 'Special Branch is less concerned with your role in this mess than Maguire's. He seems to trust you, which is good news for us. We think it would be a good idea for you to make contact with him again. Make yourself available, close to wherever he's headed.'

Even though it was expressed as a suggestion, Pearson could tell Bates had given him an order. His face hardened as he pressed the phone to his ear. 'Are you mad? Who knows where Maguire will go or who he'll meet? Are you expecting me to give up everything and follow him?'

'No, that's not what I meant. I just want you to approach him once or twice, reassure him that you're keeping the heat off his back, draw him into a false sense of security.'

'Why not send your own officers?'

'We can't risk driving Maguire into hiding or spooking him into doing something unpredictable.'

Pearson's instinct told him it was better to hang back and wait for Maguire to exhaust all possibilities, but wasn't that part of the problem – that over the years he had become addicted to watching and waiting. Unfortunately, there was no guidebook to help him control the consequences of one of his own officers turning into a traitor. Standing in the phone box, a realisation took hold of him. He had been an inattentive chief inspector at times, one who didn't watch over his officers with as much constancy and wariness as he should have, especially the troubled ones like Maguire. He promised Bates that he would do his best to keep an eye on Maguire, careful not to reveal in his voice the tension he was feeling. The Special Branch commander sounded pleased and thanked Pearson for his commitment.

'I still don't understand why Maguire wants to keep protecting his informer,' said Bates. 'Especially if it was Ruby who gave him the tip-off about the farmhouse.'

Pearson recalled that Maguire had clearly not been himself along the riverbank. He had seemed hollow inside, and exhausted. 'I don't know,' he said. 'I don't think he's able to tell the difference between himself and his informer any more. In his current mental state, there's little difference between betraying Ruby and betraying himself.'

There was a short pause. 'Betraying himself,' repeated Bates as if for the benefit of someone next to him. 'Listen, Pearson, a traitor is always a traitor, no matter his current mental state. Maguire is the only survivor of that ambush, the only one who really knew what happened, and he's not telling us the truth. Let's hope he really does track down Ruby, and he's not just looking for breathing space so that he can come up with more lies.'

FIVE

Driving west on the M1 motorway, leaving behind the crowded, watchful streets of Belfast for the twilight ahead, I experienced my first bout of spiritual vertigo. Ahead of me lay a trip to a holy island in the Irish Republic, and my search for Ruby, and all I had packed were a change of clothes, some books and three bottles of vodka.

Stories about Station Island and Lough Derg enveloped my mind as I drove, tales harping on suffering and renewal, of pilgrims emerging from the island weak and sore, but reborn from the rituals of self-purification. At school, I had learned that on medieval maps Station Island was marked as the literal gates to purgatory, earning a reputation as one of the most lonely and frightful places in the known world. I was swapping the comforts and anonymity of the city for a primitive place shrouded in a haze of rain where people starved themselves and walked barefoot all night. I was making the same torturous journey that men and women had been making for over a thousand years into an internal wilderness, determined to save their souls and find salvation in Donegal's soft, mazy bogland.

However, the idea of fleeing to the island was not my own. I had been summoned there and hence the strange feeling of vertigo in my stomach.

The traffic dwindled and the road climbed into County Armagh. In the rear-view mirror, I could see the sprawl of the

ANTHONY J QUINN

Lagan Valley, the long flat miles of Belfast and its surrounding towns, their rainy gloom and glitter, and then the gleaming surface of Lough Neagh, petering out into nothingness. Ahead of me lay a landscape that seemed changeless, while everything behind was passing. The gently sloping orchards of Armagh gave way to the wildness of Tyrone and its drumlins of blackthorn and gorse, the dark, barely cultivated hills and glens of my childhood, a hinterland that made me feel like a lonely orphan in the city, a place stripped back to muddy peat, wind-torn bushes, and deep pools of rain.

As always, I had the strange sensation that I had been someone else in Belfast, that I had found a new identity, another face, amid the busy police incident rooms, and smoke-filled bars, and that somehow I had left that face behind me. I rolled down the window and breathed in the sharp purified air of the place I called home. This was the landscape that had once defined the limits of me, and the landscape that had connected me to others; the landscape that had protected me and the landscape that had made me feel vulnerable; the landscape that constantly called me back to who I had been the last time I lived here. But I could never go back to being me. I was someone else, a third person, a Catholic detective working in a Protestant police force, who could never feel safe back among his own. I glanced in the rear-view mirror and half-expected to see the shadowy face of Ruby staring back at me.

The road guided me into the night, away from the glare of small towns, Dungannon where I had gone to school, and the blackthorn-hedged fields of the Clogher Valley where I had played as a child. I kept the window rolled down slightly, listening to the sighing of the tyres and the hum of the engine, the car headlamps jumping across treacherous bogland and in and out of motionless forests, imagining that I could hear the sounds of ghosts whispering and creaking all over South Tyrone.

On the day of the farmhouse ambush, a letter had arrived on my doormat containing the torn-up pieces of a postcard. At first, I thought Special Branch had interfered with its contents. I suspected they had been intercepting my post for months, and even had the unsettling sensation they had entered my flat and rifled through my possessions on more than one occasion. I watched as an image of Station Island formed, my fingertips instinctively assembling the pieces, the saints' beds, the stony paths, the monolithic octagonal church, the oppressive grey dormitory that looked as though it could serve as a medium-size prison, the bits of grey sky, the distorted reflections on the lough, and a piece of a dark-hulled boat packed with pilgrims. Everything was there and intact. Fragments of memory drifted into my mind. I had not visited the island for more than twenty years.

I had done the Lough Derg pilgrimage as a pale sixteen-year-old, my first trip away from home on my own. My mother, whose maternal concern was stronger than her piety, had hidden a lunchbox of cheese sandwiches in my backpack and her parting words were to remind me to nibble at them if I felt faint during the three-day fast. I set off on the bus, feeling like a hero of my own destiny, a seeker of penance and the purest values of my faith, exhilaration taking hold as I was herded with the other pilgrims into the boat at Lough Derg.

It rained the entire time I was on the island, and all I remembered was the mud on my bare feet and the soft, limpid and slightly alarming eyes of a group of teenage girls from a convent school, which seemed to follow me in silence around the prayer stations, like the unholy thoughts I failed to clear from my mind. Despite the sense of failure, I had believed and wanted to believe, to cast myself into the throng of the faithful, to forget my thoughts and lose my teenage worries on that holy island. Travelling there should have felt like a return to the values of that yearning sixteen-year-old, but instead it marked the start of a more dangerous adventure altogether.

I had concluded that the postcard must have come from my informer, or someone close to him. It had seemed an odd thing to send me, and why had the sender torn it up? Some sort of security precaution? Or was it their intention to somehow absorb me into the mystery of the island, to tease me into solving some sort of puzzle? The scraps of the mysterious postcard awoke in me a thirst for order and the truth. The message on the back was revealed when I taped the pieces together. 'Dear Turncoat, I am in Caverna Purgatory praying for your lost soul,' someone had written, followed by the confession times on the island with one of them, the last of the vigil, underlined in heavy black ink, beside it the name of a priest, Father Liam Devine, and a date, in four days' time. Even then, staring at the postcard on the morning of the ambush, I had the sense of a looming upheaval, a vague thunder rolling towards me, the threat of a moral crisis that still had no name.

Now, in the aftermath of the ambush, I concluded that the sender, either Ruby or an intermediary, wanted to meet me on the island, with Father Devine or his confessional or even the mysterious sounding Caverna Purgatory as the contact point. He or she must have believed that we could talk there in secret, in a sanctum unlikely to be infiltrated by their enemies or mine, the ultimate anonymous hiding-hole where tormented men and women had been safely sharing their secrets for centuries.

Was this the pilgrimage I had been waiting for, the journey I had to undertake in order to save my career as a detective?

SIX

The next boat to Station Island would not leave until early the next morning, so I parked overnight in a lay-by just before the border. I switched on the light above the rear-view mirror and dozed uneasily over one of the books I had packed, hoping its words would help guide me through the trials that lay ahead. However, it was hard to read and even harder to think. The word 'turncoat' played constantly on my mind, along with images from the night of the ambush. *A person who deserts one party or cause to join an opposing one.* What party or what cause had I deserted? Working as a Catholic in the Royal Ulster Constabulary, I had neither emphasised nor tried to disguise my identity, but, still, anxieties about who I was or where I had come from constantly played in the background and were now rising to the fore. Surely, there was some professional protocol I could fall back on, a way to box away the fears that haunted me, as a trained detective should.

Ever since recruiting Ruby, I had found it impossible to read fiction and could only give my concentration to books that bore some relation to my own life. I had scoured the second-hand bookshops of Belfast and managed to find several memoirs and a handbook written by former British intelligence agents and spies, most of whom had adopted pen names in order to disguise their identity. Whenever I flicked through the books, I usually found some words of wisdom or consolation, and no longer felt as lost or desperate. I pushed the images of gun-wielding paramilitaries and Ruby's shadowy face to the back of my mind, and concentrated on reading my book, determined to learn something from the author's methodical self-confidence, his lack of introspection and self-doubt.

'Spying is waiting,' the ex-MI5 agent had written, adding that he could count all the hours he had waited in the grey hairs of his head. When he was with another officer, they would pass the hours playing cards or a distracted form of chess, without ever managing to finish a game. The informers he described had roguish smiles and poison in their minds. They came and went like silhouettes in the shifting mist, and in my imagination I could see the ghost of Ruby merging with their shapes. However, it struck me that the furtive men and women he wrote about still bore the stamp of authenticity and credibility, whereas Ruby did not. I imagined the public school and Oxbridge educated agent recoiling from Ruby in horror, and because it felt as though there was something false about Ruby, I felt false, too, a fake.

Fortunately, the book was rich with secret plots and motivations, some of which I hoped Special Branch or at least the newspapers might accept as the truth. They were the sort of stories involving double-crosses and misplaced loyalties that were frequently printed in the press and the reading public could understand and believe. I tried projecting my own predicament on to the pages of the book. I read on, slipping in and out of sleep, hoping that the words of this sophisticated spy would somehow fill the void that Ruby occupied, waiting for the author to tell me what I still did not know about myself and my informer, something specific and intimate that would guide me on my journey towards the truth. But the decisive revelation eluded me and my uneasiness grew. The more I read and thought about Ruby, the more I risked descending into a paranoid delirium.

The next morning, I woke early and clambered out of the car to stretch my legs and relieve myself. I felt conspicuous and solitary standing in the dawn light. A black Audi drove past. The man and the woman inside did not even glance in my direction but, as the car sped quickly onwards, I saw them watching me in their rear-view mirrors. I walked back to my car, pretending I had not noticed their interest in me.

Pearson's sudden agreement to my little trip over the border would have sufficed to put me on my guard, even if I had trusted him. There is a brand of intimacy that goes with betrayal, and I had detected something odd in his concern for my drinking habit and the way he had kept his eyes riveted on me at the end, when he had found it so difficult to look me in the face at the beginning. He had been unable to hide his fear that the suspicions hanging over me would also tarnish his reputation.

I sat in the driver seat and meditated on the empty road that ran towards the border. How should I behave now that I suspected I was being followed? I should act like a doomed but conscientious detective, one who had one duty left, to find his informer, arrest him if necessary and hand him over to Special Branch. Once that was done, my nightmare would be over. I might even look forward to playing the role of a little mouse in this game of hide-and-seek with Special Branch along the border. However, I was unable to concentrate my mind on a fixed pattern of behaviour. Why should I burden myself with the pretence that Pearson had not betrayed me? Better to trust the spontaneity of the moment, the spinning roulette of luck, and wait for the numbers to fall into their allotted slots. I knew that the nightmare would not end anytime soon. I did my best to ignore the warning signals and forgave Pearson for his treachery. In a way, I felt he was now sharing my burden, atoning for my mistakes.

In the hour after sunrise, I crossed the border, and drove through the village of Pettigo. I stopped at a shop and, mindful of the three days of fasting that lay ahead of me, stuffed myself with sandwiches. The shopkeeper, who must have been accustomed to hungry pilgrims coming and going, watched me eating greedily and blessed himself.

Apart from the tiny main street, the rest of the village was grey and bleak, the windows and doors of its outlying houses boarded up or smashed. The final stretch of road to Lough Derg had a similarly haunted character. The car trundled along the uneven road, winding through bogland, bleak hills and mossy forests that looked to have suffered under too much rain and not enough sunlight, a landscape of submerged horrors emerging into the light of early morning – broken trees, derelict cottages in various stages of decomposition, and hillsides foaming with shanks of yellowed grasses. It was a terrain to make weary travellers founder. However, I was over the border and out of sight of the army watchtowers and police checkpoints. Weaving through the bogs of Donegal, the car grinding between third and fourth gears, I grew more relaxed in spite of the landscape's sinister cast. Several miles later, I turned down a winding forest road signposted for Lough Derg and a silver metal arch materialised out of the trees, suspended over the road, welcoming me to St Patrick's Purgatory.

There were no other vehicles in the car park next to the jetty. I got out and checked the times for the boat journeys to the island. I looked up, aware of a light hovering over the lough.

It was raining across the water, but the landscape's dripping mood of hostility was evaporating. The rain cleared slightly and I got an exquisite view of Station Island, its churches and buildings emerging into view like the relics of a long, thin ecclesiastical city, half-submerged, half-floating on the water, surrounded by spirals of mist and the gloomy shoreline of pine forest. What struck me most of all was the silence and the light brimming in the air. Even the drops of rain seemed brighter, bigger and more transparent than the rain in Belfast.

The mist cleared further, and I stared at the island, its reflections lapping along the rocky shore until my eyes grew tired and the pitch-black water began to play tricks on my imagination. The difference between land and water dissolved, and I was filled with the sensation of light descending into a dark hole in the world. I was now staring into an interior landscape trapped beneath glass, one made visible to me in extravagant detail, another tier in the labyrinth. The goose pimples tightened on my arms and shoulders, warning me that my world had been a shadowy illusion and I was heading to an island where people might swap places with their watery doubles and mysterious transformations occur.

There was a public phone box by the shelter for waiting pilgrims. My last act on the mainland was to phone the journalist McCabe. He did not pick up, but I left him a message. I told him that, in two days' time, I would meet him in Lough Derg's car park and tell him everything that I had managed to find out about Ruby.

SEVEN

Unlike Pearson's usual conversations with his counterparts on the Irish side of the border, there was no time to be deferential or cautious when Garda Commander Jack Shaw picked up the phone and said Hello, no time to sit back and see how the wind blew. Pearson had known Shaw for more than two decades, and most summers they fished together in Donegal's cold rivers for salmon. Over the years, they had developed a semi-detached form of companionship, more like acquaintances with a shared passion than colleagues or close friends. Catching fish made them more companionable and less distracted, as did the rounds of Guinness, but Pearson had never been entirely sure of Shaw's politics, nor how much he could rely on him when in a tight spot.

'Hello, Jack, Pearson here. I need your assistance. A couple of officers to do some undercover work for a few days.'

'What's up?'

Pearson wished he had been able to meet Shaw face to face. Even now, a little nod or a smile from the Garda chief would have been enough to put him at his ease. On the other hand, a second glance after his use of the word 'assistance', a slight stiffening of the expression, would have indicated suspicion or mistrust, and warned him to tread more carefully.

Pearson explained that he was interested in the movements of a suspect who was visiting Station Island on Lough Derg.

Shaw was quiet for a moment or two. 'We'll be walking on

eggshells,' he said. 'Station Island is a place of pilgrimage. My officers won't like staking it out. Most of them are practising Catholics.'

'Our target has the potential to cause considerable trouble. For me personally and the country's security as a whole. I need to have him monitored, even when he's in the confessional.'

'What shall I tell my officers? How will I convince them to follow an order like that?'

'Tell them the target is a suspected traitor. Keeping a close eye on him may prevent further betrayals.'

'A traitor? Whose country and whose cause are we talking about here?'

At once, Pearson knew that Shaw had been following the story of the IRA ambush, probably through the newspapers, and knew exactly whom he was referring to. 'A traitor who is believed to have sent three innocent souls to their deaths,' he said. 'Isn't murder always a sin, Jack, no matter your political viewpoint or which side of the border you live on?'

'You're right, Alan. Murder is always a sin, especially in a place like Station Island.'

Neither of them spoke for a while, and then Pearson said, 'Well, what do you think, Jack? Can I rely on your help?'

'I'll send two of my best officers.'

'Great. The man we are interested in is a Catholic police detective in his mid-30s. His name is—'

'Desmond Maguire?' interrupted Shaw. 'I read his story in the newspapers.'

'Correct.' Pearson told Shaw he would fax him some photographs of Maguire and a few background details. 'I need your men to follow his movements on the island. I want them to make note of anyone he speaks to or shows an interest in. Eavesdrop if possible. We understand he's hoping to make contact with his informer down there.'

'What about the informer? Any pictures of him?'

'To the best of my knowledge there are none on record.'

'What about a physical description?'

'None on file, either.'

Shaw paused. 'What's his name?'

'All we have is a code-name.' Pearson's voice grew hollow. 'The informer was known as Ruby.'

'Odd you don't have the fella's name.' The commander's tone changed. 'Or perhaps you're reluctant to share those details with me.'

'Believe me, Jack, if I had any details I'd share them with you.'

Shaw paused. 'I'd be worried if I didn't know what one of my detective's informers looked like or what his real name was.' He pressed with his doubts. 'If you've no information on this informer, how can you be sure of where Maguire has been getting his information from? Isn't that like buying a piece of art and not being able to tell if it's a Picasso or a forgery?'

'Information is information, and Ruby's intelligence was always first-rate. Besides, an informer operating at his level requires a certain degree of obscurity. He doesn't have to reveal his identity.'

'I'm not talking about revealing his identity. I'm talking about proving it. If one of my detectives had recruited Ruby, I'd insist on knowing exactly who the bloody hell he was. Especially if the intelligence was rated top grade. The informer has a duty to stand up and prove he's telling the truth and can be trusted.'

Not for the first time, Pearson felt a strong aversion to discussing Ruby, especially down a phone. He should not have revealed his ignorance so easily, and Shaw had no right to pester him with operational questions. All he wanted was a little cross-border cooperation and trust in his judgement.

'And as for your man Maguire,' continued Shaw, 'I'd demand that he also prove his informer is telling the truth.'

'Oh, Maguire will be called to account, you can be sure of that.'

A silence developed, with Pearson reluctant to give away any more information.

'Very well, Alan, you have my assistance,' said Shaw. 'But remember, this is a tense time for us all. The IRA are rumoured to be looking for a political settlement, a chance to cease their armed campaign. We have to be careful of ruffling feathers.'

'Understood. I appreciate your cooperation.'

Before Pearson put down the receiver, a thought occurred to him. 'Listen, Jack, tell your men to bring some strong booze like poteen on to the island. Ply Maguire with alcohol if he won't talk or show his hand.'

'Smuggle illicit alcohol on to Station Island?' Shaw burst into laughter. 'Christ, Alan, you'll have us all cursed to hell for eternity.'

EIGHT

As soon as the boat full of pilgrims chugged away from the jetty on to the smooth, monastic waters of Lough Derg, I felt the weight of the journey fall from my shoulders. For the first time, I could picture myself safely ensconced on my refuge, and wished that I had packed more forms of distraction such as an extra bottle of vodka.

A few seagulls escorted us as the boat spun out into the middle of the lough. The trees along the shore were mostly deformed pine, stunted alder and willow. A rugged chain of hills and mountains rose around us, covered in more trees and heather, the shades of blue and purple growing deeper towards the horizon. Across this huge vista, not a person, car, house nor farm animal could be seen. In sharp contrast, the island we were heading towards was densely packed with church buildings, and I could make out a throng of stick-like figures shuffling within its precincts.

To see as much as I could of the lough, I stood up and crossed to the bow of the boat. I was aware of the other passengers watching me with curiosity as I leaned over the railings and stared at the breaking wave. The reflection of the hidden sun shed a weak glow, creeping like an oily sea creature alongside the boat. It seemed as if I was flying, the reflections of the clouds ridging on the water below strengthening the illusion. The surface of the lough was so full of light, like a vast silver plain stretching beneath me, that I almost gasped.

The sound of waterfowl rippled out from an inlet and I felt a further stab of pleasure. Station Island beckoned to me like the perfect hiding place. If I had tried to lie low in the forests of the border, or on any other island on any other lough, someone would have eventually noticed and reported me. But here, in a boat full of pilgrims, I had cover. If I prayed and followed the stations, my presence would provoke no gossip or suspicion.

The light in the sky strengthened, giving a shine to our arrival as the boat ghosted into the island's narrow bay. On a bench by the jetty sat an elderly woman waiting for the boat to land. With a jolt of surprise, I saw that it was my mother, smiling at me with a look of joy on her face.

The sight of her sitting there patiently filled me with a serene sadness. My adventure as a detective and handler of informers would soon be over. Her gentle, happy face floated above the bow wave, welcoming me on the threshold of purgatory. It must have been she who sent me the postcard. I kept my place at the front of the boat in spite of the milling of the other passengers who were anxious to set forth on their pilgrimage. I wanted to be the first to step on to the island so that I could walk up and embrace her. Then we would stroll, arm-in-arm, and I would confess all my self-doubts and guilty feelings. Of all people, she would not be shocked by my explanations.

But there was to be no happy reunion awaiting me when I stepped on to the island. The old woman did not move from the bench. She stared at me with a look of dead indifference. I gave a sigh. She was someone else's mother with a stranger's narrow eyes and a frowning mouth. My mother had passed away six years ago, so how could it have been her? I swallowed, turned away and pretended to check my watch for the time.

The boatman entrusted us to the care of a smiling young

woman who led us to the dormitories and pointed us in two directions, men in the left wing, and women in the right wing. She performed her duties with the minimum of communication and fuss, giving me a ticket with a number on it after I had written down my name and address in a large registry book. From now on, the numbered ticket was my only official form of identity. She told me to take care of it because it would be used to allocate the single daily meal of black tea and toast that everyone was permitted.

I found my bed in a cubicle with three other bunk beds. There was a small suitcase already positioned under one of the other beds and I wondered who my roommate might be. I hoped he was a gentle and quiet sleeper. I took off my shoes and socks and placed them underneath my bed. From now until the third day, I would be barefoot.

The young woman instructed us not to sit or lie on the beds until ten pm the following evening in case we accidentally fell asleep. The opening Mass would take place in an hour's time, and in the meantime as new arrivals we had a number of things to learn. She gave us a Pilgrim Exercise leaflet, which contained a map so that we could acquaint ourselves with the paths and the topography of the island, and a list of the different rituals we would have to complete over the next two days. While the other pilgrims skimmed over the map or ignored it completely, I studied it for clues. The map was a guide, a way to read the island, and if I arranged it in my mind in the correct way, it might become something else, something that would lead me to Ruby's hiding place.

On the eastern side of the island lay St Patrick's Basilica, a large octagonal-shaped church built out of limestone, and in front of it an iron cross dedicated to St Patrick. Further west sat the six penitential beds, the remnants of beehive cells used by ancient monks, which formed the focus of the nine stations or praying rituals. However, there was no reference on the map to the Caverna Purgatory mentioned in the postcard. It sounded like a Latin name, and I wondered if its location might be marked on older maps of the island. The leaflet instructed us to walk and pray three times around the outside of each cell, and three times around the inside. At each station, there were nine points where we had to kneel, and then at St Patrick's Cross we had to kneel twice. Three of the stations were to be completed before nightfall, four during the night in the basilica, and the final two on the second day.

There was no set time to start the first day's stations, explained the volunteer, but it was advisable to begin as soon as possible, before weariness and hunger set in. The other pilgrims dutifully drifted off to start their prayers. They paced among the crosses, moving up and down the stone circles as though trying to find their way out of a labyrinth, while I hung back with my map. I was alone with the volunteer and she gave me a questioning look.

'I'd rather wait here,' I told her.

'Whatever you're comfortable with. You can catch up with the others later.'

'Well, no, I'm not going to catch up later. I came here for something else.' I glanced around to make sure no one was eavesdropping. 'I need to speak to Father Liam Devine. It's urgent.'

She paused, as if sensing the worries weighing on my mind. 'Father Devine will be hearing confessions tomorrow night. In the meantime, he's unavailable. But Father O'Hagan and Father Loughran are free.'

I smiled, but inwardly recoiled in horror. And let someone else poke their nose into my secrets? My journey had nothing to do with the other priests on the island. It was a transaction to be sorted out between Devine, Ruby, the IRA and myself.

'Father Devine is the only person who can help me,' I told her. 'That's why I want to talk to him.'

'I'm sorry. He's not even on the island. He's due to arrive on tomorrow evening's boat.'

'Do you have a way of contacting him?' I asked.

'No.'

'None at all?'

She apologised again. 'I'll ask the other priests if they have a number for him.'

'As soon as possible?'

'They're busy right now. This evening. Or perhaps tomorrow morning.'

'I see.' I sighed. What sort of transaction was I expecting to take place with Father Devine anyway? What if he had nothing to do with Ruby? I had never met him before and therefore could not trust him with my secrets. I thought of the postcard and the other clues it might contain. There was another possibility. 'Where is the Caverna Purgatory? I can't find it on the map you gave me.'

'Why do you want to know?'

'A friend told me he would be waiting there.'

She hesitated for a moment, smiled and then frowned. She looked at me as if I were emotionally disturbed. 'Your friend must be a ghost.'

'I beg your pardon?'

'The Caverna Purgatory has been blocked off since 1632.' She went on to explain that the cave had been a pit or well, through which St Patrick had glimpsed his visions of purgatory. In early Christian times, pilgrims were locked inside it for twenty-four hours so that they might witness the horrors of eternal suffering. It had never been excavated and its exact location on the island was a mystery. Some believed it lay buried under the basilica. When she saw the look of disappointment on my face, she offered to take me on a tour of the basilica and the prayer paths to help me get started.

'No, thank you,' I said. I turned my back and walked towards the jetty.

The boats came and went regularly, some full of pilgrims, some half-empty. I paced aimlessly up and down the shore. There were no barriers or fences on the island, only the symbolic one of the water. Nor was there any formal system of surveillance. Sometimes a priest or a volunteer helper took up position at one of the stone beds or doors of the buildings, but their duties were confined to giving words of encouragement.

In the little holy shop by the jetty, I bought a pair of rosary beads and a scapula to hang around my neck. I felt I was reaching into the very bottom of my bag of disguises, rummaging to the core of my Catholic identity to play the part of a devout pilgrim.

However, it wasn't religion that I needed. It was space and time to think. Rather than join the throngs on their barefoot walkabout, I returned to the dormitory. The building was chilly and austere with its bare walls and rows of bunk beds housed in cubicles, but somehow I found the dispiriting atmosphere soothing. The high lead-paned windows, the narrow corridors and the stairwells swamped in darkness gave me a comforting sense of confinement, not unlike a prison. I was now an inmate of an institution for people hankering to be good and saintly. Even the idea of giving up my shoes and socks for the next two days felt secretly pleasing.

NINE

I was now certain that there was some secret hidden in the night of the ambush, some truth I was fumbling towards. Miracle or not, there was something else, something I needed to uncover. I took out a pen and on a scrap of paper began writing down the points that still puzzled me. Special Branch's interest in my investigations over the past month. What had alerted them in the first place? Were they, as McCabe suggested, searching for a mole? If so, who had tipped the journalist off about the investigation? Then there was Pearson's reference to other miraculous survivals. How was I to interpret that?

I turned my thoughts to Ruby. Why had he never asked for payment or anything in exchange for his information? Did he know the IRA was planning an ambush on the night of the farmhouse raid? Was he involved in the trap? If not, why the silence? Was it a bargaining chip, a means to lure me to this island?

I sank into a meditative silence and went through the questions again. Was there anything that I had overlooked or forgotten about? Some connection or explanation? After my conversations with Ruby, I tended to drink heavily and lose track of everything. Perhaps I should have stayed sober more often and asked questions. I should have persisted, but I always assumed that Ruby would be more prepared to keep talking if I didn't insist on understanding everything about him and his motivations.

I got up and stashed the vodka under the bunk. Then I reached for my books and lay back on the thin mattress. Flicking through the pages, I searched for some evidence that might justify the risky strategy I had taken in telling Pearson I was determined to track down my informer. I found scenarios and fragments that were familiar to me, handlers gambling with the fate of their informers, the garrison mentality of intelligence outfits, solitary agents locked up in their own paranoia and operating without any judicial control, a world where nothing was ever very clear. I read on, stumbling through the accounts, groping in their shadows and in my past, mesmerised by the feeling that the authors were holding a tarnished mirror to my soul.

By the grey light of the window, I slipped into a doze. The stories of spymasters treading the deep carpets of Whitechapel as they fought their clever, secret wars faded on me and were replaced by images of Belfast's back streets, the dingy churches and meeting houses calling on their kingdoms to come. And then the even dingier alleyways where men and women were beaten into the twisted shapes of touts and informers, confessors and colluders, victims desperate to blame themselves and sign their own death warrants.

I was shaken out of the daydream by the tread of booted feet marching down the corridor. New arrivals, I assumed, and sat very still, hoping that whoever it was would pass by and find beds further down the dormitory. The footsteps stopped outside my cubicle, someone whispered, and then the door opened. An overly friendly voice with a Donegal accent said Hello, and two men stepped in.

I had not spoken to another pilgrim since arriving on the island and their unexpected appearance made me sit up so quickly from my books that I bumped my head on the bunk above. Had they come here looking for me and if so, what did they want? The bigger one's face was dark and frowning, but his smaller companion looked friendlier. He had an intelligent forehead.

'I'm Paddy,' he said, sticking his hand in front of me.

I shook it, reaching out at an awkward angle. 'Desmond,' I told him.

'Kieran,' said the bigger man.

'Mind if we join you?' They glanced at the bunks opposite.

'I'm a terrible snorer.'

'That's grand. On the second night everyone here sleeps like a log.'

Their physicality filled the cubicle, their glances and grins, their strong voices, the way they breathed and moved, bumping into each other as they planted their overnight bags under the empty bunk. They sat down on the bed opposite me and removed their boots and socks. Kieran's long legs stretched across the floor, blocking my exit. Their bare feet felt so close they might as well have been resting on my chest.

'So, welcome to Lough Derg, Desmond,' said Paddy, with a smile.

I thanked him and went back to reading my book.

'You must have arrived on the early boat.' He glanced at the books and the pyjamas I had laid on my bed. 'Made yourself at home, I see.'

'That's right.'

'Where are you from? Belfast, I take it?'

'Yes and no.'

'Sounds mysterious.'

'I live in Belfast, but I'm from Tyrone.'

'You don't sound like a Tyrone man.'

'You don't even sound like a Catholic,' said Kieran, with a smile.

'What do you work at?' asked Paddy.

'I'm a civil servant.'

'Which department?'

What were they circling around, prodding me with questions, brushing up against my troubled sense of belonging and identity? I had hoped that I had escaped interrogation but now I saw that more questions awaited me on this island, more labours for my conscience, more doubt. The pair glanced at each other when I did not reply. They appeared to be consulting together, deciding upon another question.

'You're welcome to hang around us for company,' said Paddy. 'Assuming you're here alone.'

'That's kind of you, but I'm perfectly fine as it is.' I was hoping that my unfriendly air would put them off.

Kieran yawned and leaned back against the wall, while Paddy lowered his head, deep in thought. He scratched his neck and then lifted his face towards me.

'Well, we're heading for a little walk around the island before Mass. You can join us, if you like.'

'As I said, I prefer my own company.'

He was not put off by my brusqueness at all. In fact, it seemed to invigorate him, heightening his good humour and bringing a glint to his eyes.

'Don't tell me you'd rather mope in here with your books.'

'Ach, let him make up his own mind,' said Kieran.

'I plan on doing some reading while I'm here.'

'About what?' Paddy's eyes fixed on the stack of books again. He could see they weren't holy books. He glanced meaningfully at Kieran. He picked up one of them and flicked through the pages I had marked. 'Do you like reading spy novels?'

'They're not novels; they're true-life accounts,' I said, taking the book off him.

'Really? I thought these writers made everything up.'

Kieran chuckled, while Paddy read the back covers of the books, his face showing more misgivings. He began to leaf through them. 'Don't get me wrong,' he said. 'I like reading books myself. But only if they help me understand something about the real world. Most of the time, I never finish them, no matter how hard I try.' As he spoke, he stared at me and then went back to reading with an exaggerated air. I felt a burst of apprehension. He came across a passage I had underlined and read it aloud.

'The elusive truth that the informer was speaking of came out slowly in a series of distorted perceptions as is generally the case in the secret underworld of haunted men.'

His gaze grew sharper. 'Tell me, does reading all these books about spying and secrets not give you bad dreams?'

I kept reading.

'It's not a serious question. Just curious, that's all.' His expression grew softer. 'We all come to Lough Derg for different reasons, and if you want to spend your time reading spy stories, then where's the harm in that?'

I took the book out of his hands and placed it in the stack. 'Why did you pick this room?' I asked. 'Did someone send you here?'

The slight stiffening of their expressions suggested my suspicions were correct. They squinted at me, scrutinising me in a different way, sizing me up like the way Pearson had done on the Lagan towpath.

'You're trying to find out whether I'm hiding something. If I'm a genuine pilgrim or not.' I kept my tone pleasant, almost as if I was complimenting them. 'I think you should mind your own business. There are plenty of empty beds in the other cubicles. Why don't you move your bags in there?'

'If it's OK with you, we'd rather bunk here.'

'It's not OK with me.' Who were they? Undercover police

officers or Special Branch agents? 'Tell me, who sent you here? The Gardaí or the RUC?'

Paddy's brow furrowed. 'We don't know what you're talking about.'

'You can pass a message on to your bosses. Get off my case.'

'We're just two farmers from Pettigo,' he said, with a bewildered air. 'We're only interested in a bit of company.'

'I've no company to give.'

'You want to be alone.'

'Yes. I want to be alone.'

'We didn't come here to disturb you and we're definitely not policemen.'

'If you're not policemen then you must be some sort of agents.'

'We're bloody farmers,' he said a final time, clearly annoyed now. They both stood up and, looking at their thick hands and bowed-over frames, I was aware of the contrast between their appearance and what I was accusing them of. They looked as though they led simple, honest lives toiling on tractors across boggy farms.

'We won't bother you anymore,' said Paddy. Their annoyance made them clumsy, and Kieran stumbled as he stepped towards the door with his suitcase and boots. He yanked the handle roughly and cursed as Paddy pushed him out the door.

I closed the door behind them and sat down on my bed to collect my thoughts. What had just happened? Who were these men? I stared through the window and watched the pair emerge from the dormitory entrance deep in conversation and walk towards the basilica.

I was convinced they were undercover police officers. Part of me wished they had behaved as coppers from the start, rather than maintain the subterfuge that they were ordinary pilgrims. But wasn't that what I was doing, too? I leaned back against the cold wall and sighed. I had hoped for a few days of respite from suspicion and surveillance on this island that had welcomed generations of sinners without question. Thieves, murderers and traitors had found refuge here, and had been allowed to hope that, with a few days of prayerful endurance and suffering, they might escape an eternity of punishment. It had been a foolish hope to share.

I was unable to keep reading and decided that I needed to go for a walk. I washed my face in the bathroom sink and put on an extra jumper. I was now a barefoot sinner stripped of my detective rank, a hunted man whose only means of salvation lay among other searching souls.

TEN

I made my way to the canteen where the staff were busying themselves setting a table of toast and dry oatmeal cakes for those on the second day of their vigil. The pilgrims came trudging through the doors with aching feet. I expected a noisy clamouring for food, but instead they were silent and respectful of each other, queuing politely and passing the plates of toast to their neighbours. Soon the canteen was filled with swarming shadows, munching resolutely and whispering, everyone reluctant to disturb the hush.

A sense of peace rose into the air like the steam from their cups. A peace that came not in the shape of thoughts or words but as a form of shared consciousness, a mood, a light that they all seemed to inhabit. A light that seemed to make their exhaustion and lack of sleep more noble and bearable. Here was an opening for me, I hoped, a space to absorb all the heavy thoughts that swirled inside my head. I could say things to these strangers that I would never utter to the living back on dry land, and I felt relieved that this warm canteen and table of toast and hot tea would be waiting for me after the long night ahead, and that I had a reward for the painful hours of walking through the island's labyrinth of prayer. I began to hope that I was no longer on a journey to the bottom or into nothingness. I had found a small tribe of people that would help me cross the void, who behaved with dignity and humility, who were angels of a sort. The feeling that arose in me felt as light as air, the notion that I might be saved and exalted, and that overnight I might undergo a metamorphosis and turn into one of them.

But then I spied the figures of Paddy and Kieran, and their clumsy gait, moving like an undercover squad through the queues, their faces set in stone. They had the determination of two police officers pursuing a suspect, their arms rigid, their heads hanging forward. Their eyes met mine, their gaze long and unnerving. The world closed in upon me again, shutting out the light, and the room grew heavy with awkward bodies, silence, and haunted eyes.

The two men moved in a wide circle around the pilgrims and took up position by the windows. I slipped out of their sight. As I passed the long food table, I grabbed some of the oatcakes and stuffed them into my pockets. Then I joined the queue for a cup of hot water flavoured with pepper and salt, Lough Derg soup as the pilgrims called it. I was convinced no one had seen me lift the food laid out for the other pilgrims. Certainly, no one challenged me or pointed an accusing finger.

I glanced up and saw Paddy staring at me. I sensed his scrutiny, the calculation behind it, the squinting gaze of a police officer sizing me up. No doubt about it.

He came up to me. 'Why did you steal the oatcakes?' he asked. 'They were left for the pilgrims on their second day.'

I shrugged.

The figure of Kieran bulked up behind him.

'You don't have to give a reason, I suppose,' said Paddy. 'I was just curious that's all. Someone will have to do without, now.'

'I thought they were extra.'

A group of pilgrims filed past and I moved to join them, but Paddy persisted, tugging me away from the procession.

'But you've only just arrived,' he said, his tone calm and

74

inquisitive. Kieran moved confidently beside him, forcing me against the wall. 'It wasn't as if you stole them out of sheer hunger, was it?'

'No,' I replied and stood my ground.

'What if one of the helpers or the priests had seen you? How would that have looked? They would have made you hand back the cakes in front of everyone.'

'Did anyone else see me?'

'I don't think so.'

'Then what's the matter?' I stared at him and tried not to waver, but my gaze roamed around the canteen, flicking between the ghosts of Belfast and the bright-faced pilgrims, from one world to another, from this simple, clearer world, the light emanating from the lough and the shimmering faces, back to the tortured nights of the city. My mind darkened and the dizziness returned. I no longer felt surrounded by kind strangers. I was beset by enemies, and the sourness of all the suspicions in the past filled the room. Why had I taken the oatcakes? It was a stupid, childish act of rebellion, a form of stealing. Somehow the intrusive presence of Paddy and Kieran had made me behave as I felt, like an outlaw.

'Nothing to do with us,' said Kieran. 'You can do whatever you like as far as we're concerned.'

He stepped back a little. A sign that I was free to go.

'That's right,' I said. 'Nor do I have to answer any of your questions.'

'Right,' said Paddy. 'By the way, someone was handing round a newspaper with your mug on the front. They were calling you a traitor.'

The word 'traitor' uttered to my face for the first time since leaving Belfast made my heart miss a beat. 'That's a terrible slur on my name,' I said.

'That's what we were thinking, too,' said Paddy.

'We thought you might want to know,' added Kieran.

'You don't have to talk about it or give any explanation about what happened.'

'I don't mind talking about it. You can ask me any questions you like.'

The truth was I could barely think straight, and I must have shown it because Paddy gave me a smirking grin and backed away. I walked off, thinking that the pair or some other agent must have produced the newspaper and passed the word around in order to expose me. In spite of the efforts to undermine me, I would go on denying I was a liar or a traitor. They had no proof. Paddy and Kieran were just two pushy but clumsy police officers. I had nothing to fear in them.

However, there was a greater problem, it occurred to me. I no longer had any control over my feelings of guilt on this island. I could feel my conviction weakening to a dull glow, the conviction that I was a helpless victim and innocent of any charges laid against me. The truth was irrelevant. It must have been all those months of secret contact with Ruby. I was a detective completely saturated in suspicion, drenched in it.

I took off and walked around as much of the island's shore as I was permitted to, and then made an exploration of its interior. I was hoping that some feature of the island would reveal a secret entrance to the Caverna Purgatory, but I found nothing at all. For the next hour, I followed the paths laid out for the pilgrims, my bare feet getting to know every sharp edge, every fault line, every pitiless loose pebble. I could see that stones and rocks were Lough Derg's obsession. They covered the entire island, carefully laid paving stones for people to kneel upon, others that were lop-sided fragments, sharp and overgrown with weeds. I heard groans and sighs as pilgrims stubbed their toes or jammed them in crevices. What exactly was the purpose of the stony paths? I could sense how the carefully measured-out walks might function as distraction or diversion, even as penance, but how were they meant to save anyone's soul or grant them salvation?

I thought of the trials that awaited me until Father Devine's arrival, the cold and hunger and the hours of sleepless walking, and my heart filled with bitter feelings. I spied Paddy and Kieran sitting on a bench with some pilgrims. They were chatting and laughing. They looked up and waved at me in a friendly way. I was tempted to join them, but my heart felt too black and constricted and I kept walking, without even wavering, not wanting to show them a moment of weakness. They had been briefed all about me, no doubt, and encouraged to gain my confidence. However, they did not know me at all.

ELEVEN

Another boat arrived, and the island filled with pilgrims and the sociable murmur of their prayers, so intense that at times it sounded as though a delicious piece of gossip were doing the rounds. I watched the swarm of men and women thronging around St Patrick's Cross and shuffling around the paths. They were following their individual stations, moving at cross-purposes but also convivially, without ever interrupting or bumping into each other or having to alter their course. Some of them were on their second day and had just consumed their meagre meal of black tea and toast. Their bodies must have been tired and sore. Yet they moved with dignity, praying under their breaths and respecting the worship of others. They were carried by their faith, like a line of figures helped along by a fresh wind. I had no faith, so how was I to follow in their footsteps? My feet fell on the cold stones, my tongue silent. How had these people managed to hold on to their beliefs when I had lost them all?

I walked round the corners of the basilica and made my way to the shore. I had no faith and no plan now other than to wait for the confession time marked on the postcard. Nor did I have any way of communicating with the outside world. I avoided eye contact with the people I met. I was on the other side. I stared across the lough at the silent pine forest and the mountains climbing above, my gaze fixing on the point where the trees were blackest. I felt drawn to the seclusion offered by the uninhabited shore, the shadows within the trees and the shadows they threw on to the lough surface, which lay grey and serene under the evening sky.

In an instant, the tree-lined mountains looked as though they were falling into the water, the entire landscape plunging towards its trembling reflection. Again, I had a strange feeling of vertigo. As though I were standing at the edge of the border, the edge of my country. I could feel the noise of Northern Ireland pouring all around me, the torrent of murderous secrets and lies that flows into the amnesia of the past. One misstep and I would be gone forever, along with all the appalling things I had forgotten about Ruby.

The bell began to sound, calling everyone to Mass in the basilica and bringing me back to my senses. The pathways emptied of pilgrims, but I was reluctant to join them. I found a way of keeping out of sight, clinging to the water's edge and squeezing myself into one of the many dark crannies with secret views of the lough. I wanted to be alone with my thoughts rather than herded in with the others.

I began to consider the possibility that my intermediary or perhaps even Ruby was hiding among the pilgrims on the island, and I would have to hunt them down. When no one was looking, I slipped into the little office by the pier. In the drawers behind the wooden counter, I found the register which all of us had entered our names and contact details in on arrival. I ran my fingers down the list. The names absorbed my attention, and I whispered each one, running them through my mind, hoping they might trigger a memory or hint at some connection to Ruby. The bell sounded again, heavy and sonorous, rolling over the island. Mass was about to begin and with all the pilgrims sequestered in the basilica, I had enough time to peruse the records.

What was the moral code on the island, and what was I risking by hunting through the names? I had already committed the worst crime, passing myself off as a pilgrim. If the priests caught me snooping, the worst they could do would be to boot me off the island. I pored over the list and tried to let Ruby speak through the names. Some of the men had written in rough hurried strokes, and I struggled to read their writing. I followed the scrawl of their handwriting as though it were a thin thread, a pattern leading me into a labyrinth. Some of the names were German and French and I assumed it would be easy to identify their owners among the pilgrims and rule them out.

The movement of a figure across the lawn made me look through the window. A young, black-frocked priest hurried along a gravel path. Suddenly, he turned and made a beeline to where I was hiding. The office entrance was on the other side of the building and I calculated that I had to act fast. I felt a twinge of guilt as I ripped out several pages. However, I was a detective, and I didn't have the time or powers to request a proper search warrant. My intuition told me that everything on the island was evidence, clues connected to other clues that might lead me at any moment to Ruby. I closed the register and slipped it inside the drawer.

I had found eighty-seven names. Now all I had to do was find the ones my intermediary and my pursuers might be hiding behind. Their names were on the list, or they were on the island with no names. Either way, I had worked out a way that might help me track them down.

I stepped out through the door just before the priest turned the corner. He stared at me with undisguised suspicion, and informed me that Mass had started and that I must hurry to the basilica.

I told him that I was not going to Mass, and would not be persuaded otherwise.

He went off and promptly returned with the elderly prior, a short man with bullish eyes, who regarded me suspiciously.

'Are you a pilgrim?' he asked.

After some hesitation, I answered. 'Yes, I am.'

'The pilgrims,' he said, 'are in the basilica.' With a confidence and authority that reflected his control of the island and all its visitors, he extended his hand in the direction of the church.

TWELVE

The only benefit I derived from the first Mass welcoming the pilgrims to the island was that, for a short while, I was able to push the thoughts of Ruby and the IRA ambush to the back of my mind. Sitting at the back of the church, I went through all the alternating positions of prayer, the repetitive kneeling, standing and sitting. I had not attended church for years but the rituals were simple and easy to perform.

When Mass had ended, I remained in my pew and pretended to be deep in prayer. The prior led the procession out of the church and looked me over, clearly dubious about the sincerity of my devotions. However, I was glad of his stern presence and the fact that he had gathered all the pilgrims in one place. A throng of people shuffled behind him, wreathed in trails of incense smoke, and I began to count them one by one, as they passed. The first twenty or so were all in moderately good spirits and appeared to be part of a large group. They offered encouraging words to each other, urging anyone that looked to be dawdling to keep up.

After that, the congregation filed past in pairs and groups of three. I kept counting them. At the rear, came the solitary souls, mostly men, creeping along the basilica walls, silent as shadows, some of them wearing expressions that hinted at inner torments. They were the kind of figures who could slip around corners or lurk at the edges of company without anyone noticing. I did not dare lift my eyes to look at them too closely, in case I saw myself reflected in their features and lost my count.

The final pilgrim stopped at the threshold of the basilica and turned towards the interior, as if waiting for me to join them. He stood with perfect stillness. For a moment, I sensed a hint of curiosity, impatience even, in the tilt of his silhouetted head. Then a vague sound from outside, a cough or a footstep, distracted him and he slipped away.

Now that I was alone in the basilica, I reached into my jacket and removed the page of names. I had counted ninety-one souls in the basilica, but there were only eighty-seven names on the list. Neither Paddy nor Kieran's name were there, so that left a further two nameless figures among the faithful. Who were they and why had they left no contact details? Were they spies, infiltrators or intermediaries sent by Ruby? Perhaps they were complete strangers and had nothing to do with me or my search for Ruby. Secretive people inhabited every sphere of life, even a place like Station Island, and there were bound to be others like me, uncertain of their credentials as pilgrims, who might prefer to slip into the island's labyrinth anonymously. Either way, I would have to unmask them, or set some bait to lure them into the open.

Outside, the prior lined everyone up to perform the act of renunciation at St Brigid's station, which was a Maltese cross cut into the church's limestone wall. I had no other option but to join the queue. When it was my turn, I reached out and touched it. I said the prayer, renunciating the devil and all his evil ways. I wanted to feel something, but all I felt was the coldness of stone.

The evening drew on and the urge to share in the pilgrims' religious experience began to deepen its hold. I was growing tired of searching for the nameless pilgrims while the others prayed and walked about in companionable little groups. I felt obliged to mumble a few offerings, and started following the set paths, surreptitiously studying the movements of the pilgrims as they shuffled and kneeled on the stones. I tried to look as if I knew what I was doing, planting my bare feet on the wet grass and the sharp stones, joining the circles of pilgrims as they followed the furrows worn out by their ancestors.

All around me were Catholics from the border counties of Ulster. I could hear it in their accents as they prayed. I saw it in their dull-eyed presence, men and women who had driven on back roads all their lives, afraid of the police and the paramilitaries, afraid of the border itself, and of being ripped off or even bankrupted by the economic vagaries it imposed, afraid of strangers in parked cars and the mysterious clicks on their phones which suggested a constant listening presence.

I thought of my maternal grandfather leaving his small South Tyrone farm to walk these very same paths. A man who walked more miles than anyone I knew. A man preoccupied with his potato crop, the rosary and his turf fire, who came here every June in a bout of spiritual adventure after dusting his potato plants against the blight and secretly blessing with holy water their tender young leaves and flowers. He dressed in his Sunday best when he came here, and put on his finest hat. This was the island for him. A man who was used to walking all day, but finding himself in the same place, surrounded by the familiar folds of his fields. A man who would not have been upset by hunger or tiredness or the fierce monotony of prayer. A man who enjoyed the rituals so much that, after leaving the island, he would spontaneously volunteer to return for another round of fasting and prayer.

I smiled at the thought of summoning his ghost by walking and praying where he had walked and prayed. My heart lightened, but then I glanced at the other pilgrims, strangers all who might not accept me as one of their own, and I grew guarded again.

The evening drew on and the heaviness of not belonging eased as my bare feet felt their way along the stones. I curled my toes around the uneven edges and shuffled onwards in the procession of forgetting. It was like a form of sleepwalking. I followed the stations, letting so much time elapse at each cell before moving on so that my thoughts might not burden the little groups of people assembled there. I placed myself in a kind of quarantine, afraid of showing my face to the same pilgrims for too long, lest they strike up conversation or enquire about my mood. Just the thought of being caught with a stranger, who might have read about the IRA ambush, of having to stand there as they gazed into my eyes or offered a kind word of greeting made my blood run cold.

So I dipped in and out of the prayers, my mind settling on a few scattered lines, mouthing the words, hoping that I would share a little of the inner light that made their eyes shine. I tried to pray like them, with a regular rhythm, not stressing any individual words because their meaning was not important, only the rhythm was paramount. But it was no good. I felt like a puppet miming empty words, and I was unable to keep up with the pilgrims, who behaved as if praying was the most natural thing in the world.

I was alone on the island, and my heart burned. I could not pray like these people. Their faith was everywhere but nothing that could be felt or absorbed by an outsider like me. It was more like a light in which they thought and felt everything, a light through which they saw each other and the world. There was no such light in me when I prayed. I was permeated with darkness. I went through my thoughts and memories but it was impossible to say where the darkness came from. It did not belong to any defined place. It was immanent everywhere, in all that I had done and said. Was Ruby the traitor or was it me? What was I concealing from myself on this island? Why was I pretending to Pearson and to myself that I could not remember the secret pacts I had made with my informer? What if the plain truth was I did not forget at all, that I was the liar and traitor?

I looked into my heart and examined my conscience. I stopped prevaricating and I considered every thought, word and deed I had formed in relation to Ruby. I could only draw one conclusion, which was that I had sunk so low in a stinking stew of secrets that I had forgotten or overlooked the true extent of my guilt. But this island was not going to let me forget. It was riddled with traps, pits opening up deep below, places set aside for souls like mine and my informer's, places where the guilty could hide no longer.

Was this why I had been sent the postcard? Dragged here and made to clamber amid stones marked by a sin that I knew would never be wiped away. Several times, I stood before St Patrick's cross, stretched out my arms and prayed aloud. I asked for mercy and forgiveness, and wondered was anyone listening to me? What kind of fallen creature was I? What sort of detective had I become?

In childhood, I had been taught that there were two types of sin. Sins of omission and sins of commission, and that I should start by examining my conscience for the former, the things that I had neglected to do or overlooked. I knew that I had slipped in my work as a detective. I had not pursued leads and tip-offs as exhaustively as I should have. I had taken risks and spoken with a general lack of prudence, neglected to intervene in murder investigations that I might have helped, and kept my commanders in the dark concerning the dangers of my relationship with Ruby, and the lack of positive results. I had done my best to present him in a favourable light. And what about the time I had wasted, waiting for Ruby in anonymous hotels and car parks, knowing he would never show, and the days lost to hangovers and sick leave, not to mention all the duty work and meaningless paperwork I had avoided? Yes, I could have done a lot more. I had not used my detective's talents to the best of my abilities, and certainly not for the benefit of Belfast's citizens. Was this my failing, the source of the darkness? Or were there other sins that I should feel more guilty about?

I stopped that train of thought and walked to the jetty. I looked back to the pier on the shore and pretended that I was waiting for a boat. Secretly, I slipped the hip flask of vodka from my pocket and knocked back half of its contents.

After a while, rain began to fall, chipping the surface of the water, blurring my vision. The downpour strengthened, beating so heavily it seemed to churn the entire surface of the lough. At last, I had found what I had been hoping to experience on the island. A force of nature that altered the view, making everything seem temporary or otherworldly, a rainstorm that threatened to wash away everything in no time at all, and make my fears and hopes seem insignificant. I stared at the flickering light and the jolting movement on the lough, the rainwater running down the back of my neck and jarring my nerves with its coldness. My legs and bare feet were soaked in no time, and I grew disorientated and detached from my surroundings. In a moment of desperation, I began calling Ruby's name in the rain, softly at first, and then louder. I cupped my hands and shouted his name across the lough, but the surface tension of the water and the smothering darkness of the forest-lined shore closed quickly over my voice and its echo.

When I limped back to the stations, the pilgrims had donned waterproof jackets and pulled out umbrellas, their shapes floating over the stone beds, as light as bubbles, as though they too were losing their moorings. Still they clung on, following the rituals, chanting the same prayers, the familiar words that stretched back into my own past. The drumming sound of the rain and the water coursing down the sides of the paths and the rocks made the words fade and die away. However, the prayers continued inside me at the same pace, so that, when I stumbled into line behind them and their voices carried in the air, their prayers rose together in unison with the ones I could hear inside.

I groped in the rain, following the pilgrims in their circular procession. Several times, I slipped and reached out for a helping hand. An old man steered me by the elbow, as though I might trip at any moment and fall into the mud. The watchfulness of the pilgrims who were on their second day of fasting alarmed me, and their hunger, the way they prowled the paths with their prayers. They were the type of people I would normally look down upon, slaves to the rituals of the Church, constantly seeking an escape from the real world. Now I felt that I was the one to be pitied. A detective who lived in a one-dimensional world, aware of only one plane of existence, one surface. I felt shabby and insubstantial next to these determined people who belonged to a world of miracles and visions. The gauzy evening light of the island drew closer, the luminous shape of the basilica rising out of the drizzle. I felt unsure of myself, an impostor carrying a palpable darkness. I leaned into the throng of praying figures, following them through the stations, drawing a sense of comfort from being part of a crowd.

The downpour thickened, forcing everyone to bow their heads. I had never seen so many old and naked feet. Swollen ankles and cracked soles with bunions angled this way and that in the mud, reddened toes feeling for leverage on the stones, arthritic joints creaking all over the place. At one point, I glimpsed a pair of slender feminine ankles and bare knees moving and kneeling deftly amid the tableau of gnarled toes and callused heels. I craned my neck and saw, beneath an umbrella, a flow of long dark hair bouncing on the shoulders of a young woman as she rose, sleek and lithe, from one of the graves and clambered over the path. When I looked again, she had disappeared. In her place, I saw the prior, staring with his dark eyes on me. What was he? Some sort of frowning troll guarding the site? I could sense his eyes inspect me, their suspicion magnified by the hushed reverence of the praying pilgrims.

By the time the station had finished, the hunger and boredom were gnawing at me again, and I knocked back another mouthful of vodka, not caring who might be watching me this time. Somehow, the prayers were beginning to feel false again, an attempt to blot out the painful reality of life, a form of words to deceive the gullible and lonely. I lurched away from the flow of pilgrims and began searching the island for some form of distraction.

A yearning was growing inside me, a different form of hunger, for human contact and company, principally female company.

THIRTEEN

The woman was standing at the end of the prayer path with her bare feet submerged in the water that lapped on to the stone steps. Like me, she was staring at the distant shore and the reflection of the pine trees. She turned and smiled in my direction, and a shiver ran through me, a feeling that something bad was about to happen. At all costs, I must control my feelings. I turned to walk away but after a few steps, I stopped and returned to linger near her.

The setting sun broke through the rain clouds and shone on the water, and I watched, transfixed, as the space between her slender ankles filled with sparkling light. However, it was her eyes that drew me towards her. They were alight with something. They looked serene and gentle one moment, and then full of a pleasurable glow the next, a glow that seemed to spread to the ends of her straight, dark hair. She stepped out of the water, a woman in her graceful mid-thirties, well beyond the flat-footed awkwardness of her youth, a woman balanced and in control as she swept her long hair and body up the steps. She stopped and turned her back to me, revealing for a moment the very pale, slightly cracked skin of her heels.

I caught fire again. It wasn't just her figure and her bare feet. It was the island. It was the enclosed space, the repetitive prayer and the effects of the alcohol. It was the watchful presence of the priests, the light the pilgrims were immersed in and the darkness that lay ahead, the long night of fasting and praying, the peaks of suffering we would have to climb one by one. But I no longer had to climb any peaks. I had found my escape.

I took up position in the shade of a tree to watch her. I was conscious that I should not behave like a pest or some love-struck teenager. I took out my rosary beads and ran them through my fingers, all the while stealing glances at her figure. She stood out from the other pilgrims; her slender body and her enigmatic eyes made her different from everyone else. There was a composure and ease to the way she walked and stood, and in her posture, a wholeness of being that began in her toes and which suggested stillness, some sort of spiritual training that no one else on the island had undergone.

I had been watching her for barely a minute when Paddy came up behind me. As soon as I saw him, I walked away.

'You're spying on that woman,' he said.

'No, I'm not.'

'I don't believe you. Who is she? Did you come here to meet her?'

I put some distance between us, and he called out, 'It's OK. I can keep a secret.'

I turned to check had the woman overheard us. She was looking at me with an expression that suggested faint disappointment, as though she had secretly wanted a strange man to stand rooted to the spot and stare at her, transfixed in admiration.

Twilight fell and I found myself following her again, hanging back slightly among the others, watching her wind her way along the paths. A gust picked up, flailing the branches of the leafy trees overhanging the prayer sites. The pilgrims around her were mostly elderly women. They craned their necks to watch the darkening sky and check for rain before adjusting their swollen feet on the stones and returning to their methodical prayer. At one point, she passed me in her rounds, and I saw how intent she was in her praying, never rushing, never pausing. I knelt at one of the crosses and tried to concentrate on the rituals, the murmurs of the Hail Marys floating above the sounds of waves, the air filled with the pilgrims' devotion and something else, something maternal and protective.

When I looked up, she was kneeling low to kiss one of the stones. She turned and caught my gaze without registering my presence in any way. She looked away and kissed the stone two more times, slowly, as if in a love scene. Then she squatted back on her haunches and blessed herself. A few drops of rain dotted the stones with grey spots. The pilgrims stretched out their hands, anxiously looking skywards, feeling more rain.

A drizzle began to fall, fading the final light on the lough. One by one, the pilgrims retreated to the basilica. I wanted to follow them and strike up conversation with the dark-haired woman. The hunger for her company intensified in my heart. However, I didn't know how to approach her, and was afraid of interrupting her so absorbed did she seem in the rituals. What was the use of all these prayers, I thought with annoyance, if they hampered communication between one soul yearning for another?

I disappeared into the soft rain and found my way down to the shore. In the darkness, I knocked back several more mouthfuls of vodka to ease my discomfort. The alcohol burned a track down my throat and made my pulse quicken. By the time I returned, everyone had congregated in the canteen for cups of hot water. I squeezed into the overcrowded room where the warmth of the crackling fire, the silence and the relaxation from the constant praying felt like a form of bliss.

An elderly nun was bending over the large black pot that hung over the fire, ladling the hot water into mugs and various drinking receptacles. My feet were muddy, and my jacket heavy and dank with the lough shore drizzle. The alcohol glowed within me, and my clothes gave off a light mist in the heat of the room. I felt I belonged to a different world from these grey people sipping reverently from their cups. I was a wild animal who could disappear at will, even from itself. I enjoyed being enveloped in the steam of my clothes and the muddy smells of the lough, but my lack of inhibition also alarmed me, and I had to suppress a wolfish grin when I saw the woman again. Catching her innocent gaze, I suddenly knew why I had come here. All the guilt I had been carrying dissolved away. I felt free and anonymous, and the sense of power that the alcohol gave me among these devout human shadows felt exciting and glorious.

Paddy and his companion entered the room and hovered behind the woman. They looked hungry and uncomfortable, and were whispering to each other. I reminded myself that my enemies were close by, watching and plotting against me, and that I would have to be careful, even though I now felt brave enough to do or say whatever I wanted. The pair stared at me with icy eyes, and before I could approach the woman, Paddy sidled in between us.

'Is it taking effect yet?' he asked.

'Is what taking effect?' Had he seen me swig at the vodka? I was sure I had been hidden in the shadows.

'The praying and the fasting.'

'I don't think so.'

'You were missed for the final round of prayers. You didn't complete the station like everyone else.' He raised his watch and tapped it. 'I timed you. You were gone for a full ten minutes.'

'What's it to you?'

He shrugged. 'Nothing at all.'

We were due to start another station, and I had missed my

opportunity to strike up a conversation with the dark-haired woman. I would now have to wait an hour and fifteen minutes for the next break.

I joined the pilgrims walking up and down the basilica aisle, adjusting my pace so that I was always a dozen or so paces behind her, while the prior stood at the altar and guided us in our prayers. My eyes kept wandering to the lift of her perfectly arched heel, the fall of her tapered toes. I wasn't praying, I was just walking as carefully as I could, hurrying to find a comfortable position when I had to kneel, trying to empty my mind of everything and holding on to that emptiness with all my determination, no longer thinking of where I was going or how long the procession would take. Somehow, the woman's presence just ahead of me made the cold church seem more companionable, the darkness perfect and complete. It felt as though the night belonged to just the two of us.

I listened to the praying, the lapping of the waves echoing through the basilica, and the soft winds of a Donegal night. My feet welcomed the coldness of the stones. I felt the chill creep through me but tried not to think about it. I focused on thinking about nothing at all, only where to place my next step. I didn't have to worry about where I was going, or how I would avoid sleep and hunger.

At one point, I stopped and examined the soles of my feet. They were cut and bruised, but I didn't mind. My soles were soft compared to the thickly padded feet of these country people, but not as soft as the dark-haired woman's. Her feet were elegant and perfectly proportioned. Following her made me forget the real source of my pain. I was leaving behind my past and the bad dreams of the news bulletins for this otherworldly island and her graceful presence. The pools of candlelight and shadows, the presence of the prior on the altar and the scrape of her feet on the church tiles awoke in me the teenage feelings of dread and desire, the excitement and fear that came with crossing forbidden territory.

I looked up and saw the prior watching me again. I realised I had not taken my eyes off the woman for a while. I could see from his gaze that he had confirmed an initial scepticism about me. To be honest, he had every right to view me with misgivings. What was I really doing here? What did I want from all these prayers and rituals? The priest glanced at the woman and then back to me. He knew the thoughts and feelings that were coursing through me and their source. That much was obvious.

FOURTEEN

The woman paused to genuflect at the carpeted steps leading to the altar and then she padded towards me. The station had just ended and I had been lingering in the basilica, keeping my eye on her and hoping for a chance to strike up conversation while the other pilgrims flocked to the canteen.

'Are you waiting for someone?' she asked. Her voice was warm and without suspicion, her body swaying slightly.

'No, I'm here on my own.' I fell silent. Had I given away too much already?

'Is something on your mind?' she asked with a teasing smile. For the first time, I saw her face close-up. Her eyes were almost too near to me, brimming with a light that made my brain give up trying to formulate a safe answer. For several moments, I stared back at her emptily.

'Why do you ask?' I said.

'Men who come here on their own usually have something on their mind.'

'I like my own company, that's all. What about you, are you here on your own?'

'I've come to get away from everyone and pray. But that doesn't mean anything is on my mind.'

'Same here. I came here to get away from people.'

'People who are troubling you?'

'I didn't say that.'

'Sorry, I didn't mean to be nosy.'

I wanted to say how lovely and deep her eyes looked in the candlelight, but I made myself hold back.

'I saw you on the morning boat,' she said. 'I'm on my first day, too.' She offered me her hand, which I shook. A firm yet gentle grasp. 'I was worried when I saw you lean over the front of the boat. I thought you were going to throw yourself in.'

'The view was so beautiful,' I explained. 'Apart from enjoying the scenery, I'm not sure why I'm here, to tell you the truth. And I don't even know if I'm doing the stations right.'

'I can be your guide, if you like.'

'That would be great. I keep wishing someone would strike up conversation or something. Instead of just praying and dwelling on all this suffering.'

'But that's why we're here. To pray and dwell on suffering.'

The less sober part of me wanted to say, 'Let's dwell on each other instead.' Our conversation felt like a form of teasing banter, except for the way she kept earnestly looking up at the altar.

'But why should people seeking God put themselves through pain and hunger?' I asked.

'Haven't you noticed all the crucifixes on the prayer paths? In Roman times, the cross was a sign of torture. Jesus suffered on the cross and by coming here we offer up our own suffering, the fasting and the tiredness, so that we can connect to God.' A loose strand of hair fell across her nose and cheek and she swept it back. 'It helps us appreciate the meaning of our lives.'

'What if we know too much about suffering in our lives?'

She flashed me a look of mild irritation. 'You might think you know too much about suffering but unless you use it as a force to bring you closer to God, you'll never understand its true nature.'

'And what is that?'

'Suffering removes our disguises. No matter what excuses we make for ourselves or the lies we tell to protect our self-image, when we suffer it's almost impossible to deceive others. We can't help showing our true faces.' She spoke with the confidence of someone who knew the secret power of the island's rituals.

'What if I have more disguises than the other pilgrims, does that mean I have to suffer more?'

She nodded and we lapsed into silence. The coldness of the breeze blowing through the open doors died away, and a drowsiness seemed to spread into every nook and cranny of the building. I resisted the ghosts of tiredness and tried to assume the role of a pilgrim, a role that was in danger of evaporating completely. Was there another part I could play close to that of a pilgrim, without actually being a pilgrim, a part that would keep me as near to her as possible?

'So how exactly do I experience the power of suffering?' I asked.

'Keep praying and doing the stations. Follow all the instructions. Perhaps you will learn something tonight or tomorrow. You might think that these prayers are simple words for simple people, but what the pilgrims are experiencing in their pain is far more complex than any suffering you've endured before.'

Her face was open and trusting, but serious. Her eyes made me think that it might soon be time to draw a line under Ruby, to acknowledge what was not true and tell the secret truth. It was a question of finding the right moment. But I was careful of not putting my foot in it and revealing too much. After all, she might be a plant, sent by Special Branch to keep an eye on me. I gave her a watered-down version of what had happened to me, sticking as close as possible to the facts that had been reported in the newspapers.

'The IRA wiped us out,' I told her. 'I was the only one who

survived. Afterwards, I ran like a rabbit in the dark. I was in fear of my life and scared at how the ambush would look to my colleagues. You can't imagine the thoughts that have been running through my head since that night.'

As I spoke, Ruby began to feel less real, a ghost confined to bad dreams and the spy books that lay on my bunk. His passage through my life had never been recorded and so would remain unknown. How could I ever be held to account for something I could deny completely? And if Ruby were a phantom, wasn't he one of many, those anonymous men and women operating on both sides, trading secrets and committing crimes like smuggling, extortion and murder at improvised checkpoints in the night. They were the phantoms no one could describe, even though they lay lurking in everyone's heart.

The curiosity in her eyes faded and was replaced by something more vulnerable, a look of pity. The story of my miraculous survival was the hook that had caught her attention. Up until now, I had the impression she was half-ignoring my presence. She turned her eyes towards me. Eyes that glowed with a self-contained light. She was the type of woman I needed in my life, someone who had a sense of moral duty, but wore it lightly, someone whose grace drew the darkness out of others, made the shadows less harsh and the inner deformities less disabling.

I proceeded to tell her about my job as a detective, and how I had come to join the police force after growing up in a staunchly Republican part of South Tyrone. I recounted the incident that had turned me into an outsider and launched me on a personal crusade against the IRA. My parents had been God-fearing Catholics, and shunned the IRA as much as it was possible to do in the early 1970s. Unfortunately, their stand against violence marked our family apart from our neighbours, who remained loyal to the cause.

'One morning, the IRA held our family at gunpoint and

hijacked our car,' I told her. 'They used it to mount a bomb attack on a local police station. For several hours, they kept us hostage, wearing balaclavas and wielding their guns. Before they left, they handed me a bullet, telling me it was for my father if he rang the police and touted on them.'

I had held on to the bullet for ages, before giving it to my mother, who placed it in the kitchen cupboard, next to where she kept the money for the milkman. Eventually the police took it away for forensic examination. I showed her my right hand and told her how I was still able to feel the imprint of the bullet in my palm, and that it would flare up at the news of the latest IRA atrocity as though raw alcohol had been splashed on to an old wound.

We had been kneeling for such a long time that my knees were beginning to hurt. I shifted position. 'When the IRA tried to kill me at the ambush, I had to get away, find a place where I could think straight. Now my commanders think I betrayed my colleagues, and that I'm a traitor. I don't know what I can do to clear my name.'

'There are priests here. You can ask them for advice.'

'Advice about what?'

'About what happened to you. Why you survived the ambush and the others didn't.'

'How would they know if I don't understand it myself? Anyway, I don't like the priests I've met on this island. I find their presence oppressive.'

'The feeling of oppression might just be in your head.'

'Granted. But they're adding to it.'

'The priests here preach forgiveness and understanding.'

'Every word that comes out of their mouths is stifling and suffocating.'

'You should try talking to Father Liam Devine.'

'Why him?' I grew suspicious.

'He was here earlier, asking questions about you.'

But I had been told he would not be arriving until tomorrow. Had he arrived earlier than planned and if so, why? 'What sort of questions?'

'He wanted to know had anyone seen a pilgrim from Belfast. A pilgrim who was a police detective.'

He must have been told about me by the sender of the postcard, but who were they? Ruby or the IRA? My heart began to pound. Out of the darkness at the back of the church, I thought I saw the figure of Ruby striding towards me, looking as though he had been marching for months. He made no sign of slowing down, sweeping up the aisle, his bottomless grin about to engulf me. An informer to drag all the other informers into the mire. What had I done? What lies had I uttered? What was happening to me?

'Where's Father Devine now?' I asked.

'He's retired for the night to the priests' lodgings.'

'I have something to confess to him. Something terrible.'

She must have seen the guilty look in my face. She spoke kindly, but with a sharp sense of rectitude. She said people came to Station Island for different reasons, and she herself had listened to all sorts of secrets, some of which had made the hair stand on her neck, violent crimes that had left no traces, held no consequences for the culprits, or had never led to punishment or misfortune. Everything had gone on as before for these people. The crime had not been enough in itself to change their lives, but their conscience had, aggravating them over the years.

'A secret crime is more of a crime,' she said. 'A crime in which the culprit's hand is hidden happens over and over again until the mystery is solved.' She paused and stared at me. 'This is an island of questions. Whether out of tiredness, boredom or the routine of prayer, no one can escape the interrogation of the soul. Everyone ends up answering eventually.'

As she spoke, the memory of an anonymous voice returned to me, threatening and scornful on the phone. *'You're ours, Maguire,'* it had said. And then on another night, *'We'll see you in purgatory, Turncoat.'* I felt light-headed. I suddenly wanted to tell her the truth, the guilty secret that I was carrying. I started to tell her the real story of Ruby's identity and how I had come to recruit him, or he had come to recruit me, but she interrupted me with a warning look.

'We have to go back to the prayers now,' she said.

'OK.'

'You can talk to me after the next station, if you like.'

'Maybe I will.'

She rose and began walking away.

'Wait,' I said. 'I don't know your name. I'm Desmond, Desmond Maguire.'

'I'm Perpetua Byrne,' she replied, and lingered for a moment. 'It's strange you didn't ask me anything about me or my allegiances. Shouldn't you be wary about talking to a complete stranger about these things? Or can you use your detective powers to see right through me?'

I smiled at the earnest look on her face and told her it was strange how the cold and hunger could make a cynical detective feel as though he had known and trusted someone all his life.

Nevertheless, when she had left I searched for her name on the register list and found it, along with contact details in Coalisland, a predominantly Republican village in County Tyrone. I pondered this for a while and then pushed my anxious thoughts to one side.

When the prayers started up again, I slipped out of the basilica and made my way to the shore. I slithered across an embankment of rocks that were treacherously greasy with algae, loping and clambering until I was out of sight. Raindrops brushed my face, softly at first, but then harder as the downpour thickened and the darkness grew dense. I sipped from my hip flask and leaned into the night, feeling the waves soak my bare feet and trouser legs, and the rain drench my face. I was smiling with relief, even though I was perched dangerously over deep water. The basilica was full of light and seemed to grow larger in the falling rain, but I belonged to the night. I felt at peace. It was the darkness of the shore, the rain, the presence of the border on the other side of the lough. It was me. A shadow staring at an invisible shore. A liar to all those who thought they knew me.

FIFTEEN

'Any reports from the island, Alan?'

'Hello, Tom. Didn't expect you to call you so soon.'

'So soon?' The Special Branch commander sounded irritated. 'Is it inconvenient?'

Pearson leaned from his hotel bed and stared at the alarm clock. One o'clock, it read. They had arranged a meeting at Enniskillen Police Station for nine o'clock the next morning, and he thought Bates could have waited until then for the latest update.

'No, it's not inconvenient,' he said. He glanced around at the dimly lit, airless room and sighed inwardly. Wasn't this the time of the night that Special Branch kept for their most important interrogations? He had to force himself to remember that he wasn't the officer under investigation, the one who had been accused of being a traitor.

'My contacts tell me that so far Maguire hasn't put a foot wrong,' Pearson told Bates. 'He's said his prayers, gone to Mass, hasn't spoken to anyone who might be his informer or one of his associates.'

'What's he really doing down there?'

'Well, it's not a bad place to seek refuge for a few days. It would be very difficult to arrest someone on church property, especially on an island. He's probably praying like mad right now, searching for a way out of his dilemma.'

'Is he religious?'

'I understand he's a lapsed Catholic.' An alcoholic who's opted for hell on earth, Pearson wanted to add. He didn't know if Bates belonged to a church or had any faith. He doubted that the Special Branch commander had any room for mystery in his life, or would submit to not understanding everything under his unremitting stare.

Bates' voice sounded aggrieved. 'If Maguire is hiding from the truth then the worst thing that can happen to him is to fall into the hands of evangelising Catholics. I think the prior should be informed about our rogue detective. By allowing his priests and pilgrims to lull Maguire with prayers and sermons on the mercy of God, they're really doing him a disservice. What he needs is a sharp introduction to cold reality.' He gave a thin laugh. 'He needs to be cut off from the rest of his tribe and the love of God, and any hope of otherworldly forgiveness.'

It was not the first time that a religious community had assisted in the obstruction of justice. Bates' misgivings might be well founded, thought Pearson. Maguire should be stripped of any soothing illusions and forced to confront the painful truth. But inform the prior about what exactly?

'As long as he is on the island, I think this is a matter for Maguire and his conscience,' he told Bates. 'We must wait and see if he can face the truth by himself. He has to the end of the vigil, another day and night. Besides, contacting the prior would risk upsetting the authorities in the South and our Garda counterparts. Their officers are doing a good job keeping an eye on Maguire for the time being.'

'OK, Alan, you know the territory down there better than I do. If that's what you think is the best way to proceed, then so be it. In the meantime, we've decided to send our own operative to the island.'

'What sort of operative?'

'Someone who will intercede for Maguire and cut away any invisible safety ropes he may still be clinging to. Such as all the lies he has told you and your officers over the years.'

There was a confidence in Bates' voice that alerted Pearson. He was beginning to realise that the true reason for the call was for Bates to update him with the latest development, rather than the other way around.

'What lies?' he asked.

'Well, let's see,' said Bates. Pearson thought he could hear the sound of fingers flipping through the pages of a spiral notebook. 'My officers have been searching through what information there is in Maguire's files and records, and we've come up with a few conclusions about his informer. A lot of Ruby's material is not verifiable and therefore it's impossible to prove if it is the truth or not. Secondly, we've collated all the information he supplied and compared it to what we know of the IRA's command structure. We've come to the conclusion that no single person would have access to this range of material. So we have to ask ourselves is Ruby fooling Maguire, or is Maguire fooling us?'

Was this the truth about Maguire? Was he part of a larger deception that had now killed three of his colleagues? If so, who was writing the script and producing it?

'We've also dug up some discrepancies about Maguire's background,' said Bates.

'His background?'

'His application for the police force mentioned an experience that had galvanised his political opinion against the IRA. According to the record, he even brought it up during his interview.'

Pearson knew the story. He had heard Maguire tell it countless times in different hues, usually towards the end of the night in a pub. At times, it would tend towards the luridly dramatic, but, generally, the story fitted with the times and no one had ever thought of questioning it. When Maguire had been a teenager, the IRA had walked into his family home with masks and guns and hijacked the family car. His parents had been staunchly opposed to the IRA's campaign, refusing to donate money to the cause or support the IRA politically, and they had paid a price for their stand. According to Maguire, the family suffered years of intimidation, death threats and abuse shouted in the small hours of the night. The IRA had even handed Maguire a bullet and told him they would use it to kill his father if he ever spoke to the police. He had held on to it carefully in his hand, knowing it contained an important message. The hijacking had ended any chance of his family having a normal life, but then who did during the Troubles?

It was a story that always won Maguire a degree of sympathy, even compassion from Protestant colleagues who would have normally ignored or even mistrusted him. Maguire would shrug the incident off as character building, saying it had turned him into a streetwise kid with a deep hatred of the IRA.

'We haven't been able to find a single corroborating fact for the hijacking story,' said Bates. 'Maguire would have been fourteen in 1972, but there were no reports of a hijacking in Dungannon or a bomb attack using a car on a police station that matched his description. So we took the investigation further. We interviewed his father earlier today in Dungannon. He has no recollection of the hijacking ever taking place. So we have to assume it never occurred.'

It was the sole incident Maguire spoke of that related to his upbringing as a Catholic. Pearson did not know anything else. Maguire's life before joining the police force was a blank, a void. It shocked Pearson that the entire story might be a sham, and that in repeating the lie, Maguire had dug himself in even deeper. But how did that false story lead him to betray his colleagues? How did one lie lead to another?

'It's hardly a lead or evidence that Maguire is a traitor,' said Pearson. 'I'd call it a childish lie, something that he blurted out on the day of the interview and never thought would be followed up.'

'A lie like that doesn't happen on impulse. He's pretending to be something that he isn't. An IRA hater.'

'OK, the hijacking might be a fake, but Maguire has a proven record as a police officer. His commitment to combating terrorism cannot be doubted.'

'It is unacceptable to lie in order to join the police force. Maguire was on a crooked road from the start.'

'What if it was just an exaggeration? Perhaps he embellished a story that actually happened.'

'A police officer should never mix the truth with lies. It's a violation of the most basic rule of our profession. A lie added to a truth is always a lie.'

'But why deceive us all these years?' asked Pearson.

Bates did not reply. Pearson sat back in the hotel bed and stared at the faded wallpaper in front of him. He had the feeling that a storm was about to burst, and that he was powerless to prevent it. Everyone at the station had been wondering how they might have been working alongside a traitor for so long without suspecting a thing. He and his colleagues had racked their brains, going over all they knew about Maguire, the troubled Catholic detective whom they had subtly closed ranks against years ago, who had to be handled with tact because of his religion and his alcohol problem, but whose inner sufferings and personal life might have been those of someone living on the other side of the country. What was his personal life? And what about his allegiances? Had they been polluted by the trivial sectarian remarks, the squalid banter in the locker room? It would be ridiculous to suggest that it was part of a concerted campaign. And hadn't Maguire been partially to blame? A more resilient detective might have laughed off the banter but the very look of his grey face most mornings was enough to give anyone a chill. Even on the pub crawls, he had generally behaved like a wet blanket, giving off little signals that generated unease. Was it his shyness or pride that made Maguire such poor company, or was it something else much darker?

Bates gave a little cough. 'He's spooked you, Alan.'

'Why should I be spooked?'

'Because Maguire has crossed the boundary. He's no longer one of us, on the side of law and order. None of us can guess what he'll do next.'

With his false story of the hijacking, Maguire had managed to convince Pearson and his colleagues that he could be trusted, and that his hatred of the IRA was steadfast. If the Special Branch hypothesis was correct, then the story was part of a clever ploy and Maguire had been a committed traitor from the outset. Certainly, that made more sense than the idea that Maguire might have changed sides overnight and been converted by the IRA. But wasn't it no less true that Catholic officers had to prove their loyalty more than their Protestant counterparts? Perhaps the story was just a white lie told to help his prospects of joining a police force that paid a good salary and was generous with overtime. A dark little tale told to colour his bland Catholic upbringing. Had the young police recruit Maguire been a politically innocent young man or had he secretly harboured a spirit of betrayal, some vestige of IRA sympathy, or worse still, an undying belief in their political violence?

This was what he would have to piece together. Special Branch was right. No one could guess what Maguire was capable of or might do next. They would have to get to the detective as soon as he came off the island and confront him with the truth.

Or rather, confront him with his lies.

SIXTEEN

In the basilica, I could hear the old people breathing heavily. They had stopped praying and in the silence some had slipped briefly into sleep. They groaned and spoke as if they were arguing with someone, searching for the right words, but all that came out were meaningless mutters. It was a collective dream, I realised. A dream of tormented conversations with their demons. The effort produced hideous expressions on their faces. Their jaws shook and their teeth rattled, until their neighbours poked them and brought them back to reality with a start. And then the praying began again, voices rising and falling through the rosary.

It was after midnight and we were on the second station of the night. For almost an hour we had been kneeling in front of the altar or filing around the church, up and down the central aisle. Everywhere I looked, I saw bare feet. Our miserable squirming toes had become as redolent of our personalities as our facial features, which we hid with our tired heads bowed. Secretly, I was enjoying this newfound anonymity. Unlike my face, my feet had not been plastered over the newspapers, nor were they marked with the haunted expression of a failed detective. My feet were those of a survivor, faltering and then steadying themselves, sharing the suffering of other feet. For the first time in months, I no longer felt like obsessively checking my face in a mirror. Instead, I concentrated on my feet and the guidance of other feet.

111

The station passed like a dream. Sometimes I saw Perpetua ahead of me. Other times I was aware that she was behind me. The night grew heavy and the older pilgrims dragged themselves along with obvious effort, but I felt as though I were floating through the gloom of the basilica. Somehow, Perpetua gave the long hours of darkness shape and gravity. I reminded myself I would have to be patient and try not to think too much about her, but the more I tried to forget her, the more I longed for her company. I said the prayers in a semi-conscious state, hovering between desire and anticipation, and the hunger and tiredness no longer felt so agonising.

Was this what Perpetua had meant about the power of suffering? That the gnawing ache in my stomach, the soreness in my knees and the coldness in my feet, not to mention my yearning for her company, might be enough to keep me afloat above the pit of guilt and self-doubt. That the physical suffering might place a limit on mental suffering or at least distract me from my fears and make them more bearable. I saw her kneel at the altar, and when she turned, her eyes met mine. We exchanged a little smile. It felt like the first honest look I'd given anyone since the night of the ambush.

I slipped out of the basilica's south door and walked around the island in darkness. I knocked back a warming mouthful of vodka and stared across at the shore. In the trees around the car park, a set of headlights appeared. The vehicle was stationary and pointed towards Station Island. I stared at the lights and wondered who was keeping a lonely vigil on that other shore. Was it my Special Branch tail or another pair of eyes? The lights touched a raw nerve in me. I felt tired of being followed and hiding in the shadows. I had crossed borders on the land and borders on water, and now I could feel beneath my feet the edge of Northern Ireland, but still I could not escape my country's sinister reach.

A feeling of tension and frustration rose out of my tiredness. Had I acceded to another lie, another flight from reality by coming to Station Island, mouthing all these prayers to replace the stories I had told in Belfast? What was I still avoiding, kneeling and fasting on these stones, and clinging to my rosary beads as though I was about to take up holy orders? Darkness welled up inside me. I was a sinner and I had something to confess, and no amount of rosary reciting could purge me of my mistakes.

On the night of the farmhouse ambush, I had placed myself in the hands of fate, but death had not wanted me. It had a more painful path in store, the path of Lazarus into this wilderness. I would have to accept its challenge. When the pilgrimage was over, Special Branch and that other world would be awaiting my surrender. My eyes turned back to the shore and I searched for the headlights amid the trees but could not locate them. The watchers, my future interrogators, had switched them off while I had been deep in thought. I slipped back to the dormitory, replenished my hip flask from my collection of bottles, and returned to the basilica.

The church seemed more crowded now that night had set in, the shapes of the pilgrims more huddled and bowed. Was it the alcohol or lack of sleep that gave me the feeling that I was levitating, drifting without a sense of identity or any idea of who or what I was searching for? I pinched myself in order to stay awake, and began following Perpetua again. The rest of the pilgrims were walking up and down the aisles in a close group, the rosary spreading in an endless ripple from their mouths.

One man, however, was not kneeling or praying. He was standing several pews away from me, with a sour curl to his lips, his face long and grey, his eyes carrying the shadows of countless sleepless nights. The dampness of the night air had matted his sparse hair in a web across his forehead. His jacket was identical to mine, and we had the same build and height. Whenever I moved, so did he. Several times he looked in my direction and seemed on the brink of saying something. He must have arrived on one of the later boats and kept himself hidden among the crowd, because this was the first time I had seen him on the island.

Like me, he had positioned himself at the edge of the small group of pilgrims that had gathered themselves around Perpetua. He was turned at an awkward angle from them, and at one point I saw his jacket flap open and reveal a bottle of spirits tucked in an inside pocket. I stared at him carefully to make sure he was real and that I wasn't imagining him. I could tell that he had noticed me looking at him. However, he didn't acknowledge my curiosity in any way. Sometimes he gazed at Perpetua and sometimes at the stained glass windows, all the time mindlessly mumbling and grinning to himself. There was something submissive yet dangerous about him, his manner more introverted than the other pilgrims, like that of a wild animal creeping across the polished tiles of the basilica.

He seemed to be mimicking my movements, walking where I walked, lingering where I lingered. Was I being paranoid? I glanced at him again. He was kneeling and rubbing his eyes, clearly exhausted. How could I make that into a sign that something sinister was afoot? I turned away but kept watching him out of the corner of my eye.

With an ugly smile, he looked me up and down. There *was* something sinister about him. Now it was my turn to kneel and pray. I pretended not to notice him. I rubbed my eyes and glanced at him secretly. Why was he staring at me with such relentless interest? I felt unable to bear his scrutiny and slipped out of the church.

When I looked back, he was striding towards me, a

determined look on his face. When he was a dozen or so steps away, he stopped, as though he wanted to keep enough distance between us so that we could study each other in silence. Was this a part of the pilgrimage, I wondered, to thread your way through this flock of sinners and find a doppelganger to measure yourself against?

Our eyes met, and I shivered. I suspected he was a police detective like me, and was immediately suspicious he had been sent to hunt me down. I was about to walk away but hesitated. Somehow, it felt pointless to ignore him. He seemed frozen by a similar thought. If I had a grain of common sense, I would have turned away, but we were trapped on Station Island, where it was common practice for strangers to strike up conversations all the time. I stared at him, willing him to explain his presence here, growing impatient when he just stared back at me, the suspicions rising and sticking in my throat. I grew afraid of his eyes, which were boring right through me.

He closed the distance between us. 'The way you were looking at me,' he said, 'I thought you knew me.'

'I was mistaken,' I replied. 'Faces seem more familiar the longer I stay here.'

He nodded as if he understood. 'For a moment, I thought I recognised you, too. That's why I came out after you.'

'Perhaps you saw my picture in the papers.'

He looked away quickly, and said what I had been through was a dreadful business. As it happened, he was a detective, too. A sergeant Peter Marley, in the Garda Síochána, based in Monaghan town. One word led to another, and in no time at all, he was telling me his life story.

Normally, he wouldn't dare divulge the details to a stranger in this part of the country, he said. You can't be too careful when it comes to matters of personal security, but he was in desperate need of company and felt there was something about my face that was mysterious yet familiar. I looked him over. His body seemed to contort with the effort of holding in some precious secret, his eyes bulging with the strain, as though he was on the verge of a nervous breakdown.

He warned me that if I had even a seed of conscience left it would awaken on the island. He had tried to build a barrier of defences but when night fell, memories of the Troubles had suddenly crowded him and he was amazed to discover that he had forgotten nothing, every maimed or dead body had floated before him with painful clarity.

A few weeks previously, he explained, one of his informers had been tortured and killed by the IRA. He and his colleagues had been close to framing a gang for a series of bank robberies across Monaghan and Cavan, and he had pushed his informer, a young man who had just got married, to infiltrate local Republican circles. Marley had used bribery and all sorts of threats to force the informer until he was hopelessly out of his depth, gambling with his own life to feed Marley's desire for incriminating information. In a terrible error, he had included the informer's address in a file of evidence sent to the prosecutor, which was then passed on to the solicitor defending one of the IRA gang. By the time Marley realised what he had done, it was too late to warn the informer.

He wasn't sure whether the murder of his informer marked the beginning or the end of his failures as a police officer, or was part of something much larger and darker that involved the mistakes of other detectives. An anonymous phone call directed him to the dead body and what he discovered in an abandoned cowshed had sickened him to the core. When he went back to the station, he tried to cover up his error but the trail of evidence clearly led back to him. Rather than reprimand him, his commander granted him a fortnight's sick leave, and told him he would not have to write a report until he returned to duty.

'I've made the worst mistake a police officer can make,' he said. 'That's what my report will be about. The one I can never show my colleagues.'

I grew more suspicious of him. His predicament so closely mirrored mine that I was convinced it was a ruse to gain my sympathy. Special Branch was really pulling out all the stops sending me this tormented soul with a plausible back story.

He said he had fretted through the early stations of the night, made repeated visits to the edge of the lough, trying to make his escape by mind power alone. His doomed words pressed upon my own defences and struck to the heart of me. What disturbed him the most was the way his police commander and colleagues had overlooked his strange behaviour and feeble attempts to hide his mistake. He could only surmise that they were motivated by a sense of camaraderie and a desire to close ranks against external scrutiny. He had been sent to a counsellor who had warned him it was time to confront this dragging sense of betrayal before it resurfaced in nightmares or depression. As he leaned towards me, his jacket flapped open again, and I saw that the bottle of spirits was almost empty.

Where had his story come from? Was it a pack of lies told to gain my trust or had it taken shape from the depths of my consciousness and somehow formed on his lips?

His eyes hovered on mine. 'What about you? Perhaps you need someone to talk to?'

'I'm OK.'

He looked at me, unconvinced. 'What brought you here?'

'I came on the boat.'

'I'm asking about why you're on the pilgrimage.'

I shrugged. 'I wanted to see what purgatory looked like.'

He grimaced at our predicament. 'Here we are, a pair of detectives trapped in purgatory. We must have screwed up badly to end up here.'

I felt an inner subsidence, as though I was slipping down with him.

'At least we can hide awhile from our accusers,' he said. 'Down here we're just another pair of sinners. They can't touch us.'

'I'm not hiding from anyone.'

'Then why are you here?'

Just to disorientate him, I decided to tell him the truth. 'I came here seeking an intermediary with my informer.'

He said nothing and looked away. We listened to the lap of the water, the sound of feet shuffling around the basilica, the wall of prayers rising from the inside of the church. He glanced at me and seemed about to say something but then he changed his mind.

'I have to go back to my station,' I said.

'Wait, I have more questions to ask you. Who's your intermediary? Can you really trust them?'

'Now there's an interesting question. Who can I trust on an island like this?'

Again, I suspected that he was a plant, and that he had been lying to me. Now that I looked more closely, I could see the shrewd glimmer in his eyes, the self-discipline and cunning of an undercover operative. He had tried to appeal to a sense of kinship, the two of us trapped together in this underworld. It sickened me that he could lie so easily. I wanted to get away from this impostor, who had almost deceived me and was intent on dragging me down to hell.

'You can trust me,' he said, looking upset. 'Haven't I told you my story? I've spilled my guts to you. Given you everything.'

'How do I know you haven't been lying?'

But wasn't I a liar myself? A police officer no longer sure of his motives, who could no longer pride himself on being better than the criminals and gunmen he pursued. How much easier it had been to believe this in Belfast, but not here on Station Island.

'You could say anything to me and it still wouldn't make any difference,' I told him.

'What do you mean?' He stared at me resentfully.

I told him I couldn't remember everything. I was burdened by another pain, the fear that I might never be able to recall the truth, that I was empty in spirit and might never bear witness to the mistakes that had entangled my career. Most of all I was afraid of dying anonymously and being found like a traitor in a ditch with a black bin bag over my head.

'A detective who doesn't remember is a detective without a conscience,' he warned. A look of fear formed in his eyes. 'And without a conscience you're doomed to wander like a ghost, trapped between the living and the dead.'

I was beginning to realise that I could never return to my detective career in Belfast, the nights spent wandering in vague circles around murderers and liars, calling out in the back streets for solace.

'Who sent you here?' I asked. 'What did they tell you about me? What instructions did they give you?'

He looked afraid of me, and backed away. He said he was sorry for having tormented me with his life story. 'You don't have to tell me anything about yourself, or why you're here. Sometimes it's better to know nothing about your fellow pilgrims.' He added that he was grateful I had listened and helped him on his pilgrimage. He said I had eased the loneliness he felt inside, but that now he must return to the stations. He walked off, slipping through the west entrance of the basilica.

Immediately, I felt as though I had attained some sort of release and lightened the burden of my conscience. Perhaps he hadn't been a plant after all, and had been telling the truth. I followed him into the church, but could find no sign of him. I waited until I was completely alone and then I removed the list of names from my pocket and glanced through them. There was no sign of Peter Marley's name anywhere.

SEVENTEEN

I must have slipped into a dream. For a moment, I felt there was no longer anything solid or substantial about the island and its pilgrims, as though the night had been reduced to the restless chant of our voices, and we were drowning in a torrent of sins, our voices shaking in desperation. I fought for air with my heart beating rapidly, my troubles entangled with the troubles of everyone else, our voices merging as we recounted our misdemeanours in all their lurid detail, each story different and full of despair. To all the sins I had committed, I added my relationship with Ruby, the lie that lay at the heart of it, and my voice rose up with the other pilgrims, thundering towards heaven in a great release of truth telling.

The touch of a hand on my shoulder brought me back to reality. I was sitting hunched over a pew close to the altar. I straightened up stiffly, my mouth open, my senses taut. When I looked across, I saw Perpetua beside me.

'I must have been dreaming,' I told her.

'You fell asleep for a moment. I spoke to you but you didn't hear. So I tapped you on your shoulder.'

I listened to the voices of the other pilgrims, and heard only the familiar monotone of their prayers. I was on the other side of consciousness now. Had I imagined hearing their confessions? Certainly, I had forgotten all the shocking details, and their individual woes seemed incomprehensible to me now. I stared at their tired faces and shuffling figures. What was most strange was the fleeting pleasure I had felt hearing and understanding their misdemeanours and misfortunes, and knowing that my own sins had been bundled up along with theirs in some collective dream or confession.

'When I touched you, you were trembling,' said Perpetua. 'And your forehead was sweating.'

'It was a disturbing dream.'

'But it only lasted a second?'

'Yes.' I shivered and looked around me. 'What time is it now?'

She held up the face of her watch. It was just past three o'clock. She smiled gently and the warmth of her body reached out and embraced me. Still, I was cold. The dream had receded but I could feel it strongly. Was it some sort of signal that I should obey? A warning that there was no escape from my sins, the lies that I had attached, one on to another, in order to advance my career, and that I was going to have to admit to them all in the confessional? But wasn't that how religious people and lunatics thought? They saw a meaning in random images, a divine message hidden in dreams, plots that didn't really exist.

On seeing me shiver, a farmer from Monaghan walked over and offered me a spare jumper. Another pilgrim suggested I could borrow a woollen cap of his. Their straightforward kindness touched me, but also made me feel bad. Had they not worked out that I was an impostor, a man with blood on his hands? They must have fallen for my act, my fabrication of being a good pilgrim. Of course, if I had told them the unvarnished truth, they would have reasoned that my duplicity was providential, that my mistakes had led me to this island so that I might find salvation by suffering and loving God. Perhaps they knew I was a fraud and were flocking around me,

Perpetua included, in the knowledge that heaven would rejoice even more for a single repentant sinner than for all the just pilgrims who had no need to repent for anything.

When the station was finished, Perpetua turned to me with her tender face, her eyes shining with an all-absorbing determination. I would have taken her away at that moment to a quiet corner of the island and told her everything, but it was she who spoke first. She suggested we follow the pilgrims to the canteen and get some hot water.

Sitting a few pews behind us, Paddy and Kieran stirred like watchdogs from sleep. When we passed them, they rose and followed us with a sour look on their mouths.

The atmosphere in the canteen, where the volunteers and nuns were serving hot water, felt hospitable and warm. Their voices were happy and full of encouragement, congratulating everyone for having made it so far. We were nearly halfway through a long night of prayer and barefoot walking, and we needed as much good cheer as possible.

The alcohol was working its way through my system and my bladder ached. I excused myself from Perpetua's company, nodded at Paddy and Kieran, who seemed to be half-asleep on their feet, and walked back to the toilets in the dormitory. The clouds had cleared and some stars were twinkling in the vastness of the night sky. I felt a measure of contentment staring at them with a lough breeze fanning my face.

After using the toilet, I downed some more vodka. Its warming effect was deep and pleasurable. In the mirror above the little sink, I stared at my face, washing my hands slowly and grinning at my secret intoxication. I thought of the sober torment of the other pilgrims, and the indelible look of suffering on their faces. Thanks to the smuggled vodka, I had slipped free of the island's bonds and was inhabiting a different world entirely. I felt a strong urge to giggle. This was no longer purgatory, it was heaven. I thought of Perpetua's soft eyes and long, dark hair. What was more splendid than the prospect of abandoning sleep and staring into the eyes of an attractive woman intent on saving your soul? The warmth of the canteen and Perpetua's company lay waiting for me like a prize for the taking.

A shape followed me as I hurried back to the other pilgrims. I could not see if it was a man or a woman. The figure drew close behind, mumbling something at me. What were they, prayers or curses? Suddenly, I felt fearful for my safety. The shadow came rushing towards me and I steeled myself, prepared to deliver a blind kick or punch to ward off the troublesome individual. But the figure moved and blended with the night, and all I could see were shadows upon shadows, the shapes of what looked to be devils and evil spirits flying towards me. I slipped into a doorway for cover, and then I saw Marley, his face looming out of the darkness, drunken and leering.

'There you are, Detective Maguire,' he said. 'You're a rotten rat trying to hide on me.'

I stepped out of the doorway and made my way to the canteen, not wishing to speak to him. Even after hours of praying and walking, he was as light on his feet as the devil, his bare feet hammering on the flagged stones.

'We're all brother pilgrims here,' he said, stepping in front of me and blocking my path. 'No need to hide or keep anything secret.' He was more forward than before, and his voice had grown cruder.

I backed away, but he pitched forward, his bare feet splashing through a puddle. His coat flapped open and I saw that he was carrying a different bottle, half-filled with a clear liquid, the label ripped off. He peered at my face, his breath foul and laden with what smelled like poteen.

'I can see it now,' he said with a grin. 'A pile of dead bodies back in Belfast.'

I kept my face blank and sidestepped him. What sort of shadowy creature was he, following me around, copying my movements, needling me with comments like that?

'I wonder who's next in line.' He bounded after me. Knowing I had a secret to divulge seemed to have made him sprightlier.

'It's been nice meeting you, Sergeant Marley,' I said. 'But I have to get on with my stations.'

'Wait. Do you know how many people I've sent to their deaths?'

'I don't want to know your business.'

'That may be, but you and I will have to be careful from now on. They've got their eyes on us.'

'Who?'

'The priests and nuns. They've been watching us ever since we stepped foot on this island.'

We crossed a patch of grass and my feet sank in the mud.

'I've a rowing boat hidden along the shore,' he said, with a slur. 'If you want to escape, now's our chance. They won't realise we've slipped away until it's too late.'

Up to this point, I had not thought of leaving the island. The vigil had seemed to stretch eternally ahead, but now that I was almost through the night, I began to wonder what lay ahead of me in the morning, and the next evening, when I was due to meet Father Devine.

'I'm a pilgrim on this island,' I said, before making a final break for the canteen. 'My only aim is to finish my stations and see the dawn.'

He shouted after me. 'I don't know you, Maguire. I mean I don't know who you are, but I know what you're definitely not. You're not a pilgrim, and you're out of sorts praying on this island. Everyone knows that by now, including that woman you've been talking to. You're not yourself at all.'

Inside the canteen, the other pilgrims watched me, while

pretending to sip water and chat. I could sense they had been talking about me, nosey for any signs of spiritual weakness or laziness, alert to the signs of someone slipping from the path, remorselessly noting every missed prayer or hurried step. I felt sorry for them and their repetitive prayers, convincing themselves they were earning a spiritual reward in heaven.

Drunkenness was a more inviting form of surrender. Unlike prayer and meditation, it withheld nothing. It offered no reward in the future. Its happiness lay in the here and now, in the depths of the body, its effects slowly spreading like a magical wave, and now that I had the lovely Perpetua in my sights, my intoxication mixed with desire felt like an admission ticket to paradise. I had heard stories of courtship on Station Island, romances blossoming because two complete strangers could be more daring with each other during a long sleepless night.

'I'm glad I found you before the prayers started up again,' I said, nestling in beside her.

'What kept you? We've only a few minutes left.' She gave a puzzled glance at my distracted state. 'I've met your type on Station Island before,' she added. 'Keeping to yourself, wandering around the island like a ghost.'

'A ghost?'

'No matter how hard you pray you can't stop thinking about your work. You're not really here at all.'

I smiled. 'But I am making an effort. Sometimes I am here.'

'No, all the time you're somewhere else. Which is commendable in your line of work. I suppose. A good detective can't help becoming over-involved in their investigations.'

Darkness had turned the windows of the canteen into mirrors. I was forced to confront my reflection, which no one should ever have to do, half-drunk in the small hours of the morning.

'Look, there's two more ghosts,' she said. 'The tall man and his short friend. I think they're spying on you.'

'What makes you say that?'

'When you went off to the toilet, they came over and asked where you were going.'

I made a mental note not to turn my back on Paddy and Kieran.

'They said you might try to escape from the island before the vigil is over. They said you weren't to be trusted.'

The effects of the vodka began to drain away, and I no longer felt that the canteen was a form of paradise. It was the opposite. I was afloat on a deep and frightening sea. My hopes of a romance on the island began to fade, replaced by cold feet as the reality of my predicament took hold, the sinister shadows, the lost sleep, and the lost leads that would never bring me to the truth about my informer.

'You're doing it again,' she said.

'What?'

'Thinking about work.'

'Listen, Perpetua, do you think you can trust me?'

'I don't know.' Her cheeks coloured a little. 'Have you lied to me?'

I could not think of a suitable reply.

'That pair know nothing about me,' I said. 'But you're right. It's time I started concentrating on the vigil and its prayers. I don't want to spend the rest of my time here brooding on the past.'

EIGHTEEN

At four o'clock, no longer able to bear the pressure on my kneesand feet, I shuffled into a pew at the back of the basilica and stumbled against the kneeling board. I was more tired and drunk than I realised. I stared at my feet and did not recognise them. They were throbbing with pain, and my toes were red and swollen. I rubbed my hands across them, thinking that, from now on, discomfort would have to be my friend, one that would help me stay alert and cautious until dawn. So far, I had kept my dignity and managed to control my feelings for Perpetua, but only just.

The strength of my desire alarmed me, and I began to worry that she had been dispatched to test my defences. Every time I glanced at her solemn figure, I felt a nauseous wave of excitement in my stomach. What plots were afoot on the island, and what role did she have to play in them? I wouldn't have been the least surprised to discover she was a Special Branch agent and not Marley.

A cold wind slipped through the double doors and crept up my back and neck. My hands began to shake and so did my toes. It was not just the breeze; it was the alcohol leaving my body and the lack of food. There was no peace nor relief in this wretchedness, I told myself, and rose to my feet with difficulty. I nodded at the watching pilgrims, as if seeking their permission to leave, and made my way unsteadily out of the basilica and into the night.

In the darkness, my strength returned, and, ignoring the cramp and deadness in my legs, I hurried back to my room in the dormitory. Alcohol was another friend, one who offered more hospitality than suffering, and I needed a private moment with it. However, when I pushed the door handle of my cubicle, the door opened slightly and then jammed against something. Someone must have barricaded it. I pushed harder but the door resisted my efforts. For a moment, I didn't know what to do. The most reasonable thing would have been to shout out and demand entry. After all, the room had been allocated to me and there were no rules forbidding my return to its comforts. I waited and listened carefully.

At first, there wasn't a sound from inside, and then I heard the weight of someone's foot pressing on to a floorboard followed by the slide of a window sash opening. I had an intruder who was trying to escape through the window. If he or she hung from the ledge, the drop to the ground would only have been ten feet or so. I ran down the stairs and hurried outside. In the dim light, the path by the dormitory stretched emptily ahead, but one of the windows, mine presumably, lay wide open.

I heard the sound of feet pounding upon gravel and I took off, putting my head down, forcing myself to run as hard as I could. My bare feet were cut and bruised, but I didn't feel any pain. The day's fasting had filled me with a nervous energy, making me feel physically stronger than I had for years. I extended my stride, pumped my arms, and got close enough to see the figure of a man dart suddenly across a lawn and slip into the old church known as St Mary's.

By the time I hurried in, I was cramped and out of breath, but I had my intruder trapped. I heard an echo of shuffling feet and then silence. I paced up the candle-lit aisle and saw what I was looking for. In the shadows, a dark figure lay prostrate before the altar. A sound like a growl or a groan came from it and, feeling more fearless than I should have, I strode up to the altar and grabbed the figure by the neck collar. The grey face of Marley turned round and stared at me with a look of surprise. There was blood on his nose and lips, and he wiped the back of his hand across his mouth.

'What were you doing in my room?' I demanded.

His eyes blinked at me. In a weak voice, he explained that he had been standing before the altar, saying some prayers, when someone had rushed up behind and struck him over the head.

I tightened my grip on his collar and hauled him to his feet.

'Are you going to attack me, too?' he complained. 'Nothing like hitting a man when he's down.' He grew unsteady, and sank back down to his haunches. A spatter of blood fell from his nose to the altar tiles.

I released my hold. 'No one's going to hit anyone,' I said. 'Not on this island.'

'Tell that to the bastard who attacked me.'

I wasn't sure whether or not to believe him. Had he been trying to hide in the church and stumbled on the step before the altar? 'Did you see the attacker's face?'

'Like I said, he struck me from behind. All I heard was his voice.'

'What did he say?'

'He cursed me and called me a turncoat.'

I almost laughed. There was a certain style to his lying, I had to admit, the way he avoided the truth by provoking my guilty conscience. 'Why did he call you a turncoat?'

Marley's eyes bulged. 'Because he must have thought I was you. You and your stupid story about the ambush.' His face was sweating and his hands shook. 'I'm sick of hearing the other pilgrims talking about it and I'm sick of seeing the newspaper clippings passed around and everyone staring at your picture, wondering what sort of detective you are.' He jabbed a finger at me. 'And I'm sick of the way you keep yourself aloof from everyone, pacing and muttering to yourself. I'm sick of the way your eyes cloud up with guilt every time someone tries to strike up conversation. What you need is a bloody good confession.'

'Now wait a minute. No one knows what I've been through. The pressure I'm under. The demands of my job as a detective.'

'I'm not talking about your job. I'm talking about what's inside you. The demons you've brought to this island.'

My fingers clenched and I reached for his collars again. He backed away, his face grey.

'You're carrying some sort of secret, Maguire. You've done something or know something dangerous, and the worst of it is you don't seem to know what it is yourself.'

He was doing a good job at tracking and interpreting my behaviour on the island, and a lot of what he said, in his rough way, was right on the mark. 'How perceptive of you.' I tried to take any threat or hostility out of my voice. 'But honestly, what were you doing in my room?'

'I don't know what you're talking about.' He challenged me with a strange grin.

'Then tell me, where did your mysterious attacker go? I haven't seen anyone leave the church. He must be hiding in here somewhere.'

For a second, Marley looked at me as though he had no intention of answering. Then his eyes gleamed. 'I think I heard him run behind the altar. He must have gone through a secret door. Why don't you go look?'

I was convinced he was pulling my leg, and he must have seen the disbelief on my face because his grin disappeared. 'I'm sure that's where he went. Or at least as sure as I can be. I must have been unconscious for a few moments.' His eyes glanced at the doors behind me. The look on his face reminded me of a criminal desperate to slip away from the crime scene.

'I'm telling you the truth.' Again that strange grin on his face. 'The man you're looking for escaped behind the altar. I even heard a door click shut.' He wiped his mouth again, glancing at the flecks of blood on the back of his hand, and then back to me. We stared at each other for several seconds, and then Marley lowered his head. 'Like I said, Maguire, I'm not the person you're looking for.' He turned on his heel and walked out of the church.

I went behind the altar and began searching for a secret door. To my surprise, I found a sliver of light along the bottom of a red drape hanging next to the tabernacle. I pulled back the curtain and touched the wooden wall behind. It turned out to be a secret door that immediately opened. I poked my head through and saw a corridor with dank walls lit by candles and painted a frigid blue, an arched roof and curving walls stretching before me. It was some sort of secret tunnel. Perhaps the priests used it as a quick passage and shelter from one church to another. I stepped through, suspicious, and then hesitated, alert to any sound or movement. A chill air pricked the hairs on the back of my neck.

Was I trespassing in sanctified space? Apart from the private accommodation of the prior and the staff, there were no prohibited areas on the island. There was a holy water font behind the door, and in order to prove to myself that I was a pilgrim with a pure heart, I blessed myself with the water and pressed onwards.

Along the left-hand side of the tunnel were several doors, and from one of them, the figure of an old nun bobbed out, startling me. She paused as if waiting for me to follow her, and then hurried down the tunnel. I called out to her to wait, but she appeared not only deaf but blind, reaching out with her hands and feeling her away along the corridor walls. I followed her with caution, wary that a shadow might pounce upon me at any moment. I called out to her again, but she continued at the same distracted pace, always on the verge of disappearing round the tunnel corner, her shape as small and light as a bird ready to take flight.

I'd never trailed a nun before, and my pursuit in that winding corridor had an odd pace and rhythm. There was something dreamlike about the way her figure kept gliding out of sight, and the lack of sound apart from my breathing and the rasping of her fingers on the walls, which seemed to curve inexorably towards some dark centre of the island.

The light steadily dimmed and soon I was feeling with my hands, too, the plaster turning colder and damper. I had lost sight of the nun completely. It hadn't helped that she was small and dressed in black. Even though the darkness deepened and my steps shortened, I pushed on and all the guilt from the past week began to melt from my chest. I no longer felt burdened. I was invigorated and fearless, ready for anything. I was ready to follow the nun into complete darkness, to march my way through the labyrinth, into the heart of the island and back into the world again.

The red glow of a cigarette hung before me and was quickly extinguished. My hands groped about, thrashing for something solid. The corridor had ended abruptly and I was facing a wall in the darkness. I held my breath and waited for a figure to materialise. I still had a vague hope that Ruby might be hiding in the centre of the island, waiting for me to find him. I coughed and heard its echo. Hearing the scuttling of a rat, I stepped backwards and fell into some sort of trench. I scrambled to my feet and felt my way round a cave-like space. I whispered the name Ruby, and there was an answer in the dark, a rustle, as though a creature had sidled out of its hiding place. I stood on something soft that recoiled but didn't offer any sound of protest. The darkness shuddered and glinted and I had the impression of being watched by a pair of twitching eyes.

'Ruby,' I said and thought I heard an intake of breath.

My eyes strengthened in the gloom. There was no one else in the trench, no informer hiding in the darkness, just shadows shivering at my feet. I listened carefully. Some sort of underground species was moving around me, communicating in a language I could barely hear. My mind sharpened upon an image that squeezed the breath from my lungs. I saw a colony of spiders that had grown huge in the darkness, trembling with a hundred furry legs and a hundred furry mouths that fastened greedily on to each other in a heavy, palpating mass.

I was back in the alleyways of Belfast, in the turmoil of countless secrets and informers' mouths reeking of alcohol and repeating words that didn't make any sense. I thought I heard the liquid lips of Ruby, the rasp of his throat, uncomfortably close and whispering my name, but the sounds were too soft and light to be human. It was the noise of the spiders eating each other and jostling for position, magnified by the echo of the trench. There was no labyrinth hiding my informer on the island, just a tangled mess of secrets floating in the darkness.

I tried taking a few steps. A thin line of light appeared and then vanished. I got my bearings and discovered a door handle at my fingers. I wrenched it open and found a set of steps leading upwards into the night. I ran up them and came out into a little moonlit courtyard that led on to the shore of the lough. On the wall opposite, hung a statue of the crucifixion. The face of Jesus, bloodied and impaled with thorns, glared at me with fierce suffering eyes, his emaciated body leaning out of the wall as though about to topple over me.

NINETEEN

Shortly before five o'clock, we began our final station of the night. I no longer walked as quickly or spoke the prayers as hurriedly. I was walking towards a new destination, and wanted to make sure that I planted each step firmly along the path. My slowness was not a symptom of tiredness, but of relief. I was staggering towards the dim light I could see softening the faces of the pilgrims, the light descending upon their figures from some invisible source above.

In a long line, we turned the corners inside the basilica, our bare feet falling softly. The mumbling sound of our voices and the murmur of the lough echoing through the opened doors soothed my anxious thoughts. Beyond these sounds, the silence of the night descended upon the island and eased my sore heart. If I stayed with these people, I would be safe. If I could not find Ruby, I could at least find protection here. The light that surrounded the pilgrims was what I had been seeking, a light that was not human, but nor was it divine. Something primitive and eternal yet also fleeting, like the mist that floats over trees and hides the darkness of the forest. These were my people and I was on my way to becoming one of them, a pilgrim.

I rested my eyelids and kept going like a sleepwalker, immersed among men and women who were carrying the dream of their faith. But I had no faith. I only wanted safety, and the thought tugged at my sense of comfort. Why could I not share their dream? Why was I so full of darkness? I opened my eyes fully and stared all around. How could these people, their figures moving and blending with each other, shadows upon shadows, have such earnest beliefs and I have none?

Perpetua appeared beside me. She must have walked around the church and lapped me during the rounds of praying. Her step was lighter and firmer than mine. She was pushing herself on towards the inescapable dawn, while I hung back, shuffling and crouching in the shadows like prey hiding from its hunter. I glanced across at her and she met my gaze. I stared at her eyes, which seemed so soft in the moonlight, but also strong and full of emotion.

She narrowed her eyes and frowned. She looked away and walked a little quicker until her figure disappeared again in the procession.

What had she been communicating? Some sort of warning that I should keep to the path and the prayers? I glanced around me but could see no sign of Paddy and Kieran, or Marley either.

Before the station finished, I slipped back to the dormitory and surveyed my room. Someone had ripped the blankets from the bed, and emptied the contents of my suitcase on to the floor. Mercifully, the bottles of vodka were still there and intact, and I was able to replenish my hip flask. The intruder had been searching for something. The question was for what? And had they found it?

I looked around again but could find nothing missing. I knocked back enough vodka to ease my worries and keep my romantic feelings for Perpetua on the boil. Then I returned to the basilica and joined the procession. I whispered the prayers, keeping in step with the pilgrims, anything to kill time until the next break, when I would have a chance to approach Perpetua again without arousing suspicion. I caught fleeting glimpses of her figure ahead but didn't join her, although I would have loved to. I didn't want to be a nuisance or make her feel uncomfortable.

My legs grew tired and I sat down in one of the pews in front of the altar. I must have nodded off because, when I opened my eyes, the basilica was empty, the aisles swimming in shadows.

I made my way to the canteen where everyone was chatting and turning red-faced in the heat of the fire, but there was no sign of Perpetua. I sipped from a cup of hot water flavoured with salt and pepper. The tingling of sleep evaporated, and the detective in me awoke. More people drifted into the canteen, but still there was no sign of Perpetua.

I looked around the overstuffed room at the specimens of humanity my destiny was now yoked to, their faces grimmer and more exhausted-looking in the harsh electric light, old men and women who had used up all their energy in waiting for the dawn, their faces pale and creased like those of drunks who stay in bars long after everyone else has gone. I listened to the crackling of the fire and the bubbling of the pot, the soft pad of more bare feet trailing gravel and mud into the canteen, a few wheezes and coughs as the faces bunched together. I watched the floor fill with the weary life of their feet, wriggling toes, callused soles, swollen ankles, like larvae promising larger, uglier things when daylight returned.

No one could doubt we were on the other side now, lost souls dragging ourselves through purgatory, a silent flock that in the darkest hour seemed to have increased to an uncountable number.

I looked up and saw the face of Marley, motionless, watching me intently, his eyes like two knots in a plank of wood. He glanced at the door. Perpetua appeared and my heart lightened. A path seemed to open up before her as though she were life itself returning to chase away the grey squirming creatures of death, her feet so slender and elegant amid the clumsy, hoof-like feet of the other pilgrims. I wanted to gaze at her without distraction, but Marley was nearby and I did not want to excite his curiosity.

She handed me a cup of hot water and I thanked her. The pilgrims nearby heard the excess of emotion in my voice and turned to stare at us.

'The final station is starting now,' she said.

'I'm tired. I'd rather stay here and talk to you.'

'Come. If you think you can't pray anymore, I'll help you.' There was a hunger in her voice. 'I'll say your prayers and then you can tell me your story.'

'That's not necessary. I can do my own praying.' Her offer felt unusually familiar and intimate. Who was she? Another spy? She rose with the others and I stole a glance at her figure, her slender waist and her long legs. I was mad to be thinking these thoughts, sitting here among the devout, staring at her firm thighs, imagining a wilder version of her in bed. It made me weak and disorientated when I needed to be on my guard. I dragged myself to my feet and joined her in the procession.

As we entered the basilica, she pressed her body close to mine. All around the mumbling of prayers began again and intensified. I felt a bolt of lightning pass through me, her softness leaning into me, a softness that I needed and invited and wanted to embrace. Was her devotion to the rituals and her interest in my soul a disguise or was it the truth? Whatever the answer, I was too weak to withstand her charms. Her scent opened in the air and I breathed it deeply.

'Tell me something about you,' I asked, during a gap in the praying.

However, she was more interested in steering the conversation back to religion. We sat down on a pew and she asked had I discovered anything new about suffering and the path of the pilgrim?

I said no, I was still ignorant and searching.

'Our relationship with suffering has to develop through the senses,' she said. 'It has to be a total experience. Hence the cold, hunger and pain. And the more you suffer, the stronger the force propelling you to God. Do you understand?'

She seemed buoyant and full of energy, unlike the others, who were so drab and subdued. There was an intense softness about her lips as she spoke. The more I looked at them, the more the night felt gentler. The backdrop of limestone and glinting crucifixes lost their sharp edges, and even the stiff faces of the pilgrims still scrupulously praying seemed to grow mellow. Her pretty face and long hair, the slimness of her body and the strength of her gaze had hooked me completely.

The wash of the waves rose through the opened doors, and I grew restless. There were questions I wanted to ask her. Wasn't there a gentler way of engaging the senses than starving oneself and walking barefoot all night? Might not love as well as suffering bring us closer to God, or at least closer to each other? If two people could open the channels between them and God through the tender emotions of the heart wasn't that the same goal the pilgrims were searching for through harsh discipline and renunciation?

I felt an overpowering urge to take her hands and drag her away to a private corner of the island. Instead, I reached out to stroke her face, but she immediately turned towards the altar.

'You're so beautiful,' I whispered.

A primness took hold in the corners of her mouth. I stared at her ungiving lips and fell back to earth. She moved a little further away on the pew. Her buoyancy, the energy around her, had been that of an evangelist trying to convert an unbeliever.

'Sorry, I forgot myself,' I said.

'Are you mad?' she whispered.

'It just feels so good to be at your side.' In a burst of desperation, I mumbled that I was falling in love with her.

She shot me a glance. 'What did you say?'

I repeated the words, a little louder.

'But you know nothing about me.'

'I don't need to know anything.'

'You're wrong.'

'I just want to hold your hand, Perpetua. Please don't say anything more.'

But we were strangers, our lives completely different from each other's. Only the act of praying had brought us together. We knew each other in the darkness of Station Island but nowhere else.

'You sound drunk.'

'Yes, you're right. Drunk on you.'

Her body contracted away from mine. How foolish I had been to imagine that I could hold her against the forces gaining on me; Special Branch, the ghosts of my murdered colleagues, and Marley.

When she turned to me, I half-expected a stern lecture on my ill-judged advance but there was no hint of criticism in her voice when she spoke. 'You're lonely and frightened, and that's why you can't find the path.' Her voice was graceful and gentle. 'Keep trying with the prayers, and when you think you're ready, go and make a good confession. Father Devine is expecting you.'

She rose and left me. It was almost dawn. My only purpose now was to stay awake and see in the new day. I kept repeating the prayers, but they didn't matter any more.

I was a blind worm lost in darkness and searching for the light.

TWENTY

The sound of Pearson's knocking, discreet but urgent, echoed along the corridor.

'Tom?' He spoke the name clearly and loudly, but there was no answer from behind the heavy oak doors.

Pearson had slept badly in the hotel and was now deeply sorry he had agreed to the Special Branch request to follow Maguire into border country. Why wasn't Bates using local staff, officers who were already on the ground? He assumed that the commander wanted to keep a tight lid on the operation, and that could mean only one thing. Politics were involved, which suggested to Pearson there would be repercussions for the careers of those caught up in the investigation, serious repercussions.

And now this meeting in the top-floor of Enniskillen Police Station. He had been stationed here during his first posting in the RUC, and driving through the steel reinforced gates had awoken in his stomach the sour tension of those years. The place had looked deserted and rain was shrouding the watchtower, the way it always had. He got out and glanced at the frogspawn grey of the bulletproof windows, nodding at whoever was watching him. The only sign of life was the echo of his footsteps rattling back from the empty walls of steel.

Pearson waited at the oak doors and knocked more heavily. He shouted, 'Tom,' and this time, a voice barked, 'Come in'.

His stomach flinched at the memory of his old boss rollicking him across the same threshold all those years ago.

The doors swung open with a slight push. At the far end of the room, Bates was on the phone, leaning forward in a thickly upholstered chair. He looked up and waved Pearson in. He had taken over the office for the meeting, and looked at home. Typical that, always a bit of swank about the Special Branch commander.

In spite of the plush surroundings, there was a hollow look to Bates' face and Pearson's eyes widened a little. Serious repercussions, indeed. He walked towards him and almost tripped over the deep pile of the carpet. The Special Branch commander finished his conversation and replaced the phone on the receiver without taking his eyes off Pearson, who hesitated and then advanced again, closer to the desk that was as wide as a snooker table. Everything about Bates' narrow face and angular body suggested tension and alertness, as though the chair he was sitting in had sprouted nails.

His voice, however, sounded friendly and normal. 'Well, Alan. Sleep OK?'

'Not too bad, Tom.'

'Any more updates on our pilgrim detective?'

'Only that Maguire is being slowly tortured in purgatory. The Gardaí are keeping a close eye on him until he comes out the other side.' He forced a smile. 'They say that, if he gave as much attention to hunting his informer as he does to chatting up women, he would have him found in no time at all.'

Bates gave a little nod. 'I hope we're not in error by allowing him to stay there and avoid arrest.'

'Maguire has backed himself into a corner. We have the upper hand. He may as well have locked himself...'

'Look, Alan, we can't have him hiding on Lough Derg like a rat under a rock, waiting for him to emerge with the truth. What does he want? The scandal of a public arrest in front of all those priests and nuns? I want you to use whatever influence you still have over him. As far as I understand, he can leave the island anytime he wants.'

'I've told you already. I have no influence over him and I don't know what he wants.' Pearson gave up forcing a pleasant smile. His mouth frowned.

'What's on your mind, Alan? I can see something is troubling you.'

'I'd like to be removed from the operation, Tom.'

'Removed?'

'Yes. I want to get back to running the station. My team has a lot of investigations that are nearing a critical stage.' He tried to keep his voice calm and earnest.

'The hunt for Maguire and his informer is the most crucial operation we have right now. The chief wants this entire mess cleared up as soon as possible. He wants answers, Alan, and I'm under pressure.' Bates' voice was equally deadpan and sincere.

'I understand the seriousness of the operation, but I think there are others better suited to the role.'

Bates kept his stare trained on Pearson. 'You're still keeping something from me. I can see it in your face.'

Pearson said nothing and returned the inspector's stare. There must be a dark thought in there somewhere about my role in all this, he thought, but out of gentlemanly respect, he is hiding it from me.

'As you know,' said Bates, running the palm of his hands over his notes, 'I've been examining the operational details of the raid on the farmhouse.' He paused for a moment, and lowered his voice. 'I've also had a look at the role you may or may not have played in this debacle.'

An ache took hold in Pearson's stomach. 'What are you implying? I followed all the procedures and checks.'

'I'm implying nothing, at this moment in time. However,

ANTHONY J QUINN

if you want to clarify the record of events leading up to the ambush this would be an excellent opportunity to do so.'

Pearson heard the note of contempt thicken in Bates' voice. He realised that the Special Branch officer had been merely concealing his hand during their earlier conversations. Hence this grisly puppetry, the two of them gaunt-faced, going through the motions with each other, circling the dangerous zone of suspicion that had opened up between them.

'I don't need to clarify anything.'

'When did Maguire first mention to you the plan to raid the farmhouse?' Bates' question came out cold and clear, as though it had been recorded on a tape.

'Saturday evening. March 22, about 4 pm. I was at home.'

'The raid was organised to take place the next night, but at the last minute you postponed it until the following Tuesday.'

'That is correct.'

'A little unusual wasn't it?'

'To postpone an operation at the last minute? Not at all. Have you forgotten how busy we are at Crumlin Road? We're overworked doing our best to follow up every tip-off and lead. Operations are cancelled or delayed all the time. Check the paperwork, take down the file for any week you want. There'll be at least several operations aborted. So don't try to trip me up with your questions and insinuations.'

'But how many postponed operations end in bloodshed? That's what's troubling me.'

'What are you suggesting?'

'On the Sunday evening, Special Branch Detective Ian Robinson rang in to say he was sick and couldn't make it into the station. He was due to accompany Maguire that night.'

'I wasn't on duty. I didn't know that until Monday morning.'

Bates nodded and made some notes. 'Naturally, I respect your last-minute decision to abort the raid. All I want to know is why you made the call. What information did you have at your disposal? I want you to share it with me so I can understand your rationale.'

'I've got nothing to hide and nothing to add. I suggest you abandon this line of inquiry.'

'Think of our officers who were riddled with bullets. Don't you want to get to the bottom of this and nail the bastards responsible?'

'All I can remember is that I had a conversation with Maguire on the phone. It was sometime on Sunday evening. By the end of the call the decision was made.'

'What did Maguire say to you? Was it his proposal?'

'Yes. It was his proposal.'

'On what grounds?'

'He said he needed time to check that the tip-off was worth pursuing. He made an appeal to me. He was concerned that Ruby might be giving him useless information. What else could I do but concede to his concerns?'

'Did you make a record of the conversation?'

'No.'

The Special Branch commander paused as if weighing up the value of Pearson's testimony. 'And neither did Maguire,' he said. 'You can see the concerns I have with the chain of events? Robinson was investigating Maguire and his operations at your station. It would have been convenient for all concerned to have him silenced.'

This was Bates' way. He had the facts and the growing misgivings. Against such relentless probing, there was little protection, least of all for an inspector who had allowed one of his detectives to run amid shadows and lies, a detective who was now in danger of disappearing right off the reservation. He knew that this would be the first of several interrogations he would have to withstand.

'You've read all the files,' said Pearson. 'You've read my notes and Maguire's. I also suspect you've been checking my correspondence and monitoring my calls. There's nothing else I can tell you that you don't already know. Most of all, you should know by now that I have no way of influencing Maguire. For months, my officers and I have been stifled by Special Branch's constant snooping and prying. If Maguire's informer does exist, I would advise Maguire not to give up his identity to Special Branch. It would put both their lives in danger.'

'That's very irresponsible of you, Alan. I'll pretend I didn't hear your accusations and paranoid exaggeration. If Maguire can be persuaded to bring his phantom informer forward, you can be sure no one would jeopardise his life. We're all deeply curious to meet this Ruby character. Both he and Maguire will be guaranteed their safety.'

The Special Branch commander's tone softened. He expressed his regret for the intrusion in the day-to-day investigations at Crumlin Road station, and any annoyance this may have caused Pearson and his team. He hoped that it would soon end, but in the meantime, he still needed Pearson to keep applying pressure to Maguire. 'What I need are your impressions about him, his current state of mind, and what he might do next. That's why I need you down here on his tail. By all accounts, you were the one closest to him. Everything you tell me will be treated with the utmost care and consideration.'

Pearson said he was grateful for the reassurance. He said he would write up a report summarising his impressions and conjectures about Maguire and his informer, and explain the events leading up to the ambush, also the rationale for his own role in managing Maguire. It had seemed that the wisest course of action had been to allow Maguire to get on with it, and trust his judgement. But in hindsight, it had been naive of him. The practice of allowing detectives to run their informers with little oversight had been encouraged throughout the force, but it was time now for more careful scrutiny. 'To answer your primary concern, I don't believe I can shed any further light on Maguire or his state of mind, nor do I expect to be able to do so. All I know is that he has not told me the truth.'

Bates thanked Pearson for his cooperation, but made no comment on what Pearson had just said. He told him that he would be in contact soon.

TWENTY-ONE

I felt the dawn before I saw it. At six o'clock, we murmured the last prayers of the night and the air grew quiet, so still that a mist formed around us as we waited at the doors of the basilica for the darkness to peel away. A silvery plume rose in the east, and the mist thickened so much that I could feel it nuzzle against my cold cheeks. The figures of the other pilgrims melted in and out of the murk. Slowly, the plume stretched across the horizon, dispelling the darkness. Not more mist, but the breaking of day.

The light increased and so did the mist. Our first night of seemingly interminable limbo was ending, and my fellow pilgrims became floating ghosts, a fog swallowing up the basilica and the other buildings on the island. The black-frocked figure of a priest drifted by and disappeared, otherworldly. It felt as though we had set anchor, and stalled on our journey through purgatory. Even the gaping blackness of the lough surface grew perfectly still. There was nothing solid to us anymore as we uttered in unison the words of the final Creed, nor to anything around us. We were fragments painted by brushstrokes on the whitening air. The torrents of our prayers rippled across the lough surface, and then the station ended and we stood in silence.

At that moment, it was impossible not to feel that I had boarded the boat of the dead, and that everything of my past life was gone forever, the long nights in Belfast and the convoluted alleyways of the Troubles melting away. For the first time in years, I had peace in my soul. Or rather, I became aware of how much peace there existed in the space surrounding me, and how small my soul was in comparison to it. Station Island breathed its special atmosphere into me, so immensely soothing because of all the suffering souls who had gathered there for over a thousand years. How easy it would be to get through days, weeks, and even months, just standing on this shore, staring at the lough as though the waters of heaven lay only an arm's length away.

The fog lifted and was replaced by a milky light. I sat on one of the benches overlooking the lough, sinking into the same silence that enveloped the other pilgrims, all of us gazing vacantly, our bodies resting after the night of constant walking and praying. The light of the waves began to vibrate gently. The rising motion of the lough and the flow of the waves gave the impression that the island was moving again, a little boat, an ark riding an overnight flood, its passengers the border tribes of Ulster, all of us survivors of an historic cataclysm.

I stared at the forest on the other side of the lough, the pine trees bristling along the border that tracked the horizon. Somewhere in the distance lay the fortified line of checkpoints and blown-up bridges that I had fled across just two nights previously. Again, I played with the thought that a flood had risen overnight, and engulfed all of the country, leaving only us, the chosen few survivors, on Lough Derg.

At nine o'clock, a fresh boatload of pilgrims arrived, swarming on to the island, high-spirited and uncertain of themselves, and for an hour or so the place was filled with their noisy coming and going, until they too emerged from the dormitories, barefoot and becalmed.

Surrounded by these new strangers, I began to think that

the Day of Judgement was drawing close. Another boatload disembarked, men and women charged with energy and expectation, marching on to the island with a chorus of shouts and laughter, their smiles flashing, terribly alive, and full of the desire to be saved.

They came marching like the souls of those who had been buried for centuries, and had gathered themselves with a rattle from their shattered tombs. This was the opening of accounts, my tired mind informed me, the undying of the dead, the tumultuous flow of souls, and all these new arrivals, walking with their overnight suitcases, their bottles of water and their warm clothes, so eager to begin their vigil, were the awakened dead, waiting to be judged. I scanned the grey sky, waiting for God to appear above us with his wall of angels, and inspect us one by one from His heavenly throne.

The bell calling us to the morning Mass interrupted my thoughts. I joined the crowd thronging through the black mouth of the basilica doors.

After the service, I went to the dormitory and washed my face in the sink. It was a way of reminding me that a new day had begun. Not as good as sleep, but it did the trick. I should have been exhausted but I felt thoroughly awake, ready to resume contact with the world, the breath of life flaring in my nostrils. I blessed myself and bid farewell to my old world and all its lies.

On my way back to the penitential beds, I met Perpetua. She had put on a waterproof jacket and changed her dress for a pair of trousers. She didn't acknowledge me in any way, and the expression on her face seemed subdued and distant. I felt hungry for her company again.

Somehow, in my desire for this woman, I still believed I could find a path through the island's labyrinth, a way to cleanse myself of past sins. I watched her move away from the others and step into the water until her bare feet were completely submerged. I remembered what had first drawn me to her, the straightness of her figure, her loose, graceful movements, her perfect ankles showing above the surface, the reflected light in her eyes and the ends of her long hair shining in the sunlight. This moment must not end, I said to myself. I stared at her and drank in the vision of her figure. This moment must not end. But even as I rose from the bench and stepped towards her, I knew that the surge of emotion I was riding would end with a fall.

'I want to apologise for my behaviour last night,' I said.

'We haven't much time, Maguire,' she replied, and turned away.

She had a completely different aura about her this morning. The expression on her face and her use of my surname made her manner seem cold and sinister. What did she mean? That we didn't have much time together to talk through our feelings, or much time to save our souls? I stared at the lough, black and shiny as glass. There was a darkness waiting for me in spite of the morning light. I looked at the frozen cast to her face. All those tender looks I had extracted from her eyes, had they come from me? Had I charged her with my own desire? If this bond between us were to have any meaning then one of us had to take action, something physical had to happen between us. I had to reach out and take her hand as if my life depended on it.

'I'm on my way down, Perpetua. Help me.' I stretched out towards her but she brushed my hand away.

'Can't you manage on your own?' There was nothing aggrieved or bitter in her manner. Her face returned to its fundamentally kind expression, but now I could see a sharper edge, a determination. 'Or shall I get a priest to talk to you?'

'I think I can manage on my own.' And keep an eye on me, I thought. 'Nice talking to you, again. Bye.'

I walked off. She was just like the other pilgrims, so strait-laced in her devotion to the island's rituals. My foolish feelings for her vanished, and along with them any hope that I might be saved. I thought she might have helped me offer up a complete and coherent account of my involvement with Ruby. I thought I could have leaned on her, relied on her moral strength, but now I would have to face the rest of my stay on the island alone. She was just another example of the mockery I had made of my life.

I walked through the empty air, a jilted lover, still hungry for her company. A breeze chilled me and the special light in the air grew weak, fading without a fight. The glow in the pilgrims' faces lost its lustre.

I saw Marley standing at St Patrick's Cross, glaring at me with scorn, his black stare sucking in all the light, drinking it greedily through bloodless lips that refused to utter a single prayer. The luminous morning deteriorated into another grey day on Lough Derg. I clung on to the last remnant of hope inside my heart and hurried to find a quiet corner on the island.

I glanced behind and saw that Marley was following me at a fast pace, as if he had something urgent to tell me. However, when he drew alongside, he didn't say a single word. I stopped and watched him pass by and make his way to the top of a small mound. There he hesitated for several moments. I came alongside, but he set off again, walking at the same pace as me, staring straight ahead.

A shiver of unease ran down my back. Every time I increased my pace or slowed, so did he, plodding on, so close to me I could smell the alcohol on his breath. What sort of drunken outcast was he? I glanced at his heavy brow and his cracked lips, and felt repulsed.

I made a left at the pier to a corner of the island where few ventured. I turned round and saw that Marley was headed to the right, back to the penitential beds. I gave a sigh of relief. Then to my annoyance, he changed course and by the time I reached the water's edge, he was right at my side again. I looked away. The lough heaved against the shore, dark and sluggish, and across the water, a clump of trees slipped into shadow.

'What are you up to, Maguire?' he said. 'You've still got your beady eye on that woman.'

'None of your bloody business.'

'You'd better not draw too much attention to yourself, Detective.' He clutched at my sleeve, and pulled me into the shade of some alder. 'I was hoping you would follow me here. You have to be careful. You're agitating them.'

'Who?'

'The priests who run the island. They can't work out why you're here.' His eyes darkened. 'The place is full of spies. The minute you look vulnerable and ready to spill the beans, you'll be under siege and forced to tell the truth about your informer. That's why I've been keeping to myself and discouraging anyone from coming near.'

'Who else knows about my informer?'

'All the priests and nuns.'

'That can't be true.'

'Yes, it is. They won't let you leave until you tell them everything.'

He was wrong. He was the only one on the island who knew anything about my informer.

'Tell me, Maguire, have you been saying the prayers faithfully? Taking part in the rituals, feeling something stir in your soul?'

'Yes.'

Marley nodded to himself and his eyes gleamed.

153

'How's your conscience?'

'My conscience?'

'Yes, that little voice in your head that tells you what's good and what's bad. How is it?'

My inability to reply seemed to confirm his suspicions.

'Any guilty nightmares?'

'I'm always prone to them.'

'Of course, it's Station Island, and it's normal to do some soul-searching with all this free time on your hands. That's what you've been telling yourself, isn't it?'

I nodded.

'Feeling the urge to make a full confession?'

Definitely true; my feelings of guilt had grown more uninhibited since arriving on the island. 'Doesn't everyone who comes here think about confessing?'

'But you're a detective. That would be a disaster for you professionally.'

'Don't exaggerate.'

'You're already showing the symptoms of a dangerous conversion. Another day here and you'll be completely compliant. Willing to do or say anything they ask you. That's the reason you're here. They want you completely guilt-ridden and under their control like the rest of the flock.'

I looked towards the west of the island, saw the prior's limestone accommodation, the watchful dormer windows.

Marley's eyes gleamed. 'Think to yourself, have they ever allowed you to be alone on the island?'

I lowered my head to the wet stones and thought back to the times I had tried to keep my distance from the pilgrims, or slipped away from the basilica into the night. Hadn't someone, Perpetua and Marley included, always been hovering in the background, waiting for an opportunity to approach me? 'That doesn't mean anything.'

'You're wrong detective. It does.'

'What do they want of me? My soul?'

'Detective, you don't have a soul anymore. You lost it a long time ago.'

TWENTY-TWO

Throughout my second afternoon on the island, I walked and walked, dragging my empty stomach along the stone paths. More pilgrims arrived by boat, eager and bright-faced, and I slipped among them like a lost ghost, convincing myself that Marley was wrong. The pilgrims on Station Island weren't interested in me or my informer. They were interested only in saving their souls and clearing their consciences.

Once more, the rounds of Hail Marys began, the renunciation of the devil and all his evil ways, the circular walking around the stone beds, the hands of the faithful making countless signs of the cross. I watched them with tired eyes, my body drinking in the constant din of their prayers. There were times when I nodded off, lulled by their repetitive words, their constant motion, only to awake startled when a passer-by poked me, my body sore and stiff.

I trudged the length and breadth of the island, staring at the span of reflections on the lough, dazed by the bluest and most tenuous prison barriers I had ever encountered.

At one point, the sound of low laughter and murmuring voices drew me around the wall of one of the holy buildings. To my surprise, I found a group of elderly people chatting together, their faces happy and smiling. Most of them were couples, and there was something tender and flirtatious about their closeness to each other, and the light in their eyes. Station

Island was probably the place where they had met and fallen in love during their youth. Their prayers could be love poems and the pilgrimage a return to the innocence of their early romances.

Watching their entranced expressions, I felt somewhere else in time, further back in my country's troubled history, somewhere else inside myself. My detective life in Belfast did not fit with these people, or the holy architecture of the island and the glitter of the lough as it showed between the limestone buildings. How easy it would be to let everything slip away and forget all the intervening years since my last visit to the island as a sixteen-year-old?

I left the old people and their happy chatter. I kept moving, trying to stay awake. At the edge of the shore, I gazed and listened. The lough brimmed with reflections, its dimensions expanding in every direction. I felt transfixed. The water somehow made the limestone basilica resemble a toy building at the edge of an abyss.

With the echo of the pilgrims' prayers ringing in my ears, I dipped my feet, and ventured out. To my surprise, the lough was shallow along this part of the shore, and I thought I might be able to strike out for freedom. My toes slithered over slime-covered stones, and then the lough bed grew soft. I squelched deeper in the mud, and waded further, glad to get away from the island and its reflections.

With each step, I had to pull harder against the gulping mud, but I was determined to make my way towards the light pouring into the middle of the lough. None of the pilgrims seemed to be paying me the slightest bit of attention, and I pressed on, no longer wanting to be walled in by the basilica and the lines of pilgrims. I staggered forwards, the mud gripping my ankles. I pulled up my right foot, lurched forwards and sank deep into the sediment, right up to the knee. I pushed on, hoisting my knees, swinging my shoulders and leaning forwards but it was as if my legs were being pulled from beneath.

I stood for several moments, afraid to put any more weight on my forward leg. If I sank anymore, I would be unable to pull myself out. But if I didn't struggle, I would sink anyway. In the distance, the pine trees crowded upon the mainland shore and rose like a black wall into the mountains. The lough surface shimmered, a tense bubble of silence. I could feel the mud swelling tight around my knees. Would anyone notice if I were to sink slowly below the surface?

I glanced back without moving my body and saw a few figures pacing with their heads down, unaware of my dilemma. I stared at the prior's house and wondered if he was watching me from an upstairs window through a pair of binoculars or perhaps a little telescope. If Marley was correct and they were constantly watching me, wouldn't someone raise the alarm? A chill crept up my legs and coiled around my stomach. Was I prepared to test Marley's claim by risking my life? How embarrassing would it be if I sank further and had to shout and roar for help?

The mud had taken a deep hold of my legs and the water was now up to my waist. I leaned back and waited. The distant murmur of prayers travelled across the water, but no warning calls from worried onlookers. No one was watching me and no one would save me. I tried to keep perfectly still and wait for the water to rise higher, but then a movement on the surface made me glance back. The light of the lough filled my eyes.

However, I was convinced I could see the shape of someone striding towards me, a figure light enough to float over the water without getting stuck in the mud. I waved and the figure hesitated. Was it Marley or one of the priests? The figure hovered between the lough and the island. I swivelled my hips and managed to get my forward leg out of the mud. Might it be

Ruby emerging at last from his hiding place to rescue his ailing detective? About time, too, I thought, as I stretched with all my strength and took another step towards the shore.

The figure glided towards me, weightless and full of purpose, leaving no trace on the lough surface, in sharp contrast to the commotion I was causing as I floundered onwards, water and mud churning in my wake.

I grinned with relief. He had come at last, my fugitive informer. My journey to the island and all my prayers had not been in vain. It was another miracle, but this one would save me completely and wipe away all my sins. I waved and shouted his name, stumbled and almost fell to my knees. I slowed down, panting awkwardly, aware that I had caught the puzzled attention of the pilgrims. I crouched slightly and waited for the figure to draw closer, my sense of relief tinged with fear.

The soundless approach of the shape began to feel ominous, the way it slanted so easily across the water. In an instant, the figure seemed to retreat to the shore, where it merged with the reflections of the island. I blinked my eyes and squinted. I waded towards the figure, desperate to identify it, but I never saw a face. The shape grew thin as a stick and gained in height. It trembled, and then like a ripple vanished completely.

I was alone on the water. Where I had imagined the figure of Ruby, only my reflection shivered on the surface, and then, on scrutiny, that vanished, too. A cold light hung over the basilica as I stepped back on to the island, a light with no warmth or sense of comfort. I was exhausted and shivering, and the island was full of treachery. What good did anyone ever get out of coming to a place like this?

The sun came out and dried my trousers, and for the rest of the afternoon, I rested on a bench. Sleep and a feeling of calm descended upon me. However, all it took was the tap of a stranger's hand and the sound of a subdued voice asking me to stay awake for the feeling of chaos to return, the fear that I was close to losing control. Several times, I was hauled mercilessly back to consciousness and exposed to the critical looks of the pilgrims who were somehow managing to resist sleep.

However, there was something soothing about the wind pressing upon the water and tossing the pine trees on the opposite shore, the light hovering over the island and the pilgrims pouring from the church. Something soothing about the boredom, the hunger and the tiredness. The same watchful faces and the same bare feet, groping for footholds. It all felt so hypnotic. I had said all my prayers, fasted and stayed awake during the night, and done my best to find Ruby. Did it make any difference if I dozed a little at this stage of my vigil?

Again the familiar tap on the shoulder and the soft voice reminding me to stay awake. The pilgrims were the motivated ones, the true believers. They spoke to me in voices that did not strain to be heard. They knew that I was one of the faithless and weak, and would obey their command. Was it a sign of failure to have nothing to believe in or hold against the temptation of sleep? I did not believe even in myself, which made me worse than those who fervently believed in a violent political cause. I needed to join a crusade of some sort, perhaps the movement for peace and reconciliation that the prior had spoken about during his sermon that morning. There was to be a march in Belfast city centre the following month, he had told the congregation. I could join the growing number clamouring for the end of the Troubles and the sectarian violence, but my interest in peace felt little more than a desire for personal therapy. Surely there must be something I could do, now that my detective career was about to end.

I stared at the waters and the waves riding blackly across the horizon. I had tried to recapture something of my faith last night but had failed. I felt cheated and began to formulate questions to ask Father Devine during the upcoming confession. However, my thoughts kept dissolving into a hazy sleep. It was the light on the island and the pilgrims walking in circles. It was the softness of their footfalls and their voices whispering prayers. It was the undercurrents in the water and the distant pine trees crammed with darkness. The trusting faces leaning towards me and tapping my shoulder.

I woke with a start and found myself staring straight into Paddy's eyes with what must have been an uneasy expression.

'Do you plan on sleeping for the rest of your time here?' he asked.

'No. I sat down to think and then I dozed off.'

'Keep walking. Drink as much water as you can and stay off the booze. That way you'll last until ten o'clock tonight. Then you'll sleep like a babe.'

TWENTY-THREE

The evening drew on and I watched the pilgrims, grey and identical-looking in the low light, keeping up their procession like human ants. I listened to the slap of their bare heels on the stones as they shuffled in circles. How many of them were there? They were without beginning or end, moving around the penitential beds, grouping together as if intent on surrounding me with their watchful eyes. They jostled around me, their faces merging into a grey mass in the twilight, wearing a single accusing look. The prayers rose from their mouths, were carried in the wind, and imprinted themselves on the surface of the water. The restless words churned the lough and swirled the dangerous thoughts in my head.

I walked back to the dormitory and examined my secret stash of vodka. I was down to my last half-bottle. I drank from it steadily and soon I was floating on air again. The feeling of inner warmth returned and I felt glad to be on the island. I returned to the penitential beds and watched the pilgrims. I was fascinated and touched by their devotion. I searched their faces, charmed by the humble looks I saw there. Suddenly, I wanted to cheer them on. They made me so happy, the way they kept to the uneven paths and concentrated on their prayers with such devotion. What had they done in their lives that necessitated such arduous penance, what secrets were they hiding in their hearts? I hopped around the paths and told them how good they made me feel. My coat swung open revealing my hip flask, but I no longer feared their suspicious stares. They were uncomfortable under my benevolent gaze and tried to avoid me.

At one point, I reached out to support an old man as he negotiated a difficult step.

'I'm all right,' he said, scowling, and shook his walking stick at me.

I found another pilgrim shuffling along the circular path in the wrong direction. Clearly a novice. 'You have to do it this way,' I shouted at him, and waved my arms like a police officer directing traffic. I held up the flow of people so that he could join the procession at the correct spot.

Paddy walked up to me and spoke in a low scolding voice. 'What are you doing? Drawing attention to yourself like this? You're a disgrace.'

However, I was in my element and would not be deterred. He walked away, and I plunged after him. He was clearly uncomfortable, but I wanted to disarm him with my good humour.

'You're doing a great job, Paddy,' I said, in the manner of a superior bestowing praise on an officer. 'Or is it Kieran? Either way, the two of you have been keeping a tight eye on me, which is only right and necessary. I need to be watched.'

He didn't reply. He just stared at me with a dead expression in his eyes.

'Everything is good,' I said. 'You're good and I'm good. Isn't that right?'

We were all night owls, I told myself, and the island one big party where everyone had stayed up all night and were now wandering round in states of distraction. All I needed to do was keep sipping the vodka to maintain a state of euphoria. Everyone's face glowed in contrast to the leaden grimaces from the night before. We had finished our stations, and were now free to wander around the island and strike up conversations with whomever we pleased.

I walked along the shore and soaked up the last of the twilight. Only the constant movement kept me from falling asleep. Dew descended and the grass grew wet underfoot. A light mist hovered around the island. A traveller woman, exhausted from lack of sleep, began to laugh hysterically in between her fervent bouts of praying. The sound of her laughter was eerie but it gave me a sharp sense of relief. At least someone else was close to cracking up.

I sipped from my hip flask and grew drunker. I tried rehearsing what I was going to say to the priest at confession time. I thought of recounting the strange story of Ruby as if someone else had recruited him, another detective, a colleague with a similar set of loyalties. I would emphasise the detective's human weakness and ask the priest to forgive him for his frailties. I cherished the hope that the priest would listen without surprise or contempt, and console me with his understanding as the truth flowed from my lips.

I looked up and saw a tall figure, furtive and alert, staring at me. It was that troublesome detective again, but even his constant stalking presence made me feel warm and happy. His insatiable hunger to follow me everywhere felt so reassuring. I waved at him and beckoned him over, but his name had escaped me. Was it Marley or was he a Maguire, too? My drunken namesake from the other side of the border. Tiredness was making me more confused and the alcohol did little to clear my head. Marley or Maguire, I couldn't work out what to call him. Our names and our stories were mixed up in my head with the ferment of nocturnal prayers and dream-like images of the basilica.

And what about Perpetua? Where was the love of my life? I

missed her reassuring voice and eager eyes. She was probably busy, steering another lonely man along the path, a lost soul whom she could mother and shower with her sympathy and understanding. A wave of regret washed over me. I had spent the night leading her on with my heartfelt expressions of guilt and doubt, enjoying her reverence for my troubled conscience, allowing her to play out some drama of suffering over my soul. I should find her, apologise and finally reveal the truth about Ruby and the night of the ambush. I lurched off in search of her.

In the canteen, I shouted, 'Has anyone seen my friend Perpetua?' The room was empty apart from two nuns standing around the bright oven, the lid of a heavy black pot rattling with boiling water. I felt light-headed in the sudden warmth and asked the question again, but they ignored me.

'Water's ready,' said the younger of the nuns.

Blood was pounding through me as I stepped towards them. I suspected they knew where Perpetua was hiding. I could see it in the way they glanced at each other and watched me with cold eyes. Their silence and resistance felt eerie, and the fact that I was walking towards them, drunk and full of desire for a woman I barely knew, compounded my sense of being on the edge. Was this why I had been sent the postcard and dragged to this otherworldly island? To deprive me of sleep, cut me off from my routine and set me loose with my lustful feelings among priests and nuns? I was out of control and surrendering to the darkness inside. What else was I capable of doing, intoxicated like this, pushed to the limits? The fire of lust kept burning inside me and the only thing that would quench it was a glimpse of Perpetua's pretty face.

When I was almost upon the nuns, the younger one tipped the pot and flung its contents across the floor. I stepped back just in time as the steaming water splashed across the tiles, narrowly missing my bare feet.

'You could have burnt me,' I said. 'That water's boiling hot.'

The nun shrugged and lifted a mop. 'Perpetua doesn't want you near her,' she said, walking towards me and raising the mop threateningly.

I made to sidestep her but she manoeuvred me out of the canteen so quickly and lightly that I tripped over the doorstep and fell on to the gravel path. My legs weren't functioning well and I struggled to my feet. There was something painfully degrading about my predicament. I had survived IRA and loyalist threats in one of the most dangerous cities in Western Europe, and here I was being put in my place by a nun with a mop. She followed me outside, silhouetted by the light of the canteen, a looming hooded figure.

'You're drunk,' she shouted and shoved the wet mop into my chest. I sensed her absolute determination to keep me away from Perpetua.

'All right, all right.' I said, pulling myself away. 'I thought nuns weren't meant to hurt people.'

She laughed scornfully. 'Every second you're here, Detective, is meant to hurt. You're on purgatory island now. Never forget that.'

I backed away and made my way to the basilica. The nun knew I was a detective. Was she in on some sort of conspiracy to make me suffer and repent? And why were they so determined to keep me away from Perpetua?

The moment I entered the side-wing of the church I saw my dark-haired Perpetua sitting with Paddy and Kieran. They were deep in conversation and when I heard them mention my name, my blood ran cold. She saw me and rose to her feet. Before I could call out, she slipped out the northern exit. I ignored the two men and followed her. Who was she working for? What did she want of me? Had she been tempting me all along with her soft eyes into betraying myself? Even with all these doubts circling in my head, I still wanted her company. I was drunk and capable of tricking myself into believing her intentions towards me were honourable, or even romantically inclined, and that her eyes had been egging me on since we first met.

I shouted her name and she turned towards me. I saw a tiny flicker of fear in her eyes, immediately disguising itself as a look of concern, and which in my intoxicated imagination I thought might be a passionate plea, some sort of secret signal to follow her. She hurried into the shadows towards the smaller St Mary's Church, and even at this stage, with the growing realisation that she was in some sort of conspiracy with Paddy and Kieran, I felt such a powerful attraction towards her. Her eyes were so soft and doe-eyed, yet strong and determined. She belonged to a world of light and hope, the world that I hoped to return to after my vigil on the island.

The paths were deserted and the lough heaved with waves advancing towards the shore in relentless lines. Night was upon us now, and only an hour remained until the confessions were to take place. Soon my vigil would be over.

TWENTY-FOUR

Raindrops pursued their course as relentlessly as bullets against the windscreen and roof of Pearson's car. The chief inspector lingered for several moments in the driving seat, and then he made a dive for the hotel entrance, his leather shoes getting soaked in the puddles. He was tired and hungry and wanted to take a nap for the evening. Glancing at his watch, he hoped he was still in time for a meal, one that included a bottle of something to help him sleep.

'Someone rang you earlier today,' said the receptionist. 'A detective. We told him you weren't here.'

'A detective?'

'Yes. I can't remember the name. He insisted you get in touch with him.'

'How am I supposed to get in touch?'

'He left a phone number. Just a minute.'

It was a Belfast number. Pearson stared at it, and then he picked up a phone in the lobby.

A voice he did not recognise answered immediately.

'Inspector Alan Pearson, here. You wanted to speak to me.'

The man at the other end of the phone did not introduce himself. 'Good afternoon, Chief Inspector. The committee has asked me to speak to you, again.'

Pearson mustered his powers of concentration. First the Special Branch commander and now this. What further requests and burdens awaited him? He understood the caller's secrecy and his reference to the committee, an inner circle of solicitors, politicians and high-ranking police officers operating at the heart of Northern Ireland's justice system.

According to the caller, the committee had been in a stir since Special Branch began their investigation into the group of detectives based at Crumlin Road Police Station. The committee had followed the Special Branch investigation closely, and debated what action to take. At risk was an entire network of spies and informers as well as powerful links with loyalist paramilitaries bitterly opposed to the IRA. The committee had failed to come up with a suitable strategy to protect Pearson's detectives, but all had agreed that they were facing a major crisis. It was only when the farmhouse ambush happened out of the blue that they were finally able to put in place a plan.

'The last thing the committee want is Maguire wandering drunk and paranoid in no-man's-land,' said the voice. 'They want you to take him under your wing and remind him of where his loyalties lie. They are asking for your help in this regard. They also want information about Special Branch's investigations, in particular the leads being followed by Commander Bates.'

It was not the first time Pearson had taken a phone call from an anonymous messenger of the committee. On previous occasions, under duress, he had supplied them with names and contact details, but they had never asked him to carry out an operation like this before. He needed to buy some time and ponder their request.

'What sort of information are they talking about?'

'They want to know has Special Branch talked to you about a previous attempt on Maguire's life. One which he also miraculously survived.'

'No. Why?' Pearson held the phone closer to his ear. Outside, the rain was falling in a deafening torrent. He tried to shut himself off from distractions.

'Special Branch has been investigating an IRA plan to kill Maguire at a funeral in Dungannon last June. Apparently, the gang was waiting in a car parked outside St Patrick's Chapel. They knew that the funeral was for an old friend of Maguire's and that he intended to be there. However, Maguire never showed up. Special Branch thought it was too much of a coincidence and began to dig further.'

Pearson recalled the incident. 'I suppose you could call it a coincidence that Maguire didn't go to the funeral that day. But he certainly intended to. He'd booked the day off work for that precise reason.'

'The thing is, Pearson, Special Branch is investigating your role in this coincidence.'

'What do you mean?'

'Let me ask you a question. Do you think it would be wrong for one of your detectives to have allowed Maguire to go to his death that day?'

'Of course, it would be wrong.'

'Even when by informing Maguire, the detective risked blowing the cover of a valuable informant?'

A door slammed nearby and someone scraped a chair across the floor. Pearson glanced round but the lobby was empty. Special Branch was right. It was too much of a coincidence that Maguire had also escaped death that day. He vaguely remembered the details of a tip-off around the time the caller was talking about, one involving an IRA ambush in Dungannon, but back then, he had not followed it through. His detectives came forward with so many informers and secrets, it was impossible to vet them quickly enough or verify everything they were disclosing. Pearson had been forced to turn many informers away or ignore the information they were peddling.

He felt a chill creep down his spine at the thought that one of his detectives might have known about the IRA murder plan but had neglected to warn Maguire. Worse still, was he equally culpable by not passing on the second-hand information? For a moment, he thought he heard another voice in the background, whispering to his secret caller, but he couldn't work out what the voice said, or whether he had really heard it. All he could hear clearly was the heavy knocking of his heart in his chest.

He sighed heavily. He had not just been blind to Maguire's failings. He had been blind to many things in his team of detectives. His sense of judgement had been weakened by the interminable fight against the IRA. He had not been aware of how many deceptions might be operating in his police station, how many secrets were flowing like hidden currents in the sea between informers and detectives. Perhaps he was no longer fit to be a detective, let alone a chief inspector. And here he was, trapped in the chase for an informer that may never have existed in the first place.

'Special Branch is changing the entire direction of the investigation,' warned the voice. 'Bates is collecting evidence against you. He suspects that it was you who made sure Robinson would be in the car on the night of the farmhouse ambush. Robinson had uncovered evidence incriminating some of your detectives, and by implication, you, too.'

'If that was the case, then why does he think Maguire survived?'

'Because everyone would then think Maguire was behind the plot. That he had orchestrated Robinson's death to take the heat off his own back. Bates is coming round to the conclusion that Maguire and his informer were set up as scapegoats. You're going to have to fend off some very awkward enquiries, and the press have also been given wind of the new suspicions. They're on the hunt, too.'

'I will protest,' said Pearson. 'At the highest level. Special Branch is using the ambush to hound my team. I'll get Bates stopped in his tracks.'

'You haven't got time.'

'Of course, I have time.' His hand trembled slightly as he held the phone to his mouth and tried to keep his voice down. 'It's a well-known fact that Special Branch is hostile to the work of ordinary police detectives. The chief commander will understand.'

'These are my instructions. I was to inform you of Special Branch's discoveries and request your cooperation in ensuring Maguire keeps to his story about his informer, and that you answer none of Special Branch's questions for the time being. No one must know about this telephone conversation.'

'Who gave you the instructions?'

'I cannot say.'

'At least tell me your name. Who are you?'

'I am not your enemy, Sir. Nor am I part of the plot to blame you for the ambush. I was told to remind you that you still have the support of your loyal detectives.'

TWENTY-FIVE

In the confines of St Mary's Church, I told Perpetua I'd had enough of praying and now I wanted to speak. The island was turning my soul into a bottomless pit, and the only way to stop myself going mad was by telling someone the truth about my informer and the night of the ambush.

For a moment, I thought she wasn't going to listen and instead keep reciting the rosary. She flashed me a look that might have been fear, or was it secret anticipation.

'What exactly happened that night?'

'I led three men to their deaths. It was my darkest hour.' I turned and stared at the altar.

'Is that all you have to tell me?'

'No, there is more. Much more.' I glanced at her imploring eyes and felt my inhibitions return. What if telling her my sins left a shadow on her heart and made her cold and unforgiving? What if I ended up dragging her into the abyss, too? Perhaps I should say no more. She didn't need to know everything about that night and probably knew too much already. It would be better if she knew nothing at all and completely forgot what I had told her. If she wanted to leave the island safely and go back to her own life, she would have to forget everything about me.

'Perhaps I should talk to a priest, first,' I said.

'You can talk to me.' Her eyes were bright, eager.

'It always feels good talking to you.'

'It's good to listen, too.'

The candles wavered as a gust of wind entered the room. I did not want to leave the tiny church. I wanted to stay here with her, to be enclosed by the solid stone walls, and gaze at her face, which was lit up by the soft amber glow of the candles and the metal grate covered in dripping wax. I felt so grateful for her company, grateful for her sharing this part of my journey and alleviating the loneliness I felt on the island. But somehow, the closeness of her body, the intimacy of her gaze made me feel more alone, and the more time I spent with her the worse it got.

I looked at her face and noticed her eyes had lost some of their dangerous glow. An enviable serenity had taken hold there. She watched me intently, and I lowered my gaze, feeling studied, hemmed in by her scrutiny. I released my clasped hands. I hadn't noticed I had been clenching them so tightly. I could no longer hold back or stop myself from talking. It was time to confess my sins in this hushed sanctuary. Time to tease apart the web of lies that had claimed my soul.

Her gaze flickered across my face, as though she were reading every secret thought and emotion expressed in my features, alert to every drop of guilt and anguish in my soul. She leaned forward, her knees touching mine. 'You have to set the record straight,' she said.

The door tugged open behind us, letting in the wash of the waves, and then slid shut with a slam. The candles went out and we were suddenly in darkness. I had the odd sensation of the island's shadows constantly sniffing me out, finding me in these gloomy nooks and crannies. A small sound echoed from behind us that might have been a door handle clicking, or something more sinister, a revolver setting.

I turned round and saw an extra shape in the darkness that

shifted slightly as one of the ancient floorboards creaked and then the shape slid back into the shadows. Someone else was in the church, monitoring our movements, listening in on our conversation. The whiff of candle smoke filled the air, and a cold prickling sensation ran down my spine.

I rose and crept down the aisle to challenge the eavesdropper, but the shadow disappeared, or rather, it seemed to grow so large that it filled the back of the darkened church. I reached out for the pews and clawed my way forward. There was just enough light for me to make out a looming headless figure waiting near the door. I glanced back to Perpetua, and as I turned, a sudden blow to my head knocked me to the ground. I gave a grunt and my body went limp.

When I came to, I was lying on the floor with Perpetua leaning over me. Someone had lit the candles again, and the church ceiling was full of flickering shadows.

'What happened to you?' she asked.

'I don't know.'

'You must have fainted. It's the lack of food and sleep. Come with me to the infirmary.' She smiled as if to reassure me, but I did not feel reassured.

'I'm fine. Don't need help.' Every turn of my head was agony and my neck felt numb. I had trouble putting together words to explain what had happened to me. I felt the back of my skull and found a large bump matted with blood. Someone had struck me with a heavy object. Was the blow a warning? A reminder not to let the truth slip out?

When Perpetua saw the blood, she gasped and hurried off to get some disinfectant. Rather than remain in the empty church on my own, I rose and stumbled outside. My attacker was still on the island and I intended to hunt them down.

I heard someone call out my name, low and accusing, and hurried in the direction of the ghostly voice. Perhaps it was my imagination and the lack of sleep playing tricks with my mind. Then I heard the voice again. A figure was leaning against the south wall of the basilica. Not Marley or anyone else I knew. I could feel the scrutiny of the figure's gaze, sizing me up. I was growing used to being the object of calculating stares on Station Island.

When I drew closer, the figure took off. I made chase, my shoulders dropping into a boxer's crouch, ready to defend myself if needed. I rounded a corner of the basilica and ran into a group of nuns, passing by in a line with their hooded heads down. There was no sign of the figure anywhere. I asked the nuns if they had seen anyone but they ignored me. I asked again, louder, and the last one lifted her head and pointed to a low door in a building adjoining the church.

The door refused to budge when I pushed it. I listened carefully and thought I heard the sound of footsteps echoing inside and then fading away. Had my attacker found sanctuary within? There was no handle to grasp, just a keyhole. I ran my fingers along the cold edge of the door, searching for a gap that might help me prise it open, but found nothing. I ran round the building and came to a set of double doors on the lough-shore side. They were locked, too. I knocked and rattled the doors and then crept along the narrow windows, pausing to stare through the panes, seeing only a darkness moulded by the reflections of the waves falling on to the shore.

I toured the building twice, and then the futility of what I was doing began to penetrate my anger. I wasn't going to find my attacker, and even if I did, would anyone believe me? The only evidence I had was a bump on the back of my head and no eyewitnesses. Perpetua had evidently seen nothing and I had only been dimly aware of a fleeting shadow. Nevertheless, I stood under an old tree and watched the double doors for a while. Eventually, they opened and a figure emerged. An elderly nun, bent over and walking slowly. I waited a while longer but the building remained sunken in silence.

I went to the dormitory and drank some vodka to calm my nerves. I did not feel like reading, but nevertheless I picked up one of my spy handbooks and forced myself through several chapters.

Perhaps it was my agitated state, but I began to feel cheated by the author and his air of comfortable self-possession. I could no longer share his enthusiasm for code-names and cover-ups. The way he stalked the bars and corridors of gentlemen's clubs seemed so old-fashioned, a grey man of catchwords and familiar clichés, lacking a soul or any degree of conscience. The narrative that had gripped me when I first started reading the book ran into several meandering trickles, leaving many questions unanswered and plots suspended in the air. Perhaps the author was leaning heavily on discretion, or was recounting events many years after they had taken place, and could only circle around the truth. Unfortunately, nothing in his words stirred me to the truth about Ruby. His story was completely alien to me on this island of prayer, and I found his descriptions of informers pretentious and suspect. I threw the book down and returned to the comfort of alcohol.

By the time the bell rang for confessions, my head was swimming. I drew myself up tall to create a sober air, and then, marching grimly, made my way back to the basilica.

TWENTY-SIX

Just before ten o'clock, an elderly priest appeared and walked past the line of pilgrims waiting at the confessional box. He stopped to look in my direction, as if he knew me. I paid no attention and stared straight ahead. The priest stiffened slightly, as if detecting a threat. He blessed himself, glanced back in my direction and then slipped into the confessional box, but not before hesitating again as though reluctant to step into the darkness of that little room.

I waited until I was at the front of the queue. I was about to enter the confessional for the first time in twenty years. My body froze, so deep was the aversion to entering that wooden cell, but the thought of escaping the island and its purgatorial rituals shone brightly before me. I wanted to be free of darkness, and that narrow door was going to lead me to the truth, or at least give me an answer that would return me to a brighter world.

I stumbled as I crossed the tiled floor. I hated my unsteadiness, and for the first time on the island, wished that I was sober. Inside, I squirmed and squinted in the semi-darkness. A light slanted from the metal grille separating me from the priest. All I could see of him were his thick square hands folded in his lap.

His whispering began as soon as I entered, reciting the familiar opening lines of the ritual. As a boy, I had enjoyed the seclusion of the confessional box, the shadows that fell over

178

the priest's face, and the shadows that fell over my heart. It had felt like a refuge, a secret place to bury and forget one's misdemeanours and failings.

I knelt down, blessed myself and asked the priest was he Father Liam Devine? When he said yes, I told him that I was Detective Desmond Maguire. A week ago, I had survived an IRA ambush and now I had come to Station Island seeking the truth. His hands retreated a little into the shiny black cuffs of his soutane. I could sense his dark shape crouching on the other side of the confessional, contracting like a mollusc in its shell.

'What are you doing in my confessional?' he asked.

'I want to speak to the IRA.'

All traces of pleasantness disappeared from his voice. 'You've no right to come here and make a request like that.'

'A week ago, I received a postcard from the IRA with your name on it and the time of this confessional.'

'Why would they send you that?'

'I don't know.'

His breathing grew sharp and heavy. I feared that my first visit to the confession in more than two decades was going to end with him dragging me from the box and marching me out of the church.

'I need to speak to them, Father. I have to find out why I didn't die on the night of the ambush. The only way I can prove my innocence is by getting the truth from the IRA. I came here hoping you might help.'

'Did you indeed?' His tone remained cold. 'And what makes you think I can help?'

I stared at his worn cuffs and imagined his stubborn, wary face in the darkness. A country priest, who was used to hearing the confessions of children and pious old men and women. It had probably been years since he'd threatened the torments of hell.

'You're the only link I have with them. I suspect you have a way of contacting them in an emergency.'

'Before I give you what you want, you should tell me what is burdening your conscience. Are you blaming yourself for the murder of your colleagues?'

For several moments, I did not speak. Had someone else put him up to the question? I resisted the temptation to deny any responsibility whatsoever. 'Tell you the truth, Father, I have no idea what happened that night. All I want to do is speak to the IRA.'

'Surely there are easier ways of contacting the IRA than coming to Station Island?'

'What do you mean?'

'Why do the rituals if all you want is to speak to the IRA?'

Had he been watching me, as well? 'I had to fit in and not draw attention to myself.'

'Somehow, I doubt that's the only reason.' He slipped into the glibness of a sermon, and suggested that my presence on the island was a spiritual quest, borne out of the ambush, and that God had arranged everything because I needed direction and meaning in my existence.

'It's not working, Father. Whatever the reason you think I'm here, or what the island might do for me.'

'Everyone who comes here is on a quest.'

'But I'm not on a quest. At least, not the one you are talking about.'

'I believe you're mistaken. You're here because you want your conscience healed.'

In the darkness of that wooden box, seeing only the priest's still hands, I felt blindfolded. The temptation to speak garrulously and seek reassurance grew strong.

'Finish the vigil, first,' he urged. 'Tomorrow, when you board the boat, I'll give you a telephone number to ring. Leave a message and the IRA will decide where and when to contact you.'

'Give me the number now, Father. Let me get off the island tonight. This place is getting me down. Another night here, I'll crack up completely.'

'I know the vigil is not easy, but you are so close to finishing it. Everything will feel different when you wake up in the morning after a good night's sleep.'

'That's exactly what I don't want. I don't want to wake up on this island. I just want to get back to the real world. Make contact with the IRA.'

'It's normal for pilgrims to feel low at this point. Hold on a little while longer. Say some prayers and then go to bed. Give sleep a chance, that's all I'm saying.'

'You don't understand. I want off this reservation. The prayers, the fasting, the constant walking. All the pointless bloody trials.'

'The life of a Christian is a trial.'

'But does it have to be? The rest of the pilgrims can suffer on. I've had enough. I've tried my best, Father. I've tried to be good. I've followed the stations. But I've stumbled along the way.'

'You sound like an honest man. A decent Catholic.'

I lowered my voice. 'Sorry to disappoint, but I'm no longer a believer or any type of Catholic.'

'Then why do the rituals? There must be something you want off your chest. This is the darkest hour of your vigil. Self-doubts and anxieties are at their height. Would you rather have fear and guilt lodged in your heart forever, or get rid of them?'

'I don't have a choice.'

'Tell me what is troubling you; do your penance and then see how you feel. You can decide to stay or leave afterwards. Before you go, I'll give you the telephone number.'

'You promise to do that? Let me leave tonight if I make a full confession?'

'If it's your wish.'

And so I came round to it tentatively, the dawn of all my lies, the guilty disorder of what I could never admit to anyone, the Ruby thing.

'Bless me, Father, for I have sinned.' I started telling him everything that had happened to me in Belfast and in the dark, little alleyways of my soul, where the story of my informer had grown and closed itself around me, slowly burying me alive.

Gradually, Ruby came out into the open, into the light, and I saw him as he was.

Who was he?

A shadow that had taken shape within me and had no right to exist.

TWENTY-SEVEN

As the day darkened, Pearson drove his car south of Enniskillen. He felt as though he were floating along the grey border roads, stateless, his body without substance. He received barely a nod of recognition from the RUC and army patrol at the fortified border checkpoint, and further down the road, the sleepy-looking Garda officers showed him no curiosity at all.

Once he was in the Republic, the axis of his world tipped slightly, adding to his sense of weightlessness. Road signs with the names of unfamiliar towns flashed before him, and he tried to place them on a mental map of the country but failed. He hesitated at crossroads, crouching over the steering wheel. Soon the signposts disappeared and he was threading his way through a maze of potholed back roads dwindling into nothingness. All he had to guide him now were the low hills and the deadening light of the western sky.

The family home that welcomed him an hour later was warm, busy with children and smelled of cake. He glanced around, wary as a wild dog, as Commander Jack Shaw led him into a dimly lit room with a fire in the fireplace and two comfortable armchairs arranged around it. He could see that someone had moved one of the armchairs recently. The imprint of its feet still marked the carpet in a corner.

'I was beginning to worry you'd taken the scenic route,' said Shaw. 'Such a lovely day for a trip round Lough Erne.' He bustled around Pearson, taking his coat and hanging it in the hall. 'On days like this I wish I was back on the beat. Roaming up and down the border.'

'Sorry for the tardiness,' said Pearson. 'I got lost. What smells so good?'

'My wife's been baking all morning. We're celebrating our granddaughter's first Holy Communion. Hence the madness all round.'

Shaw closed the door and suddenly it was quiet in the room. A grandfather clock ticked loudly in the corner. Pearson glanced through the window at a bouncy castle planted on the lawn and the tumult of young children playing. He sat down awkwardly on the armchair offered to him. He had disturbed a family occasion, forcing Shaw to rearrange things and retreat to this hushed room at the heart of his home to talk about traitors and murderers. Pearson had been strictly raised in the Presbyterian faith, and he had the unnerving sense that he was in a strange place, a strange country, surrounded by people with strange beliefs.

However, there was nothing strange or unfriendly about Shaw and his welcome. He leaned back in the chair, reassured by the Garda commander's hospitality. His visit threatened to ruin what was clearly an important family celebration and Shaw could just as easily have reacted with bad temper. Instead, he appeared to be treating their meeting as a happy reunion, a chance to reminisce over old times.

'How are things, Alan?'

'The journey was fine.'

'I'm not talking about the journey.' Shaw settled into his chair and gave Pearson a heavy stare.

'I'm doing all right.'

The Garda commander leaned across and lifted a bottle of whiskey from a tray. 'Are you sure you're all right?'

'Yes. As long as I get your assistance with something.'

'What's up?'

'Still the Maguire situation.' Pearson sighed. 'I need to speak to him as soon as he gets off the island. Before anyone else gets to him.'

Shaw's eyes were small and grey. He lifted a fistful of ice and dropped it into two glasses. Was that a look of doubt Pearson saw creeping into his face?

'He's left such a gaping hole behind him,' said Pearson. 'So many unanswered questions.'

'Well,' said Shaw, and began pouring the whiskey.

The mood in the room changed subtly. He could feel it in the air and in Shaw's expression. A sense of wariness. What did the Garda commander see as he handed the tumbler of whiskey to him? A hollow-eyed chief inspector unable to manage the repercussions of his poor leadership? In a moment of painful lucidity, he felt the shine of his professional charm dim in Shaw's eyes. Perhaps all the suspicions Pearson felt circling around him had been spun from the threads of Maguire's lies and someone with a more arrogant disposition would have broken through or completely ignored them.

'I'm afraid someone might want to harm Maguire,' he said.

Shaw stared at him for a moment, the look of tension hardening in his eyes. 'Harm him on my side of the border?'

Pearson nodded. A feeling of unease, not unlike guilt, uncoiled from the pit of his stomach and climbed into his chest. 'Nobody knows what to do with him and his lies,' he said. 'He's a complete liability, which is why I need to warn him, ensure that he takes the right course of action. It's imperative that I speak to him as soon as he comes off the island.'

'Really?'

He nodded again, and Shaw rose quickly. For a second, Pearson thought he had angered the Garda chief, scuppered his chances of cooperation, and was now about to be hastily ejected from his home. But Shaw had risen with a gentle smile to greet a little boy who had run into the room.

'What are you doing in here, Granddad?' said the child. 'You're missing the party.'

Shaw embraced the boy. He glanced at the child and then at Pearson, straining to cover up his unease. He looked old and tired. Then he chased his grandson out of the room with a wave of his arms, but not before the boy threw Pearson a look of annoyance.

Shaw spoke again. 'You know there are official channels for this sort of thing?'

'You're not going to give me a lecture on cross-border bureaucracy, are you, Jack?'

'No. For Christ's sake, I don't want to bore you with rules you already know. I just want you to be aware of the political sensitivity around this.'

'Of course, mustn't ruffle any feathers.'

'No, that's not the reason. I want to see Maguire sorted out like you and your colleagues in Special Branch do. I want to help you get the truth out of him.'

'I appreciate your efforts.'

Shaw was distracted by a scream of laughter from outside. Another group of children ran by the window. The Garda commander stared through the glass for several long moments, watching his grandchildren, their buoyant cries trailing through the garden. There was a musicality to their voices, a pattern that wove itself around the house, the vanished innocence of childhood. By the time his gaze returned to Pearson, it had softened. 'Sounds to me like Maguire has been through a lot of soul-searching,' he said. 'Perhaps a different, gentler approach is needed.'

'I understand what you're saying, but I think I know my own

186

detectives. I've already talked at length to Maguire about his mental state. He can't be spared a rigorous interrogation. Not when he's implicated in the deaths of three police officers.'

Pearson followed Shaw's gaze through the window. He saw a girl running in a Holy Communion dress, drawing a gang of children behind her. The scene seemed unreal, like a dream an old man might carry in his heart. Shaw had his family around him, and his faith, but he had neither. All Pearson wanted was to have his reputation restored, or at least its polished outward appearance. To be impervious to criticism once again, to bristle with indignation at any negative assessment of his character or judgement. He had never been preoccupied by family or religion before. He had never felt the need. But now, seeing Shaw ensconced in the deep heart of his home, he thought of the invisible protective walls a man could build around himself, the comforts of loving children and a merciful God that might be more effective than rows of jagged glass, metal grilles and security cameras.

He took a swig of whiskey and gritted his teeth, trying not to feel too ghoulish.

Shaw said, 'So you want to speak to Maguire because you think he knows something that would endanger his life when he returns to the North?'

Pearson nodded.

'You suspect Maguire of betraying his colleagues, but you also suspect his colleagues might betray him. Is that correct?'

Pearson accidentally crunched on a lump of ice. 'I didn't say that. All I can say is that Special Branch now has proof that Maguire's survival is down to more than just good luck.'

'What proof are you talking about?'

'I'd rather keep you out of this, Jack. Bad enough that I'm mixed up in it. I'd much rather steer clear of this mess, but that's no longer possible.' He pressed on with a question before

Shaw could reply. 'What about your officers on the island, have they anything new on him?'

'No. He's giving them the complete runaround. Whenever they try to engage him in conversation or challenge him, he becomes evasive, and doesn't make sense at all. He spends most of the time muttering and reading spy stories.'

'What sort of spy stories?'

'Airport thrillers. Trashy tales about the Troubles written by Englishmen. He keeps a stash of them near his bed.'

What was Maguire doing reading spy novels? Were they somehow linked to his own story? What connections existed in Maguire's mind between his lies and the words of fiction? Pearson took a deep breath and looked at Shaw with his most frank gaze, and then he spoke. 'Maguire invented Ruby.' He sighed. 'I'm almost sure of it now. It was too good to be true. Looking back, I always had my doubts. But Maguire was a Catholic and I wanted him to be a good detective, an officer I could trust. I'm going to give him one final chance to tell the bloody truth, head-on and in all its gory detail. I want him to blow the lid on Ruby, once and for all. That's why I need to speak to him.'

Shaw poured them both a fresh measure of whiskey. They raised their glasses and gave each other a forced smile, as though acknowledging that alcohol had always been their secret intermediary when the official channels of communication proved inadequate or suspect.

Pearson hunched over his glass and stared at Shaw. 'Policing in Northern Ireland is screwed, Jack. There's a ceasefire and a peace agreement coming soon. When that happens, we'll all go down the drain. None of us will be spared.'

'No,' said Shaw, sipping from his glass. 'You're being too pessimistic.'

Pearson leaned across and clinked his drink against Shaw's.

'I'm afraid it's true, Jack. When the IRA get their political deal they'll start making the laws and rewriting history. The barbarians are already at the gate.'

'You're getting poisoned, Alan. You're catching the informer's disease. You're beginning to think and act like a hunted man.' Shaw sat still, twirling his glass in his large hands, staring at the whiskey.

'I need to speak to Maguire. It's what I've got to do.'

'I don't think Maguire will give you the reassurance you're looking for, or help you understand what is going on.'

'I'm just asking for a little time with him. A chance to save him from his demons. If he is playing some game with the IRA, I hope to be able to uncover it.'

Shaw kept studying the contents of his glass. Both men fell into a companionable but melancholy silence, and then Shaw looked up at Pearson. A flicker of light had taken hold in his eyes. 'Very well, Alan, my officers will be waiting in the car park when he comes off the island tomorrow morning. They'll escort him back to the border in one piece, but I'll ask them to hold back and let you speak to him first. But you must promise me to be discreet. There are reporters on the prowl. Wear a raincoat or hide under an umbrella.'

'Don't worry, I always carry an umbrella in my car. It rains a lot in Belfast.'

'Rains a lot on this side of the border, too. Haven't you noticed?'

TWENTY-EIGHT

The darkness of the confessional box and the power of the ritual sorted out the truth from my lies. Kneeling at the grill, whispering into Father Devine's silence, I was able to order all the fragments of my story, the drunken memories and stray conversations into a narrative that began to make sense.

I explained to Devine how I had invented everything about Ruby, or at least I believed I had.

The idea of my informer was born after I started receiving anonymous phone calls late at night, taunting me with bits of information about IRA operations. My persecutors, for that is how I regarded them, had neither face nor name. The first time I answered, I thought the call was a wrong number or crossed wires. A series of voices spoke to me in broad Tyrone accents, bragging about the bombings and shootings they were planning. There were pauses and muffled bursts of laughter in the background. At times, the voices descended into a wordless rumble and I had the impression of the phone being passed from person to person in a packed drinking club. The call ended as abruptly as it had begun, and I put it to the back of my mind.

A few nights later, the phone rang again, and the voices began where they had left off. I held my breath and listened to the flow of their stories, the hints scattered amid the drunken banter, the curses and laughter and threats to kill and maim, all the time waiting for a precise picture to emerge so that I might drop everything and act on the tip-off as a good detective should. Then the phone call ended just as suddenly as the previous one.

A pattern took hold. I had several more calls that week, late at night, the voices always speaking in the familiar accents of home, accents that stung an antenna deep inside my body and left me feeling uneasy and powerless.

Why were they contacting me, and what were they hoping to do? Were they young fanatics or cynical old-timers? The ringing of the phone late at night became an aggressive summons and I would rush to answer it, even though I was certain that nothing clear or coherent would emerge. Unwittingly, I had become their hostage. Sometimes, when I picked up the phone, it would fall silent and I felt relieved until the ringing began again. For weeks, the voices kept me on edge, locked into a process, an underground flow of secrets and whispers. They turned my flat into a prison with the phone their means of torture, ringing and ringing at the centre of my nights.

Were they from the IRA, or one of the mushrooming groups opposed to any form of political solution to the Troubles? The Republican movement was riven by internecine struggles and constantly breaking into rival factions. Or perhaps they were secret informers, motivated by their consciences, but too afraid to reveal any details about their identities? They kept alluding to upcoming IRA operations, bombings and shootings, and details of criminal rackets such as smuggling and extortion. Whatever they were, the warnings they whispered to me often proved correct in the days following the phone calls.

My mind began to step in and plug the gaps, joining the different strands of their conversations and working out what types of operation they were talking about. However, as soon as one picture began to form in my head, with a time and place, intended targets and means of transport, the voice would break off and someone else would begin describing a different attack, and before he had proceeded very far, a third voice would begin and then give way to a fourth. I took notes and waited, following the news reports over the next week or so, trying to match the latest atrocities to their stories, trying to get to the truth in their jumbled accounts.

Several times, I threatened to disconnect the phone, but the voices told me that I had a duty to listen. I was a police officer, a detective, and they had secrets to share. They were urgent yet patient with me, explaining and commenting on what they were doing as though relaying the moves of a complicated game of chess. I had a responsibility to listen, they said, a moral responsibility to take the phone calls and learn from them. I felt the palm of my hand burning like a wound as it held the phone, the old imprint of the bullet the IRA had given me for my father. What was I to do with the knowledge? Keep pretending to be deaf and mute, locked in ignorance and procrastination?

During the daily briefings with Pearson, I could no longer look him in the eye. I was now the possessor of vital information that might save lives, and I worried that questions would be asked if I ever blurted out the truth. Why had I been so shy about coming forward with the information? How exactly had I uncovered it? I kept going for weeks, keeping the phone calls secret, in the grip of a rising panic, the fear of being found out, that I was holding on to dangerous secrets, which might prevent injury or death if I had only shared them with my colleagues as soon as I received them.

The voices grew more serious and coherent, and I began to see more clearly the links between what they were saying and the activities of the IRA. I was on the verge of being able to predict where their next attack might take place, and my uneasiness grew. Out of the tangle of information, certain clues kept filtering through. The Belfast wing of the IRA was planning something special. A major incident in which many people would lose their lives in the city centre. The car used by the volunteers, as the voices called the IRA members on active service, would be a green Renault with a distinctive dent in the bonnet and a Tyrone registration plate. I hung on to my end of the phone, enthralled by the flow of information, tormented by the fear that the mysterious truth would never be revealed. I began to remonstrate and argue with the voices.

'If you've something important to tell me, say it,' I told them. 'And when you're done, I want you to stop calling me. Do you understand?'

However, they did not pay any heed to my outburst and the phone kept passing from person to person.

'You know, there's nothing stopping me from getting these calls traced and you all arrested.'

I heard laughter and then a voice spoke slowly. 'Trace them and you'll find empty phone boxes and the backrooms of bars. Anyway, what law are we breaking? We're just chatting to one of our own, a Catholic boy from Dungannon up in the big smoke, making a good name for himself in the RUC.'

'I'm not one of your own. And I don't want to hear from you again.'

'But we've got clues for you.'

'I don't want your clues anymore. I don't want anything from you.'

'You're a detective. You can't turn down clues.'

'I don't trust you. You've some secret plan in mind and I don't know what it is. No one gives away information for nothing. Especially not the IRA.'

'You don't know what our plans are, and you haven't the slightest idea who we are.'

'I know enough to work out this is some sort of trap.'

'You're wrong detective. We're trying to help you. We want to see you get promoted and earn the plaudits you deserve.'

'You're mad. You're nothing but a bunch of thugs puffed up with dreams of murder and revenge. Most of this is in your heads.'

'The only mad thing would be for you to turn down our offer of help.'

'Rubbish.'

'Think of what you're passing on here. If not for your sake, then for the innocent lives that will be lost. We want you to use the clues in whatever way you see fit.'

'And then what?'

'Nothing. We'll keep giving you clues and you keep making a name for yourself as a big detective working with the top brass.'

'I'll be in your debt, won't I? That's your secret plan, isn't it? Once I start acting on your information, you'll think you own me.'

'Own you?' said the voice with a sudden brutality. 'Why would we want to own a little turncoat like you?' At that, my callers erupted with laughter and hung up.

I put the phone down and stared through my bedroom window at the street below. I watched as the dark shape of a car with a dented bonnet pulled on to the other side of the street. It was a green Renault. The driver switched the headlights off, but no one emerged from the car. The driver was waiting for something. Was it some sort of warning intended only for me, or were they planning an attack? Should I phone the station and tell Pearson about the phone call? What exactly were my persecutors doing and did they have any connection with the world out there, the real city of Belfast and its daily roll call of violence?

I would have to make up some sort of story to explain my suspicions. I'd have to tell Pearson something about the phone calls otherwise he'd think I was making it up. But if I told him the true story, he might ask why I hadn't mentioned the calls before, especially when valuable intelligence might have been gleaned from them. To tell Pearson the truth now would tarnish my reputation, and that would mean my persecutors had won. I could not let them win. I sat for a long time staring at the car, and then I went to bed. My only option was to wait for them to make the next move.

The following morning, the green Renault sat parked in the same place. I drove down the street and saw two men inside, both of them averting their faces as I passed. When I turned into the busy traffic on the Ormeau Road, the Renault was following me. In my mind, there was a direct connection between my tail and the phone calls, and the shadowy men inside were the embodiment of the voices that had been tormenting me for the past month. In reality, I didn't understand anything. I was drawing conclusions from whispered words and the random flow of traffic, a set of coincidences that might not belong to the same story.

I stopped behind a bus waiting at a set of traffic lights, and watched the Renault in my rear view mirror. I considered radioing in to the station and asking for assistance. A call could be sent through to the officers operating the checkpoints around the city centre, asking them to detain the vehicle and question its suspects. But on what grounds? The paranoia of a detective who hadn't slept properly for weeks. I closed my eyes and told myself I was overreacting.

When I opened my eyes, the lights had changed. The engine of the bus in front coughed and took off in a spurt of heavy black smoke. I drove towards the city centre. Smoke shrouded the road, and the cars behind me were hidden from view. I cut across the traffic and swung into University Street. I accelerated up the empty road, glancing several times in the rear-view mirror. I kept expecting to see the Renault scuttle around the corner but there was no sign of it.

I manoeuvred my way back through the morning traffic towards Great Victoria Street. A fire engine passed on to Sandy Row, its siren roaring, and then fading. The clatter of a surveillance helicopter rose above the rumble of traffic. It hovered over the city centre. Then an armoured Land Rover went careening after the fire engine. I looked at my watch. It was almost nine. I pulled on to Bedford Street where a group of schoolgirls was getting off a bus, full of excited chatter. They spilled on to the pavement. Then I saw the Renault again, parked about twenty yards from the city-centre security barrier.

A young police officer, wearing a bulletproof vest and carrying a gun, was checking the incoming vehicles. He had just cleared a car, which was inching forwards under the security barrier. My eyes swept back to the Renault. Two men wearing hoodies jumped out and made their way through the schoolchildren. As soon as they turned the corner at City Hall, they sprinted away. The traffic kept moving forward and the schoolchildren made their way along the pavement. As far as everyone was concerned, it was still a normal morning in the city. I was the only one aware of the secret signs.

I swung my car on to the pavement, jumped out and waved at the police officer. I pointed to the Renault and shouted, 'Suspect vehicle!' Then I took off after the two men, who were running against the flow of commuters. I pushed on. A flock of pigeons exploded under my feet. Distracted by their flapping, I lost sight of my quarry. The pigeons settled, and then I spotted them again. They were fifty yards away, standing motionless in a shop doorway and staring at me. I drew closer. What were they waiting for? Their faces were thin and very pale. They looked more like truant schoolboys than dangerous terrorists. They watched me with blank expressions.

Then a bomb went off. The contours of the shop buildings gave a slight shiver and a deafening roar filled the air. The two suspects disappeared from the doorway. I turned round and watched the shaking at the edges of the buildings continue until the street was obscured by billowing smoke and debris. The vibrations shook my body, and then I was running back to the site of the explosion.

I turned the corner, and, for several moments, the street appeared deserted and lifeless, the blown-out shopfronts breathing clouds of dust. A man with a blackened face rose from a pile of rubble as though it were a makeshift bed. He pulled on clothes that were no longer clothes, just shreds that kept falling off him. He kept looking around him. I saw others wearing the same blackened face and bewildered expression, floating like ghosts through the street.

The silence ended with the strange sound of rain. A crunching rain of dust and bits of rubble that blocked the light of day. People gathered in small groups, gesticulating and shouting, carrying the wounded, unrecognisable with their injuries and ragged clothing from the smartly dressed pedestrians I had passed moments earlier. I ran back to the security checkpoint. The green Renault was now a flayed and twisted lump of metal. The young police officer's body lay where it had been flung against a shattered shopfront, his blood clumping on the dusty pavement, broken glass everywhere.

The wail of an ambulance sharpened and the falling dust deepened. A woman's face appeared before me, one of her eyelids torn and streaming blood. The exposed eye peered at me, and then she was sucked back into the dust that swarmed everywhere. The burnt tang of it filled my nostrils and tightened my throat, a swallow of pounded Belfast, bitter and suffocating. The dust got everywhere, even into my eyes, inflicting a form of blindness.

I spent the next week almost permanently drunk. The first thing I did on waking each morning was to reach out for something to drink, and keep going from where I had left off the night before. Anything to prevent the images of the bomb repeating in my head. Alcohol was my tunnel through those weeks, a tunnel with chambers full of ghostly visions of my detective's life, the incident rooms at Crumlin Road Police Station, grave-faced colleagues coming and going, their words of shock and sympathy echoing around me. I had narrowly missed being killed by an IRA bomb, and had rushed back to help the wounded and dying. They treated me with a new-found respect, but I was completely anaesthetised, alone and careless in my desire to keep drinking. Surviving the bomb had given me a special status and set me apart. No one mentioned my drinking, at least to my face.

I no longer had any limits, sipping from a bottle of vodka in my desk drawer, taking little naps during the working day whenever the opportunity arose, going straight to the pub as soon as my shift ended and staying there until early the next morning. Some nights I only went home for a change of clothing and a shower before heading back to the station. I could not escape the phone calls, however. They continued at the same pace, filled with more clues and information about upcoming attacks.

One morning, Pearson called a special meeting for all the detectives based at the station. In the assured monotone he used for rallying calls, he urged us to make a big recruitment drive for new informers.

'Throw money and fast cars at them, if you have to,' he said. 'I sense a change in the Catholic community, a desire for peace. Whatever bits of information you come across, no matter how slight or flippant, make sure you share them with your colleagues. There's always careless conversation and someone drunkenly boasting about a plan. It's your duty to come forth with what you hear.'

I felt that Pearson was addressing me directly, wearing his sternest official face, not a muscle moving, his eyes fixed on me, and his jaw tight. I tried to return his stare but failed. I thought of the phone calls and found myself breathing heavily, my face hot. Behind me, I could hear a low murmuring take hold.

'What did you say?' I asked the detective behind me.

'Nothing,' he replied. His face was expressionless, but I could feel the suspicion radiating from his eyes. I adjusted my body, tuning my ears to what was being said behind my back.

I needed a drink, something to take the edge off my paranoia. I staggered as I rose from my seat, drunker than I realised, my body full of confidence, but somehow unbalanced. I grasped at a chair to steady myself, uncertain of the most direct path to the door. A silence that felt uncomfortably like embarrassment filled the room. I took a few paces forward, hesitated and changed direction towards the door.

'What's wrong with Maguire?' someone asked.

'He's a drunk,' was the low reply.

'Takes one to know one, George.'

'No. Maguire is a Fenian drunk. I'm a loyal Protestant drunk. Big difference.'

It had been ages since I'd had a proper break between bouts of intoxication and I could not remember the sequence of my drinking that day or if I had bothered to line my stomach with food. I was switching between spirits, beer and wine, and sometimes eating nauseated me and weakened the numbing effects of alcohol. Somehow, I had overestimated my consumption. I groped my way to the door, praising myself in a whisper when I successfully exited the room. I shuffled through the back corridors of the station, impatient now, the comments from the meeting ringing in my ears, officers passing me like shadows. I stumbled on, savouring the wave of relaxation and warmth that would pass through me as soon as I got the next hit of alcohol.

At my desk, I gulped down what was left of the bottle stashed there. Later, in a city-centre bar, I talked to anyone who would listen, rambling from one incoherent story to another until I could no longer speak, my tongue as heavy as a deadweight. I stumbled through the crowd, smiling at strangers as though they had just told me a wonderful joke. When I found myself alone at the end of the night, I drank myself into darker depths, muttering all the time, tripping through the streets, gasping and lost and just at the point I felt I was drowning, I awoke in my bed, my body at an awkward angle, sweating and remembering in the light of a new day.

It was late and I had to get to the station. Through the window, I could see washed-out buildings and a rain-tortured street. I watched a youth with a scarf covering his face spray-paint the words 'Ruby is a tout' on to a gable wall, and then run away. I closed the curtains and stared at my bed. How easy it would be to give the day a miss, but I soldiered on, hunting out a fresh bottle of whiskey for breakfast. I gagged as I swallowed but enough went down to ease the hangover. My thoughts dimmed and I was ready for work again.

Another week passed before I emerged from the drunken tunnel my mind was falling through. One afternoon, I found myself in the back of an armoured police Land Rover, surrounded by colleagues from Crumlin Road. I must have been napping and tried to remember where we were going. We were in heavy traffic on Sandy Row. For some reason, we had come to a complete standstill. The minutes ticked by and I felt a weight of tension build in my chest. The pain in my forehead told me that the effects of the vodka were wearing off. Through the metal grill of the side window, I watched a woman with a young boy venturing out from a butcher's shop and then retreating into the doorway, dragging the child with her.

Suddenly, a crowd of people was rocking against the Land Rover. Moments before I had been half-dozing but now I was fully alert. We had strayed into the middle of a loyalist march. Angry men in bowler hats marched past us while their drunken hangers-on swarmed around the police vehicle

I ordered the driver to push through the mob, but he didn't respond. I shouted again, hearing in my voice the cranky desperation of an alcoholic needing his next fix, but the driver refused to move. I peered out at the striding men and women, fitted out with their sashes, playing flutes and drums. A bald man with tattoos smashed his fist against the glass and I cowered.

'Fuck the pope and the IRA,' he roared through his twisted mouth. 'Kill all Fenian bastards.' His insults fused with the swaying motions of the Land Rover. The crowd and the noise of their band instruments felt like a black wind funnelling down the street, throbbing with the beat of Lambeg drums and the trill of flutes, raised like lances in the air. The shouts of the loyalist street flowed through my body, sickening my stomach. The crowd rose, a mock militia, lifting their banners higher. Another heave rocked the Land Rover, and the light from the grilled windows darkened.

'Drive through them, you bastard,' I said to the driver. The marchers now had the Land Rover in their grip like a young bully with a toy. They yanked at the doors. The vehicle's security locks strained and howls of frustration rose from the mob. My colleagues sat like shadows, murmuring in low voices. They were picking out relatives and neighbours in the crowd, with no sign of fear in their voices. I, however, was the only Catholic in the van, and felt like a trespasser who had strayed far from his tribe. I grew more sober than it was possible to imagine, frightened and sweating, expecting at any moment to be dragged from the vehicle and pounced upon. How much more of this would I have to endure? If only I could get back to the station, I'd be all right. All I needed was another surreptitious swig of spirits and the fear would pass. I closed my eyes, breathed deeply and told myself to calm down. But I had a bigger problem than sobriety. What if I had no control over my drinking and was now immune to intoxication? I worried that the weeks of non-stop drinking had saturated my liver and that I would never be drunk again.

The ugly light and the sea of angry faces rose against the Land Rover's windows. I clawed my way towards the front of the vehicle and ordered the driver to reverse and find an alternative route. I grasped the back of his seat and gave the order again.

An hour later, when we arrived back at the station, I took the bottle of spirits from my drawer, and poured its contents down the toilet. I wanted the act to be a ritual rather than a futile gesture, a deliberate renunciation of alcohol and all its false comforts. If I sacrificed the drink that I so desperately needed, I might get my wish to be in control of my life again.

Then I made an appointment to see Pearson the next morning. I planned to be abject before him. I would arrive at his office sober and tell him everything about the phone calls and the car I had followed to the city centre on the morning of the bomb. I would tell him about my alcoholism, how it had given me an edge to get through the working day, but now I wanted to make the painful journey back to sobriety.

I had a story to tell him about the secret phone calls and the green Renault, but the story I eventually relayed to Pearson was not the confession I had planned. It was the story of Ruby, and I told it after downing my usual morning measure of vodka. I walked into the station that morning feeling shakier than I had ever done before. Now that everyone had guessed the truth about my drinking habits, the alcohol no longer galvanised me. Instead, it left me feeling like a patient whose sickness was at the centre of everyone's attention. My delicious routine of secretly drinking spirits while on duty was over. I was now the most conspicuous person in the office, a spectacle, a failed detective. I would have to begin another masquerade if my career as a police officer was to survive, another deceit, another trick.

I thought that the information gleaned from my late-night callers would be more credible and useful if I pretended I had recruited an informer, a man of flesh and blood, rather than this crowd of ghosts who had recruited me. What I needed was a verifiable, paid-up character, one who conformed to the normal patterns of behaviour of an informer, a person who wouldn't raise too many eyebrows from my commanders. I remembered the name of the tout that had been painted on to the gable wall on my street, and Ruby, secret, mysterious Ruby, was born.

When Pearson had listened to my lies, he shrugged and grunted, and said nothing. I was puzzled by his reaction and disappointed. I had been expecting him to cross-examine me on Ruby's identity, or talk eagerly about how we might manage him, verify his story and his details. I had come up with a vague back story about Ruby's life and his great need for secrecy. Pearson, however, showed a clear lack of enthusiasm. Instead, he called attention to my dishevelled state and the poor state my shoes were in.

Yet, I persisted with my story, and from that day on, I began passing on the secrets relayed by my callers, not knowing what the repercussions might be, whether I would get a medal or a bullet for my efforts. After the information led to some breakthroughs, Pearson put me on a special course on security and communications, and exhorted me to get more intelligence from Ruby. He told me to report directly to him and no one else, not even Special Branch.

To my surprise, a wilful blankness overcame him, and he never once asked me for proof of Ruby's existence. In fact, Ruby seemed to be the answer to all his prayers, never mind that his identity was a complete mystery, or that his handler was an alcoholic Catholic detective who had never really fitted in with his team. Pearson set aside a fund to reward Ruby when his intelligence proved useful. He insisted that I make payments to my informer, even though I told him that Ruby wasn't interested in money. I paid the money into a secret bank account and used some of it myself, drinking in pubs, waiting for my lies or a figure like George Smiley to catch up with me.

Even though I grew to trust the information relayed by the voices, they remained remote and inaccessible, and I had no way of contacting them myself. I took precautions to maintain the lie about Ruby, organised visits to hotels and car parks, made payments into secret bank accounts whenever the tip-offs proved valuable. I used all the euphemisms of intelligence gathering and pretended that I had to protect Ruby's identity at all costs. Somehow, the level of secrecy and my extreme caution added to the credibility, made the lie more effective and powerful.

My fellow detectives acted on the information, trusted it, and from time to time it prevented killings. And yet I sensed that there wasn't a single police officer in the station who truly believed in Ruby's existence, that they all harboured some doubt, or deep misgiving, about him, and about me. Perhaps they didn't want to know the truth and preferred to operate in ignorance. Secrets are powerful weapons, and hard to argue against, especially when they save lives and advance careers. But it was also true that my commanders, Pearson in particular, didn't even try to seek the truth. I knew the truth but concealed it out of pride and fear, and those who didn't know, didn't ask questions. That was the code that operated in my unit. I protected the identity of Ruby, and the others protected their ignorance. We were no longer police officers operating out of a heavily fortified police station. We were prisoners locked together in a fortress of ignorance.

I justified things to myself at the start by telling myself that subterfuge was part of my work in Belfast. There were no certainties or cast-iron guarantees with the country on a war footing, just thin mad whispers carrying the chaos of sectarianism. Lies ran in every direction, turning the city into a labyrinth peopled by aliases and double-crossing agents. The Troubles forced me to develop my own resources, my own stories. It was the mother of many duplicitous things, including Ruby.

I hoped I was doing enough to ease my conscience. I was passing on the information that had come my way, and I should no longer feel guilty. I was doing what the voices had asked me to do as well as protecting my own reputation and career. Perhaps they might even stop bothering me and let me go in peace.

There were times when I came close to revealing everything to Pearson, but the words always seemed to stick in my throat. I tried to spit them out, the way the priests had taught me to during confession, but my voice was no longer my own. It was the voice of a man who had killed his career and reputation, and was about to do the same to his colleagues.

TWENTY-NINE

After my confession with the priest, I made my way back to the basilica and walked around its octagonal shape several times. Bats swooped and darted, catching insects above my cowering head. There was no sign of Perpetua or the others on the prayer paths. The pilgrims from the first night had retired to the dormitories, intent on sleep, and the new arrivals were settling down to the first station of their long vigil. I was glad to be alone. I had seen enough bare feet to last me a lifetime. My stomach gurgled with hunger and my legs felt weary, but I kept walking in a fog of fatigue and discomfort.

Just beyond the path, the waves broke in swirls over the rocks. Another monotonous night of waves and winds and forced walking awaited me on this island prison. I had confessed to the sin that had been eating me for months, but still I felt restless. How much longer would I have to carry the burden of my guilt? I decided I couldn't keep walking forever. Someone would be watching and wondering what I was doing. I crept back to the dormitory and slipped into my cubicle.

I put on my shoes and socks, and was stuffing my books and clothes into the suitcase when the door opened.

'What are you doing?' asked Marley, from the door. He was wearing a black raincoat, and his eyes gleamed with a feverish light.

'Going to bed.' I lay down on the mattress and pulled the

blanket over me even though I was fully clothed and wearing shoes.

'I don't believe you. Where are you going?'

I swung my feet out of the bed and sat there. 'Into hiding,' I told him. 'There are plenty of buildings on the island. I'll find a safe corner somewhere.'

'How long do you plan on doing that?'

'Until morning. When the first boat leaves. I'm going to treat this as my final penance.'

Marley removed a bottle of spirits from his coat and held it aloft. 'Before you do, shall we drink a toast, Detective? To you and your miraculous informer.' He slurped from the bottle and passed it to me.

I assumed it was poteen and ignored the offer. I leaned against the wall and grew aware of his dreadful curiosity, his eyes glinting at me. We stared at each other as from opposite ends of a narrowing tunnel.

'You're suspicious of me,' I said.

'I'm not suspicious of you. It's you who's suspicious of me.'

'Were you sent to watch me?'

'Put it this way, I'm not here to stare at the feet of fucking sinners day and night.' He spoke in an ugly and sarcastic manner, and I had a bad sense of foreboding. What else was he hiding under the cover of his drunkenness?

'If you want off this island,' he said, 'we can work on an escape plan together.'

'What do I have to do?'

'I have a rowing boat hidden on the eastern side of the island. All you have to do is tell me Ruby's real name.'

I grabbed the bottle from him, wiped the mouth with my sleeve, and drank from it. The raw alcohol cut my throat. Definitely poteen.

'Who exactly is Ruby?' he asked.

'An informer.'

'But did you ever meet him in the flesh? What does he look like?'

I took a deeper drink.

'Easy now,' he said, grabbing the bottle back from me. 'Don't drink it all at once. You're going to leave us without a drop on this island of holier-than-thous.'

I lay back in bed again and pulled the blanket over me.

'What colour are his eyes? His hair? Does he have a beard or a moustache?'

'Don't you ever get tired, Marley? All these endless questions.'

'Special Branch doesn't believe that Ruby is real. They say you can't be trusted.'

'Leave me alone.'

'Just give me a name and I'll take you to the boat. Then your purgatory will be over.' He stumbled closer. My gaze switched from his greedy eyes to his bare feet, all sinew and gnarled hairy toes.

'I can't say. It's a secret.'

'But why keep it secret any longer?' He leaned closer. 'Why be loyal to someone who has betrayed you, or whose cover is already blown? You can't stay loyal to a doomed spy forever.'

'I can. You don't understand anything.'

'What don't I understand?' His feet padded closer like the hooves of a restless animal.

'I need Ruby to stay in the shadows. At least until I'm off this bloody island.'

'But there are too many shadows around Ruby. Nothing about him is fitting together. Can't you see?'

He gave a throaty laugh and drank from the bottle, concentrating on each sip, as if every mouthful was precious.

I recognised the familiar habit of an alcoholic. Booze was his consolation, his only friend. He handed me the bottle, and I raised it to my lips, but it was empty. I threw it to the floor and he laughed again, louder.

I'd had enough of his drunkenness and his shuffling feet. I rose up out of bed and bundled him out the door. His body was inert and sullen, and he did not attempt to resist me. His eyes were lost in his drunkenness. I shoved him into the corridor, shut the door and then crawled back to bed.

I lay awake, clinging to my thoughts, determined to see the night through. I had stopped caring about everything else. Beyond this intention, there was no other goal. Mercifully, Marley seemed to have given up his torture of me, and the other men in the cubicles had fallen asleep with the exhaustion of slaves. I could hear their snores and the murmur of their sleep-talking rise into the vault above us, confessing their stories in garbled words.

Hunger and tiredness ran in shivers through my body. Every time my eyelids drooped, a dream erupted with tantalising images of Belfast and home, the genial babbling of a pub packed with police colleagues, the joshing and the infusion of high spirits and alcohol, everyone giving each other wink winks and nudge nudges and roaring with laughter at the latticework of lies and betrayals. Other images came whizzing towards me, Pearson's face, tense and bright, asking for the latest update on Ruby and then marching past without waiting for an answer, and then I saw the faces of my murdered colleagues trudging towards me in single file, their faces so relaxed that I envied them their peace and solitude.

Finally, it came, a soft knock on the door of my cubicle.

The door inched open and a light fell on my face. 'The prior will see you now,' said Father Devine quietly.

He handed me a religious booklet and without saying

another word, escorted me to the prior's residence. I opened it and found in the back, hastily scrawled, a telephone number. I thanked him but he made a dismissive gesture. He led me to a building beside the jetty and up a flight of stairs to an oak door. He knocked sharply and we entered. I stepped into a large study, its windows covered in purple drapes, the walls lined with heavily varnished shelves and methodically arranged lines of books, every thing bound up and tucked away in its place. It took me a moment to realise there was someone else in the room, sitting with his back to me in a deep armchair next to the fire, an open prayer book propped on his black-frocked knees.

The prior seemed as secure of his place as everything else did in the room, but in the moment he turned and fixed his gaze upon me, he looked uncertain, as though I were some sort of burglar or bailiff intent on extracting him from his comfortable little nook. Devine led me to the fireplace and gestured towards a smaller armchair next to the hearth, and then he left the room.

'I was about to have supper,' said the prior, 'but out of respect for your vigil, I've chased away the cook.' He closed his prayer book and tapped it several times on his knee in the manner of a man with pressing subjects to discuss. 'It's not my normal practice to invite pilgrims up here. Usually there are plenty of priests to handle confessions.'

'I thought I was here for a private chat. Not a confession.'

'Call it whatever you like, Detective Maguire.' He smiled softly. 'Tell me, do you believe in purgatory?'

'Have you ever seen the effects of an eight-hundred-pound bomb during rush hour?'

The prior opened his prayer book, reached for the gold-tasselled bookmark and pulled it tight. 'What I'm trying to work out is your true purpose in coming here.'

'To be blunt, I'm more interested in leaving.'

'What happened to your trousers?'

I looked down and saw they were scuffed with dirt. 'I was attacked. Knocked to the ground.'

'Did you see this attacker?'

'No. But I'm convinced they are hiding somewhere on the island and wish me harm.' I bent forward and showed him the wound that had matted the back of my head with blood.

He held up his hands. 'It's quite possible your presence here has agitated one of our pilgrims. Not you personally, but what you represent. You are a serving member of the Royal Ulster Constabulary, after all.'

'So that makes it OK to attack a fellow pilgrim?'

'No, it doesn't. We're all responsible for our actions.' His voice grew colder. 'This afternoon, some of the cleaners discovered empty bottles of vodka in the dormitory. Also, complaints have been made about a male pilgrim looking the worse for wear and harassing a female.'

'Really?'

'Yes, really.'

'Was it the female who made the complaint?'

'No.'

'Any other complaints about this male looking the worse for wear?'

'No.'

'Sounds like it might be spiteful gossip.'

He leaned back in his armchair and paused. 'Father Devine has suggested we grant you special permission to leave the island. When do you want to go?'

'Right now, if that's possible.'

He gave a frosty smile. 'The boatman has gone to bed.'

I returned the cold smile. 'Then we'll have to get him up.'

'Before I do that I want to make you an offer.'

'What sort of offer?'

'A chance for you to do something noble with your life. To take away this guilt that burdens your conscience.'

'What do you know about my guilt? You're prying into my secrets. You and everyone else here.'

'No, we're not.'

'I can see it in your faces. The strange looks you give me. You know more about why I'm here than you're letting on.'

'We've read the newspaper reports. The looks are merely human interest and sympathy. Your plight has moved us and it is in our nature to reach out to lost souls.'

I watched him closely, his glassy eyes, the skin of his plump cheeks, pillow-soft, not rough and weather-beaten like the pilgrims. Could I trust him? I heard him catch his breath and then he spoke.

'I can help you, Detective. You see, I'm part of a special network.'

I watched the tremor of a vein on his forehead. For the first time with him, I felt a spark of danger in the air. 'What sort of network?'

'I have secret links with the IRA. They tell me you've proved capable of passing deniable messages, important information upstairs to your commanders in a way that protects the source and your own reputation.'

'Who told you that?' He could have been setting a trap and I was on guard.

'Let me explain. The Republican movement is trying to pursue more peaceful methods, and I belong to a group of trusted individuals who have known the IRA leaders since the early days, and are trying to help them move in the right direction. I'm not a kingpin, or anyone significant in the network. I don't have any powers or influence, and there's a lot of danger in what I do.'

He moved in his chair as if he was going to rise, but he didn't. 'The IRA has asked me to make you an offer. They want you to act as a go-between, help them find a way to the peace table.'

I made no reply. The prior's face grew relaxed again. The ease of his smile was completely alien to the suspicions rising in my head. I thought of the ripped-up postcard and the message on the back, my lonely vigil on the island and then the confession with Father Devine. Was this the reason I had been summoned to Lough Derg? 'Jesus Christ,' I said. 'You're... they're serious about this?'

'Yes. They think it would be easy for you to come up with a reason to keep coming and going to Station Island.'

'My meetings with them would happen here?'

'That is their plan. Anywhere else would be too conspicuous for both parties. As the prior, I have guaranteed them confidentiality. I believe that their intentions are honourable.'

'Why would I risk my career and personal safety to become a messenger boy for the IRA? I've worked my way up through the ranks. It's taken me eighteen years.'

'Remember, you are here to save your soul, not your career, Detective.'

'Dear God, you must think I am mad.'

'Are you?'

'No.'

I took a deep breath. I could almost taste the raw fumes of Marley's poteen in my mouth. I needed another drink. 'So the night of the ambush, I was spared because I was their asset?'

He shook his head firmly. 'The IRA has told me they did not shoot your colleagues. They had nothing to do with the ambush.' He turned to the fire and began to stoke the coals, his plump face enveloped in the burning glow.

'What are you saying?'

'They wanted you to know.' He put down the poker and leaned forward as if to see my reaction better. 'Your colleagues' blood is on the hands of some other organisation.'

I laughed.

'What's the matter?'

'I'm confused. Why would they lie about the ambush? By all accounts it was a great success.'

'Precisely. They've more to lose by telling you the truth.'

And what did they have to gain by lying to me, rather than torturing me with more doubts and suspicions? I let the news sink in, going over the events that led up to the ambush, Pearson's postponement of the original operation, the previous threats to my life, realising that other forces may indeed have been at work, and the truth might be something completely different from what I had believed.

Slowly, I came back to the prior and our conversation. 'I see. This confirms a lot. It explains why I was sent here.'

If it had not been the IRA, then neither I nor the voices were to blame for the ambush, and all that guilt should be heaped elsewhere. A new terrain revealed itself. The fiction of Ruby, the IRA, and the secret interplay between the three of us. While I had been creating the cover story of Ruby, the IRA had been fashioning me into their instrument, their agent. The symmetry left me feeling disturbed. The way the IRA had lured me into a no-man's-land, a moral limbo, the powerful physical presence of which was this island of purgatory. I stared at the prior. Did he and the IRA really expect me to sign over my career with such ease and ignorance? Was this why they had forced me to compromise myself with the lies about Ruby, so that I would be glad to sacrifice my career and forge ahead with their plans?

'Well, Detective, what do you think?' asked the prior.

'No,' I said with belligerence. 'I won't do it. I can't do it.' If there was some political game being played by the IRA through the prior, then chances were the both of us would know only a small part of it.

The prior sighed. 'All they want to do is open a channel with the RUC. They probably might never use you, but they want to know that the possibility is there. Someone who might help them gain concessions, enough leverage to take Republicans to the negotiating table.'

I remained stony-faced.

'Think of it as an experiment. A chance to become a good detective and play a dynamic role in bringing peace to this country. Is it possible that you are the person they are looking for?'

'What they are looking for is a sacrificial lamb.'

'That is quite possible, too. Would a further stay on the island help you clear your mind? Another opportunity to do the vigil?'

'Definitely not. Is that what the IRA is suggesting?'

He shook his head.

'Then I've heard all I need to hear. I can't say I trust the IRA any more than I did before, knowing now their plans for me. I'd like you to arrange for me to leave the island. As soon as possible.'

The prior appeared to relax. 'The workings of the IRA are impenetrable really. This might all be a game they're playing, dragging a detective like you down here, torturing you with guilty doubts, encouraging you to step across a dangerous line. They might just be enjoying themselves with the hold they have over you.'

'You sound very cynical for someone striving for peace.'

He laughed ruefully. 'Perhaps I'm not the conduit they think

I am. In a way, I'm glad you've declined. I would have felt responsible for you and your safety. I'll pass your decision on to the IRA; tell them you're not the man for the job. Hopefully, they'll drop their interest in you.'

'I appreciate your efforts.'

'Like I said, this is a dangerous role for me. I'd prefer if you kept this conversation confidential.'

'Of course.'

'In return, I shall do my best to get you back to shore and to what you regard as safety.' He clapped his hands, signalling that the matter had been concluded and a deal struck. He smiled, more warmly than before. 'Now, let's see if we can get you a boat.'

I returned to the dormitory to collect my things and then we walked down the path that led to the jetty. I looked left and right to check that no one was waiting in the shadows. I took a covert glance at the prior, noticing the look of tension that had returned to his expression. What sort of connections did he have with the IRA and what was the secret network he had referred to? What sort of powers could they summon up to fulfil their goals?

'Perhaps your time here has brought you closer to God?' he asked. His question seemed absurd with the threat of the IRA hanging over both of us.

'Last night, I thought I felt something. But it might just have been nostalgia for my Catholic upbringing.'

The prior lead me through a gate that had been locked earlier and pointed me to a private jetty out of bounds to the pilgrims. He quickened his pace. Was he setting me free or banishing me from a place of refuge? 'An honest answer, Detective. Sometimes, I suspect many of our visitors from the North are using their faith to defy the Protestant state of Northern Ireland.'

The boatman was waiting for us. He touched his cap respectfully and nodded at the prior, but did not say a word to me. I turned back to the prior who stood on the pier like a gloomy sentinel, waiting for someone or something, it seemed. Into my mind came the sound of my late-night callers and I suddenly felt afraid of the dangers that awaited me back on shore.

The boatman dropped the mooring line, fidgeted with the controls of the boat, and grew preoccupied. He mumbled to himself and went below deck. A while later, he emerged, face frowning, his hands covered in oil. The stink of diesel rose with him. He showed his palms in a gesture of futility. 'Someone's cut the fuel line.'

I turned to the prior, who was frowning. 'What shall I do now?' I said. 'Swim for shore?'

'No, Detective,' he replied. 'I think you should pray.'

THIRTY

I left the prior at the jetty, determined to find a safe hiding place on the island until morning. Wandering along the prayer paths, I heard someone shout my name, shrill and accusing. I sought comfort amid the nooks and crannies of the penitential beds, their cramped stones and crosses now reassuringly familiar to me, even in the moonlight. I grew spooked when I heard the voice call my name again. I listened carefully, trying to locate the direction of the voice, and then I set off.

At the doors of the dormitory, a figure stood, waiting for me.

'We need to have a little chat, Maguire.'

It was Marley. I thought I had confessed to everything, wiped my internal slate clean, but his gloating eyes reminded me of the unanswered questions still dogging me.

I gave him a searching glance. I couldn't make out if he was smiling or sneering. 'A little chat about what?'

'Let's go somewhere private.'

He beckoned me with a swift jerk of his arm. The moon disappeared behind a cloud. Even in my exhausted state, I seemed to have a limitless capacity for following others in the darkness of this cursed island. I took off after him, along the black edge of the lough, careful not to slip into the water, orientating myself to the sound of his breathing. I thought of all my solitary investigations, the cases without beginning or end, the vast geography of betrayals, the lies that blended into other lies, the suspects and informers who blended into other suspects and informers, the countless shadows like Marley, and all of it extending throughout my life, the unremitting suspicion of it all. Was it because there was only one true shadow hiding behind everything else, one source of darkness, unchanging and eternal, the darkness cast by me?

We reached a secluded part of the shore, and Marley began pacing up and down in an agitated manner. There was something dangerous yet vulnerable about his unsteady body and flapping coat, his shoes slipping and sliding in the soft mud. 'You're a marked man, Maguire,' he said, breathing hoarsely. 'It's time you knew that. You have to leave the island with me right now. I've a boat hidden nearby.'

'You can't drag me out here and threaten me like this.'

'I'm not the one you need to worry about. You've far more dangerous enemies waiting for you tomorrow.'

'Who are you talking about?'

'Chief Inspector Pearson, for one.'

The name jarred me. It was the one I least expected to hear. 'I wouldn't trust Pearson as far as I can throw him, but he's not a dangerous enemy.'

Marley stopped pacing about. He panted with irritation. 'Have you ever thought about your commander's role in the ambush? Did you ever wonder why he insisted on postponing the visit to the farmhouse?' He walked back and forth in front of me, trying to get under my skin. 'You went to him for help after the ambush and he betrayed you by tipping off Special Branch. You're a detective, why have you never questioned his motives and his loyalties?'

'Pearson's not to blame for anything. Leave him out of it.'

'Not to blame? Of course, he's to blame. Don't you know?' There was an edge of scorn in his voice. 'About a year ago, there was a funeral back in your hometown and you were meant to show up, but you didn't. Pearson was informed that the IRA was planning an attack against a police officer that day in Tyrone. He should have warned you, but he didn't.'

'Why would he not warn me?' I stared into his unstable eyes.

'You must know why. Stop playing the innocent with me.'

'Obviously, I'm not as well informed as you by your commanding officers.'

'Pearson kept silent because he didn't want to blow the cover of a top-level informer. The IRA would have realised you'd been tipped off. As indeed you may well have been, but from a different source.'

From the greedy look in his eyes, I could tell he was talking about Ruby. I felt chilled by the implications of what he was saying. 'I knew nothing of any plot to kill me. No one tipped me off. I came down with a heavy cold that morning and decided to stay in bed.'

'Is that the truth? So either Ruby knew nothing of the IRA operation or he was prepared to let you die that morning as well.'

'Look, Marley, what you're saying is rubbish. Pearson would never have allowed one of his officers to be sacrificed like that.'

'It's not the first time he was prepared to sacrifice a police detective. On the night of the ambush, Pearson made sure Robinson was in the team because he knew Robinson had uncovered incriminating evidence against him and his officers. It was all a set-up orchestrated by someone close to Pearson.'

'If that's the case, why did I survive?'

'Because everyone would then think you were behind the plot.'

A sick feeling crawled through my stomach. Had I been blind to Pearson all along? What Marley was saying certainly fitted with the IRA's claims that they had nothing to do with the ambush. I had been blind to many things. My sense of judgement had been weakened by my lies about Ruby. I had not been aware of how many deceptions might be operating at Crumlin Road Police Station. And here I was about to embark on an escapade with Marley to guide me, relying on him for the strength and inspiration I had hoped to find from other sources on Station Island. I shivered with the cold.

'We need to talk to Ruby, Maguire. And find out exactly why he tipped you off about the farmhouse.'

'Yes, we will talk to him.'

'Then shall we proceed to the boat?'

'OK, let's go.' I took the bottle from him and drank greedily from it.

He watched me with a slowly spreading grin. 'That's it, Maguire. You'll be a different man altogether with the poteen in you.'

The alcohol burned in my empty stomach as we set off. The night sky swung above us, full of stars and swollen with darkness. I tried to follow Marley, but kept turning corners that weren't there, correcting my unsteady progress along the dimly lit path. Marley swiped an arm at me and pulled me towards a clump of bushes. He shoved me forward and I fell into the front of a small boat hidden under the branches.

He spoke in the firmest voice he could muster. 'You will take me straight to Ruby when we land on shore.' Then he loosened the mooring rope, pointed the boat into the night, and stumbled in beside me.

The boat smelled of rotten wood and was thickly coated in damp. I lay still as a rabbit caught in a trap. 'Whatever you do, don't drown us for Christ's sake.'

Marley wielded the oars and strained against them with the clumsiness of a man embarking on a reckless drunken adventure. 'Now we're off, eh, captain,' he said. 'Soon all your trials with Ruby will be over.' He splashed the oars in the water.

'Just keep rowing in a straight line,' I replied. I found the bottle of poteen and downed another slug of the fiery liquid.

Thereafter, I moved as little as possible, while Marley rowed vigorously, rocking the boat from side to side. Sometimes the oars missed the water or skimmed the surface, splattering water over my feet and knees. I warned him to be careful again, but without much hope. He rowed like a champion of the condemned, propelling us into the vastness of the lough, a grin glued to his face. I leaned back and listened to the creak and splash of his rowing.

'We'll soon be there, chum,' said Marley.

I nodded.

'Both our trials are almost over.'

'Yes.'

'We'll slip away into the night.'

He kept rowing, marking each thrust of the oars with his heavy breathing. I looked back and saw the basilica and its lights retreating. The mainland had seemed inviting with its thick forests and empty mountains, but the shore we were rowing towards looked like a hellish place in the weak moonlight, full of dark jutting things, rotten tree trunks and upended roots, a landscape half-drowned by rain and the rising levels of the lough.

A thought occurred to me. 'Maybe I did die in that ambush and this is purgatory or worse,' I said.

'Worse?'

'Yes. Worse. I'm beginning to think that I'm headed for hell. Cheers, Marley, you're the first person I've shared that with.'

Marley seemed deep in thought as he rowed. The night air was uncannily still, disturbed only by the plop and splash of the oars. 'What makes you think you're going to hell?'

'The island and the fact that I'm trapped on this boat with you.'

'If we're on the way to hell, then who am I?'

'One of the devil's agents.'

'Sent to punish you?' asked Marley.

'Yes.'

Marley took out the poteen and began sipping from it. 'You're absolutely right, Maguire. I work for the devil.' He appeared not to be taking my claims too literally.

'And what about the others on the island? Are they in league with the devil, too?'

'Most probably.'

'And the woman I was talking to?'

'Definitely.'

'So, I'm a lost soul doomed to eternal torment?'

'Take a sip, Maguire. I think you need it.'

'Where are you taking me to?'

'Like I promised, I'm taking you off this island to meet Ruby. Ask yourself this, Maguire, if this is hell or purgatory, how will you go about freeing your soul?'

I drank from the bottle and did not reply.

Marley spoke again. 'All we need now is some assistance from your friends. A safe house, some money and a car.'

I straightened up. 'What friends?'

'Come on, Maguire. You're still playing the innocent.'

'I don't know who you're talking about.'

There was a long silence, broken by the slap of the waves against the boat. In the distance, I could hear the whirring of a low-flying helicopter. Marley laid down the oars and pushed the bottle back to me.

'Don't worry,' he said. 'If you've changed your mind we can always row back to the island straight into the arms of Special Branch and the Gardaí.'

The sounds of the helicopter rotor blades grew louder but still it was invisible in the sky. What sort of trap lay waiting for me? A cast of satanic tormentors, Pearson, Special Branch, the journalist McCabe, and my IRA tormentors? I cursed them all.

Marley's face loomed closer. He leaned back and began rowing again, grinning at me all the time, his breathing hoarse, more strained.

Was this the disgusting finale of my pilgrimage to Station Island? Trapped in a boat with this foul double of my life shuffling me towards the gates of hell?

'I want you to turn back,' I said.

'But this is our escape route. We had a plan, remember.'

'I don't care. I don't want to be part of it anymore.'

'You still haven't told me what Ruby looks like.'

'He stays mostly in the shadows.'

'But is he short, tall, fat or thin?'

'Medium build, I'd say.'

'How do you communicate with him?'

'He communicates with me. Usually by phone. I have no way of contacting him.'

'Has he ever told you anything about his role in the IRA? Is he involved in high-level decision-making?'

'I never asked him.'

'So, all this time he was telling you secrets and still you don't know his role or rank in the IRA?'

'What I knew, which was very little, I deduced from the information he gave me.'

'Is he married? Any children?'

'Questions like that are getting us nowhere.'

'That nicely sums up our predicament right now.'

'I never questioned Ruby about his role or his private life.'

'Did he ever mention another mole, someone working for Pearson?'

'Nothing like that.'

'What about the steps the IRA would take against a suspected informer? Did he ever mention that?'

'No.'

'Why are you so shifty when I ask questions about him? Ruby gave you the information and you passed it on to Pearson. You acted in good faith. He's the guilty one, not you.'

'I'm used to guilt. I can handle it on my own.'

'When I get my hands on Ruby, I'll extract the truth from him. I'll make him pay.'

'I'd rather you leave him alone.'

'You're too attached to your informer, Maguire. He's your real torturer. Not me, nor anyone in Special Branch.'

A hesitant breath of wind wafted from the shore, and then a more certain gust, pushing the boat slightly off course. Marley rowed with more purpose.

'Why won't you tell me what he looks like?'

'I want you to turn back to the island.'

'This is our escape route. We had a plan remember.'

'I don't care. I don't want to be part of it anymore. I was only pretending to go along with it.'

'You've been lying to me all along.' His voice lowered to a dangerous growl.

I could tell I was in trouble but I had been in worse situations. I had a good view of my enemy and he was encumbered by a set of oars. In a strange way, I found it soothing to watch him puffing and heaving at the oars with the manic energy of an evil spirit.

Marley spoke in an injured voice. 'All I'm asking is for you to be honest with me.'

'I don't think I can do that.'

'Why not?'

'I don't like you and I don't want to escape with you.'

'You're mad, Maguire. All this talk about hell and purgatory.

225

You've been mad for months, but somehow you convinced everyone that you're sane.'

'I was just trying to be a good detective.'

'Enough now, Maguire. It's time you started telling me the truth. No more lying words.'

In the moonlight, the shore seemed to have receded. I could see that we were off course. Either Marley had rowed the boat back into the middle of the lough or a powerful current was carrying us sideways. Perhaps he had just been rowing blindly in the dark and never intended to reach land.

'Come on you little rat, you lying bastard. Do as you're told and tell me the truth about Ruby.'

To prove his point, he removed a revolver from his inside trouser belt and waved it at me. He had swept aside all pretences, all scruples. 'You see this?' he said. 'You're going to answer my questions now or I'll shoot you and dump your body overboard.' Brandishing the gun in one hand, he seized me by the arm and dragged me closer.

'You can't kill me,' I said, staring into his gloating eyes. 'Not if I'm in hell already.'

I grabbed one of the oars, and swung it, aiming to wind him in his chest, but it struck him on the arm. The force of the blow made him drop the gun. It fell overboard and sank under the waves without a trace. Marley stared at the water, and then at me, his face white. I prodded him to the back of the boat. He groaned and raised his face towards me, supplicant, like a cowering dog, mumbling apologies and calling me by my name. I lowered the oar, relaxing my grip, and in the same instant, he reached forward with a violent thrust and grasped the other end. I held on grimly. We were now half-standing, half-crouching in the middle of the boat, battling for possession of the oar.

'This is your last chance, Maguire,' he said. 'It's Ruby they want, not you.'

His foul breath aroused an acute hatred in me. I pushed the oar into him, but he retaliated with greater force, lurching sideways and attempting to wrench the oar from my grip. I levered myself into a more commanding position and forced him to his knees. I could feel the fight in him slowly wane and his hold weaken. I had more reserves than I suspected. I swung the oar out of his hands and bore down upon him with the gravity of months of frustration and loneliness. Anger flooded through me as I knocked him into the prow of the boat. I swung again, striking him on the head, and this time he tottered towards the edge. It was the weeks of pressure building in my chest. The lashes of guilt against my ego. With another swing of the oar, I propelled him closer to the water. Stupid, evil Marley. We had nothing in common and he was not my double. He was nothing to me. Just as everything on the island was nothing to me, except the guilt and the cold suspicion all around.

His eyes rolled back and his arms swung in the air. He gave a loud gasp and fell into the lough. A wave washed over him, and then he sank from sight. Moments later, his arms reared out of the water and groped for something to hold on to. I watched him struggle and then plunge from view. The boat drifted. A cloud of bubbles broke the surface, and then his head and shoulders emerged further away before disappearing beneath another wave. I waited for him to appear again, but nothing happened. The waves were smooth and black. I leaned over the boat's edge, and saw the dark shape of his body slanting below the water's surface. Once more, his head tipped out of the water, his eyes like lumps of jelly, his mouth spluttering water, and then he sank again.

It seemed a just ending for him, a man who was prepared to send me to my doom, but the vengeful feelings within me changed shape and faded away, leaving behind the familiar spectre of guilt. Wasn't Marley only doing his duty, as I had done, obeying the people who had organised my downfall but did not have the courage to implement it themselves? I looked up and saw Station Island with its basilica shining above the waves, and my thoughts slipped out of darkness. Who was I to send this Judas to his death? A traitor like Marley should be allowed to decide his own fate, as Judas had done, and as I was about to do. I reached out with the oar, hoping that Marley would reappear and grasp it. I fished it through the water and then I felt it strike against something.

Marley rose out of the depths, tugging at the oar, spitting water and curses at me, his coat swelling around him. He clung to the oar, but he was too heavy to pull back on to the boat, and I was afraid he would try to haul me down with him. An inflated life jacket lay at my feet, and I flung it towards him. He let go of the oar and grabbed the jacket, hanging on to it for dear life as the waves lifted him up and down, his mouth gaping at me. A small, rocky island appeared in the moonlight about twenty metres away and I convinced myself he would be able to reach it with the help of the jacket.

I rowed back to the island and the light of the basilica, a chasm opening up between me and my retching double. The underside of the boat grated upon the shore and I clambered gratefully on to dry land with Marley's bottle in my hand. I lost balance and fell back into the water. I found myself slithering upon a terrain of rocks covered in mud and slime. I abandoned the bottle and hauled myself towards dry land, loping and slipping down the sides of an embankment. In my drunken imagination, the mass of rocks resembled a crowd of faces wedged together, their eyes and mouths protruding from the water. I could make out furrowed eyebrows, twisted lips, and flared nostrils. I jumped from one rock to another, careful not to fall into the pools of water. What a pity it would be if I allowed myself to be submerged with these doomed souls.

When I reached firmer ground, I hoisted one of the smaller rocks upon my chest and clambered up the path towards the basilica. I unloaded it at the door of the confessional box and returned to the shore for another. I began to understand how burdensome a pilgrim's conscience could be, the interminable guilt and submission. I was a sinner again, a slave of the church, and this was my penance. I worked in silence, hugging the rocks along the paths. It wasn't an easy task I had set myself. The effort of lifting and carrying the heavy stones left me gasping for breath, but I felt I had to keep going. I puffed and wheezed like a steam engine.

A crowd of pilgrims began to gather at the doors of the basilica. They made angry hisses as I pushed through them with my load. However, no one was prepared to stop me. I was utterly exhausted and unsteady on my feet, but it seemed to me that I was finally accomplishing something of importance. I was proud of my handiwork, the rocks piling up in front of the confessional box like a congregation of gargoyles. I felt at peace with Ruby and myself. For the first time since the ambush, I was free and unencumbered. Every vestige of my detective's life had vanished completely. My spiritual awakening, begun in the sober rituals of prayer and assisted by the guidance of Perpetua, had been brought to its conclusion by Marley's poteen and this final bout of drunkenness.

The last rock fell with a thud to the ground. My knees collapsed after it. I knelt down, my head bowed, gasping for breath. I was finished. I would carry no more rocks. All my efforts and exertions would not change the course of my fate by a single millimetre. All I could do now was sleep and wait for morning.

Later, voices woke me from my slumber. When I looked up, I saw Paddy and Kieran standing over me. I tried clambering to my feet, but the darkness spun around, adding to my sense of vertigo. I felt as though I were falling into a pit that opened up into infinite blackness.

'Easy there, Detective,' murmured Kieran.

I lunged away from them, slipped again. I was drunk to the core of my being.

'You're away with it,' said Paddy.

Speaking with all the authority I could muster, I said, 'I'm not away with it.'

They shook their heads and hauled me to my feet.

'What the hell is wrong with you?' said Paddy. 'Writhing about in front of the basilica like a blind drunk.'

'I'm not blind,' I said.

In fact, blindness was the opposite of what I was feeling.

THIRTY-ONE

I woke to birdsong and a patch of water reflections fluttering in front of my eyes. I turned towards the light, my face throbbing with a heavy band of pain. I tried to get my eyes to focus, but all I could see were bright shapes floating on a misty background. The washing sound of nearby waves and all the light made me think I was entangled in the rigging of a boat far out on the lough.

A face flashed before me. I heaved myself into an upright position and tried to get my bearings. Slowly the figure of the prior became visible. I was still on the island, in some sort of white-painted room with a window open to the lough.

'Are you sober?' asked the prior. His face was taut, pale.

I moved and my head swam. 'I think so.' Not completely, but better than last night.

'Follow me.'

For a moment, I saw the blue uniformed figures of Paddy and Kieran standing in the doorway and then they disappeared.

'Marley,' I said with a croak. 'I hope he made it to dry land.' A new wave of nausea overcame me as I remembered how much poteen I had put away the night before.

'Don't worry, your friend washed up fit and well with an empty poteen bottle.'

The sky was completely blue and the low sun glinted off the surface of the lough. Paddy and Kieran were standing at the jetty. They leaned into each other and laughed as if sharing a joke. As I crossed the distance towards them, their expressions changed, growing impassive and flat. I could live with their aloof manner. I stared at the far jetty on the mainland, and breathed in the air. The world that awaited me on shore felt more deranged than the world I had left behind three days ago. It had expanded with threatening shadows and conspirators.

'You're in no fit shape to go anywhere, Maguire,' said Paddy, 'but the prior wants you off the island as soon as possible.' Suddenly, he had the bullying, convivial manner of a country sergeant. 'A police launch is due shortly. We've been instructed to hand you over to the officers at Pettigo Station.' He winked at Kieran in a deadpan way.

When I gave him a questioning look, he shrugged and said, 'For your own safety, Detective, and that of the pilgrims on this island.'

I cleared my throat. 'Am I under arrest?'

'Like I said, it's for your own protection as much as anything else.'

Kieran moved in front of me, his tall figure blocking out the light. Was he my jailer or my guard? I sat down wearily on a bench.

Meanwhile, the pilgrims were congregating on the other side of the jetty, inching towards the edge of the lough like a funeral procession gathering around a grave. They belonged to another world now, and already I could see looks of worry and concern etched on their faces as they prepared themselves for the return to their everyday routines. There was no longer an unearthly light around them, no sense of a strengthening wind passing through them.

Kieran leaned towards Paddy. His voice was quiet, confidential. 'Did you experience anything on the island?'

'I felt nothing and saw nothing.'

'Same here. That's the way the island works, though. Only some people get to experience it.'

They looked at me in an unhappy way, as though I were to blame for their lack of spiritual awakening.

The prior made a short, impassioned speech to the departing pilgrims. I was too distracted to listen to what he was saying, my thoughts on edge from the poteen and the prospects that awaited me, but then I saw the look of concentration on the pilgrims' faces, and a light intensify in their eyes.

In a calm, genial voice, the prior told the pilgrims they now belonged to the holy traditions of the island. They had entered the world of a two-thousand-year-old faith, and during their night-long vigil, everything about their daily lives had disappeared, their everyday worries, wants and dreams, to be replaced, he hoped, by a shared experience of a living faith. It was exactly the same faith nurtured by St Patrick and St Brigid and all the other saints during their years of renunciation and discipline. The prior added that he didn't need to remind them about this, but they should all now focus on returning home; other people depended on them and they had duties to fulfil in the real world, in their families and communities. He reminded them to look after the flame of their faith, and that love and suffering were the keys to understanding all the mysteries of life and death, the bonds they had with their spouses and families, their neighbours and communities. When you have faith and love, he told them, you are ready to learn everything in life.

I managed to summon up some courage from the priest's words, and even a little bouyancy in my heart. I listened as the priest started the rosary one final time. I mouthed a few prayers in unison with the pilgrims until I was interrupted by the chugging of an outboard engine. The police launch boat swung into view and a long, gurgling wave rose against the jetty. The sound of the pilgrims' prayers grew incomprehensible, and I lost my connection to their voices and their faith. I was close to tears and cursed the arrival of the boat for ruining my final moments on the island. With a minimum of fuss, Paddy and Kieran escorted me down the jetty to where the boat was waiting. I could tell from their upright postures, their refusal to make eye contact or engage in any small talk, that they were in official mode, focused on removing a difficult drunk from the island.

For some reason, the boat was not yet ready. I glanced across at the pilgrims. They stood perfectly still, as though they were waiting to enter a different state of being. I turned towards them and gave a little wave to Perpetua, and she waved back. However, I could no longer see her clearly. I was staring through her at the light, feeling a strange sense of happiness stir within. I told myself this was nothing to do with the fact that I still might be drunk. This was all about being on the island, the light that reflected off the vibrant surface of the lough, the light that glowed within the pilgrims, and made their faces seem transparent, their eyes bedazzled. I felt a prickling awareness crawl up my back. The island was the engine of the light, and if I just reached out, I could invite it inside me. The light high up in the sky, and the light on the surface of the lough, the light that surrounded me on all sides with its beauty, and which was giving me this sense of joy mixed with pain because I was separated from the light and might die without ever touching it. Suddenly I wanted to be with Perpetua and the other pilgrims, to stand on their side of the jetty and listen to them chat about the lives to which they were returning. I wanted to hear their voices praying again, to see the light in their eyes, to board the same boat as them, even though they all knew I was an impostor and had failed in my vigil.

I understood that the praying and fasting were symbolic rituals, and the faithless could not partake of them, but just to be able to stand among the pilgrims would be a blessing. I stared at them with the hunger of a ghost watching the living eat and drink. Then, I lurched forward and stumbled. I tried to make a break from the police officers but slipped and banged my head on the wet jetty. When I opened my eyes, Paddy and Kieran were standing over me, seemingly indifferent to the state I was in. They looked ready to let me slither away like a poisonous snake.

I hauled myself to my feet and turning, saw Perpetua hurry towards me from the other side of the jetty, her feet in sandals, and a confident litheness in her hips I had not noticed when she was barefoot. Had she heard about my drunken escapade with Marley?

She stood silently beside me.

'Hello,' I said, and made some space for her on the bench. She did not sit down. She glanced at Paddy and Kieran and asked could she have a moment alone with me. They moved away slightly. She had heard about last night. I could see it in her eyes and in the tightness of her mouth.

'Know them?' I asked, nodding towards Paddy and Kieran.

'Only that they're the police. Is it true what they're saying about you? That you tried to drown a man last night?'

I couldn't tell her the truth with Paddy and Kieran hovering so close by.

'I can't talk about it until I see a solicitor. What about you? Are you connected with the security forces?'

She glanced at me as if I were mad and shook her head. 'I don't have any secrets.'

It was a stupid question. Wasn't it clear that her energy was directed elsewhere, towards the brightness of the basilica and the glow around the island?

'When I heard they had arrested you, I burst into tears.'

'Why?'

'From the moment I first saw you I was so intrigued by your story and the newspaper reports that were being passed around the island. I wondered if something good might happen to you on Lough Derg, and after I watched you I wanted something good to happen to you.' She described how the prior had stared at us on the first evening, at me and then at her, and then back to me. 'I thought there was something hovering in the air between us. And the prior was acknowledging it, but I didn't know you and I had to tread carefully.'

'What do you mean by something good happening to me?'

'A sign from God. Something to help you on your way.'

I nodded. 'It was good to have you by my side. I appreciate what you tried to do. Sorry if I disappointed you.' I was conscious that my breath probably stank of booze.

'Is there anything else burdening you? Something you want off your chest before you leave the island?'

I could not speak. My burden was that I only knew half the truth.

'Look,' she said, 'I don't know what's burdening your soul, whether it's really serious or if it can be healed or not. I don't know your secrets, but I can see that your job as a detective has tainted you and darkened your view of yourself and the world. A heaviness surrounds you. You carry it around with you all the time like a shadow. It's the burden of working with dangerous criminals and paramilitaries. I know you have to perform your professional duties and go back to that world. I can see that. But don't let the evil of that world creep into your life and knot itself to your soul.'

As she spoke these words, I studied her face and my heart lightened. A form of blessing descended on me, a wave of tenderness and compassion mixed with confidence and power. Here was a person of dignity, steadfastness and goodness who believed I could be saved. I felt afraid yet also released. Perhaps my purgatory was finishing and I was finally heading back to my old life, the one I had before the late-night phone calls started. I had declined the IRA's plea to help them negotiate a peace deal and perhaps they would now leave me alone. Let them find a new intermediary, a well-meaning fool who would help them negotiate peace terms with other violent men.

I looked up at the clear blue sky filled with exhilarating sunshine and the only strain I felt in my heart was the tension of ending the lies. My punishment was over. The weight of the shadows surrounding me dissolved into the fineness of Station Island's light.

Paddy leaned over me. 'Come on, Detective Maguire,' he said. 'The boat is ready to leave now.'

Perpetua gazed at me. I thought of reaching out for her hand and kissing it, but she said, 'You have to go now.' Then she walked away with her elegant stride back to the huddle of pilgrims.

Kieran lined me up in front of the boat. 'Watch your step,' he said, pawing at my sleeve.

The boat pulled away from the island, and the waves grew choppy on the lough. We pitched up and down, tossed from the comforting light of the island and its perpetual hum of prayers.

I turned to Paddy. 'There's a journalist waiting to speak to me. He arranged to meet me this morning in the car park.'

'Good luck to him. Everyone wants to speak to you this morning.'

'Who else are you talking about?'

But he refused to answer me.

THIRTY-TWO

A rain cloud looked ready to burst over the car park when we docked at the jetty. A Garda car sat waiting for me and behind it a fresh group of pilgrims was assembling from a hired coach. I recognised the figure of McCabe emerge from the crowd and take up position at the end of the jetty. Behind him, near the entrance of the car park, sat a blue Cavalier with two silhouettes in the front, keeping surveillance, it seemed to me. Had someone been keeping watch for the entire time I was on the island?

A light sheet of rain skimmed over the car park, blurring the figures congregating at the jetty. When it passed, I saw the figure of Pearson emerge and walk past McCabe. His face looked grave and weary as though he had completed a long journey to get here. What was he doing? Did he think that his presence could intimidate me at this late hour? I watched him scan the Garda officers waiting by the car, the journalist McCabe standing behind with his notebook out, and the new batch of pilgrims waiting for the boat to the island. Everyone wore a look of uncertainty, as though they could feel a dangerous stand-off developing. Only an elderly nun sitting on one of the benches, her cowled head bent forward in prayer, seemed oblivious to the unfolding drama.

I took a final look around to be sure that the island was still there, the solid basilica and the crowded mass of religious buildings floating on a wide sheet of silver, vibrant yet tranquil. A pilgrim boat docked and the new arrivals clambered on board. I sensed how this had been happening for thousands of years, pilgrims departing and arriving, a changing of the guard as ordinary and repetitive as the waves rising and falling on the shore.

As soon as I stepped on to the jetty, Pearson marched coolly towards me.

'Will we walk, Maguire?' He was carrying an umbrella, pushing its point into the wooden boards as though it were a walking cane.

'No. The best thing you can do is take me back to Belfast. But before you do, I have to speak to McCabe. Then I'm going to make a full report to Special Branch on the lies I told about Ruby and the events leading up to the ambush.'

'What lies?'

I told him about the late-night phone calls and my dread of the voices whispering secrets. I told him how I had invented Ruby to hide my failures and live a different life as a trusted detective, to process the phone calls and their secrets and protect myself from their sinister influence. I also told him that I had new information to share with Special Branch, information about a planned IRA murder bid that Pearson or his detectives may have known about in advance. I had been the intended target but, mercifully, I had managed to escape death on that occasion, too.

Pearson did not appear surprised by what I said. 'I'd rather you keep going with the story about Ruby being your informer,' he said, with a frown.

I stared at him, puzzled. 'What do you mean?'

'The matter is out of your hands. Ruby was your informer and he set up the ambush at the farmhouse. That's all Special Branch need to know.'

I turned away from him. 'I'm going to speak to McCabe. I'm going to tell him the truth.'

Pearson put his hand on my shoulder. 'Look, Maguire, we've both made mistakes, and I know I've been an inadequate commander.' His frown trembled slightly. 'Granted, I allowed my officers to treat you badly and possibly endanger your life. I allowed them to forge links with loyalist paramilitaries and all sorts of criminals. My officers blurred the lines between investigating the wrongs done to citizens and the wrongs that law-keepers decided should be done in revenge. But I'm asking you to think of the force's reputation and the moral victory you beating your breast in public would give the terrorists. Let's have no more detectives fleeing like fugitives, Desmond, no more careers tarnished, no more suspicions hanging over us.'

'No more suspicions? But if I don't tell Special Branch the truth, I'll never clear my name.'

Pearson removed his hand. 'You've been lying about Ruby for months. What's so terrible about maintaining the lie? Why end it here?'

'I made up the lie about Ruby, but you helped me stage it. It would never have worked without your silence. You kept turning a blind eye, letting me get on with the charade, organising meetings that never took place, making payments into a false bank account.'

'And I thought about bombarding you with questions many times, demanding that you hand him over to Special Branch, let them work with him directly.' Regret lined the features of his face. 'I didn't know what the ending was so I decided to play along with your deception.'

'But it was an honest deception, told to pass information that might have been true. It was your moral duty to end it if you suspected Ruby did not exist. Instead, you allowed me to keep playing it out, to run here and keep the lies going. He who pretends to be deceived is just as dishonest as he who deceives.'

'I've staked my reputation on you and Ruby. I allowed you to play out the delusion that you were a trusted handler of a top-class informant. This is your last chance to save us both from professional humiliation. Think how hard Special Branch will come down upon you.' Pearson rubbed his brow and glanced down at his watch. Was he wondering how much longer he had with me? 'If you can't agree to this, I'll have to take you with me.'

'Are you threatening to arrest me?'

'You're out of my jurisdiction, unfortunately.'

'Then what are you threatening?'

'Tell me this, Maguire. Who else do you have on your side? Look around this car park and tell me if you see any friends or allies. I'm not threatening you with anything, but everyone else is.' He glanced at the Garda officers, McCabe, the unmarked car by the gate. 'You should never have come off the island. You've left yourself badly exposed. You've done everything wrong. But it's not too late to change your plans.' Holding out his hand to me, he gave me his most forthright stare. 'Let's shake on it, Desmond. Sometimes it's not only acceptable for a detective to lie, it's his duty. Everything you told us about Ruby was the path to the truth. In some ways, you're the most honest detective I know.'

He held his hand in mid-air. 'Take it, Desmond. This is your last chance to save yourself. Come with me and we'll both brazen it out with Special Branch. Deny everything. Your lies about Ruby will save you, but the truth will kill us all.'

'I can't live with a lie anymore.'

'Yes you can. Just accept that Ruby is a reality now. Keep the lie going for a while longer.'

'There has to be an ending. The lie was meant to end on Station Island.' I pushed past him, but he blocked my path.

'Listen, it wasn't me who started this. It was Special Branch.

I never wanted you to choose between the truth and a lie.'

'But why did Special Branch start it?'

'I've been told they're investigating every detective's track record. Including mine. All our links with paramilitaries, loyalist and republican, as well as criminal gangs.'

'What have you to fear but the truth?'

'It's the wrong time for internal investigations. The country is stumbling towards peace. The population needs to keep its faith in the police force and know that we would always do the right thing by them.'

'Sorry, Pearson. It's not that easy.' I moved to sidestep him and this time he grabbed me by the arm.

'Why?'

A car engine started in the car park. Pearson raised his voice above the revving engine. 'You can't change your story now, Maguire.'

'You're wrong. I am the story.' I shrugged off his grasp. 'I can change it as I wish.'

Pearson began prodding the umbrella at the jetty walkway. He needed to assert his control over something. However, I could no longer live the stories I had read in my spy books and keep inventing Ruby out of lies. The rules of those books were different from the rules of life. I could not let Pearson trap me in my lie like an insect in amber, drowning forever in cloying guilt. He was the monstrous one, not me. I could see it in his stubborn jaw and haunted eyes, his enraged sense of superiority when I refused to shake his hand. His face turned grey and his eyes hardened.

I would no longer be drenched in suspicion and the bleak light of betrayal. I inhabited a different light, the gem–like light of the pilgrims. On Station Island, I had leapt from one to the other, and now I felt collected and calm as I stared into Pearson's eyes and wished him good luck.

I walked towards McCabe as though gliding across a silver surface, the shadows weaving with the brightness of a new day, hoping that the feeling was not just a passing illusion. Part of me had thought that I would never leave the island, and that I would be bound all round by the night and gloomy water of Lough Derg forever, with no hope of ever reaching beyond my lies. Now that I had reached the shore, I wanted to spend the rest of my days in the service of the truth, even if it brought me to some terrible and lonely place I could not yet imagine.

Ahead of me, the nun on the bench stood up suddenly, knocking over her little suitcase. She bent down to grab the case. I looked back and saw that Pearson had not followed me. He stood exactly where I had left him at the far end of the jetty, gazing keenly back at me, lonely and insignificant with his umbrella against the backdrop of the lough, like someone waiting for the final curtain to fall. I smiled and reassured myself that I was no longer in purgatory or some bad dream. Everything about the morning felt too real.

At that moment, the car near the entrance took off and accelerated, bumping across the uneven surface towards McCabe. Who were they? Pearson's cronies in Special Branch, the Gardaí or a squad of IRA men? A sixth sense made me glance back at the nun. It bothered me that she had reached for her case with such agility. She was bent over, rummaging in her gown. The car rolled towards the jetty and a passenger door flew open. The nun came elegantly out of her stoop, sweeping her arms upwards. She was holding something firmly, raising it and pointing it towards me. It was a semi-automatic gun. I found myself staring at the pale, composed face of a young man dressed in a nun's garb. His gun began firing and I turned away abruptly, trying to dismiss the ugly transformation I had witnessed. My back arched and I shuddered as the bullets struck my chest.

I stumbled away from the black figure towards the light of the lough. I fell at the water's edge and there I remained. Nothing else mattered but my view of Station Island and the lough, brimming with its eerie rays of light and reflections, offering me a cure for all the mistakes I had made, the lies I had told, the betrayals and the countless nights of guilt. I was bleeding and in great pain, but somehow I felt blessed by the lough, its overflowing cup of life raised to my lips as I lay there on the shore. I clung to the vision of Station Island, its buildings like the remnants of a once substantial city still inscrutably afloat, an island that had the secret power to disappear into eternity but did not, lingering instead on the threshold between this world and the next.

The world we live in is the stories we tell ourselves, and mine were all ending. The light slowly dwindled from the lough, shadows draping themselves around the distant basilica, and the island's floating façade sank before my eyes. The shadows passed over me and a vague rain began to fall. If I could only hold on for another minute or two, the rain would probably pass and the day would brighten again, but a coldness had already set into my bones. The lough was brimming with death and I gulped greedily from its cup.

THIRTY-THREE

Afterwards, there was little Pearson could remember of the killer and his face, or of the gunman's movements as he cast aside the disguise of a nun, raised his weapon and fired at Maguire. He hardly saw anything, and in the moments following the attack, he was stunned and numb with shock. He watched Maguire submit himself to the hail of bullets, as though ready to be sacrificed, and stumble to the ground. The shooter then ran to the waiting car, which took off in a plume of gravel and dust. The Garda officers rushed over and prodded Maguire with ignorant fingers and tried to resuscitate him but their hands were soon covered in blood.

He stood over Maguire's dying body and stared at the heavy shadows under his eyes. Someone dashed off to phone for an ambulance, but it was too late. The story of Ruby would go to the grave with Maguire. Pearson was in the clear and yet not in the clear. Maguire's lies about Ruby could never be disproved, yet they were as flimsy as smoke. Maguire was a turncoat, but he was also an innocent pawn. Had the IRA killed him in revenge for the recruitment of an informer, or was his murder part of a more fiendish plot to cover up the tracks of corrupt police detectives back in Belfast? Either way, there would be enough to keep the conspiracy theorists busy for months on end and new layers of deception would be added to the old.

Pearson decided that he should not feel guilty about anything.

Unlike Maguire, he would live with and eventually overcome these shadows on his conscience. Maguire's relationship with guilt had been quaint, comical even, a neurotic Catholic unable to shake off the fear instilled during his youth. Maguire had possessed the conscience of a second-class citizen, an outsider detective. The slightest misdemeanour was capable of having him beat his breast and torture himself with recriminations. Pearson belonged to a different class, a different breed. He would always be an insider, a member of the establishment.

Like a ghoul, the figure of the journalist McCabe hovered at the edge of the scene, and then he came up to Pearson, his notebook at the ready.

'Come for a comment, McCabe?' said Pearson. 'Something to flesh out yet another murder of an RUC detective?'

'I've a couple of questions for you, Pearson.' Gone were the usual courtesies between a hack and a senior police officer.

'Officially or off the record?' He was troubled by the steadiness of McCabe's gaze. There was nothing downward or shifty about it.

'What did you find out about Maguire and his lies?' said McCabe.

'Nothing. It seems that he was telling the truth about Ruby all along.'

'You're not telling the truth. Maguire was an alcoholic and a liar to his boots. Anyone could see through his deceptions.'

Pearson grimaced. For several moments, he glared at McCabe. 'What about you? You were meant to be investigating Maguire, too. What did you discover?'

'A rumour of a conspiracy more disturbing than one man's lies. Something more monstrous but more grubby, too.'

Pearson made to leave but McCabe blocked his path.

'The rumour has it that you knew all along Ruby was a lie,' said McCabe. 'You or someone close to you set up the ambush

246

to protect your detectives from Special Branch investigations, and Maguire was the unwitting fall guy. You needed Maguire to keep fabricating his lies, to keep up the smoke, so that you could stay ahead of Special Branch and their search for corrupt police officers.'

'Do you really believe there's more to this than Maguire and his pathetic informer?'

'I don't have the slightest doubt. That's the terrible thing about the Troubles. You can never stop investigating and probing for the truth. If you stop probing, you're screwed. If you think you've worked out the betrayal and unmasked the traitor, you're screwed. There's always another mask behind the mask, and the real traitor is always running in the shadows.'

'You're adding conspiracy to conspiracy, McCabe. The worst I did was turn a blind eye to Maguire and his schemes, but I'm not to blame for this mess. End of story.'

But even as he said the words, he knew that the story would have no end, that it would keep unravelling in darker alleyways of Belfast among the shadows of his flawed police officers and their downtrodden informers, in the deals that were traded with criminals for information and the cover-ups that were meant to hide all the traces.

'I've made mistakes,' said Pearson. 'But hasn't everyone? What about journalists and reporters like you, who fall for every piece of propaganda and misinformation sent your way. Haven't you passed on lies and people suffered for your mistakes?'

'Wrong. We make the lies public. We show that people in power don't care for the truth, or don't want to know anything about it. If you had cared for the truth why did you not investigate Maguire's informer, why did you let Maguire's explanations pass?'

Perhaps McCabe was right. If he had been less arrogant and more humble, more cautious and less sure of his place in the world, he might have been alerted to Maguire and his lies much sooner. He had got into the habit of convincing himself that he and his detectives were always right and on the side of truth. Some excuse or mitigating circumstance could be invented to ensure that his officers would emerge unharmed from any controversy, and his reputation unscathed. He had never behaved in a way that was wilfully dishonest, at least in the moment of committing the act, and so much of his detectives' investigations had to be conducted in secrecy. It had always been possible to convert the truth into a more palatable form, to add things or distance oneself, or, even better, never to speak or write about it in the first place, to let the truth slowly slip from memory into nothingness.

'Listen, McCabe, we'll never know what happened to Maguire and why he was killed. So many things have happened in this country without anyone realising the truth and in the end everything is forgotten anyway.'

'Special Branch is on the hunt for a traitor. They want to know who set up the farmhouse ambush and they won't rest until they find out.'

'Maguire was the traitor. He was about to confess everything but the IRA shot him before he could reveal what he knew. That's all you and Special Branch need to know.'

'But what about the people? How will they interpret what happened here?'

'Who are the people? The readers of your newspapers? They haven't a clue what is really going on.'

'I have the utmost faith in my readers. I have to stick to the facts but they will understand what I'm not able to report. They will understand the lies as well as the truth.'

Pearson saw it clearly now. The truth would have to be indefinitely postponed. Maguire was dead and would not return, and the story of Ruby would have to be buried with him.

The dead could never be called to account for real or imaginary crimes. He would continue his job as a police chief in Belfast, and give the people what they wanted most. Not light but darkness, a comforting darkness to hide away all the crimes and sins of the past, all the lies and punishments, the betrayals and humiliations, the vengeful underhand actions of the Troubles and its heyday of henchmen and psychopaths. What sort of victim would want the light of day to play constantly over their suffering, to be trapped and half-drowned by the truth and forced to accept the apology of their enemy, everyone carrying on in the rut they were in for years afterwards, a ghostly territory of bitter confrontations and DIY amnesties. The wrongdoers singing their sins but never easing their guilt, and the victims singing their sorrows and suffering all the time. Nothing would ever change. Those who wielded guns could never take back what they had done, and to ask the weakest in society to fight their pain and forgive seemed very cruel. What the people of Northern Ireland needed most wasn't forgiveness and the endless baring of troubled souls. They needed normality and peace, or just enough peace and normality to let them live in the modern world again, have democratic elections and punish the loudmouth politicians by not voting for them, to leave behind the half-life of the Troubles without having to inspect its carnage, and no longer be subjugated by paramilitaries and soldiers carrying guns. Wasn't this a future worth burying the past for?

'You're wasting your time,' said Pearson. 'Now that Maguire is dead, Ruby and all the speculation about his existence will go into the official secrets tray. The answers you're hankering for are fifty years away, and no matter how robust your investigative techniques you can't make time go faster.'

'I'm putting together the story, Pearson.' McCabe was blinking hard. 'I've got bits of the conspiracy and I'll uncover the rest. I've got the names of officers on your team suspected of receiving payments from criminals. I've already talked to one of them and I've got promising leads.'

'OK, McCabe. Keep me posted on whatever you discover. I'm always happy to deny a rumour or a piece of gossip.'

'A deal, then,' said McCabe. 'When I uncover anything you'll be the first to know. How's that?'

Pearson walked off without answering. He was keen to get away before Shaw or a senior Garda officer could turn up and ask trickier questions than the ones McCabe had posed.

He drove through Pettigo and headed straight for the border. His eyes kept flicking at his rear-view mirror but the road behind remained empty. He focused straight ahead with a tunnelled gaze. He reassured himself that Maguire's story was over in spite of McCabe's threats. The truth about Ruby would never be told. Did that mean he had won and that Special Branch would end their interest in the fictitious informer? That he had no obligation to pursue Maguire's killers and uncover the truth about his death? The murder had happened in Shaw's jurisdiction and was not the RUC's responsibility, but did that mean he could give up the search for the truth?

He arrived at the border sooner than expected. There was a long queue of traffic, and soldiers were stopping and questioning the drivers of each vehicle. A soft rain began to fall as Pearson waited at the end of the queue. The checkpoint fortification was lit up by the fuzzy orange glow of sodium lighting, but the mist and the rain blurred everything so that the only fleeting shapes visible were secret and military. He saw a soldier walk down and inspect the line of cars. He stopped a short distance away. The snub nose of his gun was pointed at the ground, but his eyes stared hard at Pearson's car, noting the registration. Something awoke in Pearson, a growing uncertainty, a conviction of impending doom.

The car ahead inched forward, but Pearson kept the engine idling for a few moments, trying to work out in his mind the strange fear that was coursing through his veins, this precarious sense that the border was balancing on the edge of time and space, that he was about to cross some sort of knife-edge in the landscape, one with an overhanging and bottomless drop on the other side, stretching steeply all the way to his police station in Belfast. It struck him that, if Maguire was the fall guy for the first ambush, then he was the fall guy for Maguire's murder. Was this why Bates had dispatched him down to the border to tail Maguire in the first place? Or was he a pawn in someone else's game, the secret committee of police officers and politicians, who had requested him to take Maguire under his wing and encourage his silence?

He put the car in reverse and retreated back down the road he had come. He turned off at the first side road available and pressed the accelerator hard. He drove north into the bogland of Donegal, skirting the border. He made slow progress, reversing out of dead-ends, and inching across blind crossroads. He passed the huddles of derelict cottages descending into nests of briars and nettles, all the time hoping that the roads would rearrange themselves into a familiar pattern or a sign would appear to direct him over the border.

The pine-forested hills parted to give views deep into Donegal, tilting towards the evening sky, but never into Tyrone on the other side of the border. That view was sealed off completely. He spent a solid hour manoeuvring the car over potholed roads and humped lanes with weeds growing down the middle, the view from his windscreen filled with low cloud and bogland threaded with tortuously thin fields and pine forests, the perfect setting for a ghostly fairy tale. He kept to the centre of the road, fearful that his car would slip at any moment from the winding narrowness of the civilised world and be lost forever. Only when he was over the border and back into Northern Ireland could he count on feeling halfway safe.

The countryside changed. The bogland gave way to pasture and neatly hedged fields, and the farms grew more modern and tidier, the farmhouses comfortably off in appearance. A subtler shade of green took over. Shiny new livestock silos and feeding towers emerged from the rotting stumps of ancient byres. He felt a kinship with this new landscape. It mirrored his taste for the orderly and new. He had left behind the straggle of slovenly farms and unlovely bogland that characterised Donegal and was now back in the North, travelling through Protestant farmland, a sense of calm at every level, from the trim hedgerows to the freshly mown grass and the mud-free farmyards.

The sight of the Garda checkpoint in the middle of the road made him brake sharply. He was disorientated, believing he had already crossed the border, slipping across one of the back roads he had once known like the back of his hand, but he was as far away from home and safety as winter is from summer. He felt faintly dizzy, some sort of geographical vertigo taking hold.

The figure of Commander Jack Shaw appeared out of the drizzle and waved at him. For a cosy moment, he thought he was being welcomed back to Shaw's home, where a comfortable armchair and fine whiskey would be waiting for him. Perhaps he no longer had to keep outrunning the devil and his guilty conscience.

Then he saw the cold weight Shaw was carrying in his face, and his anxiety returned.

He rolled down his window and asked, 'What's up, Jack?'

'Good afternoon, Alan. We want you to come down to Pettigo Station. We have a few things to tidy up, answers to some questions about Maguire's murder.' His face was slick with the drizzle, as was everything, his uniform, the narrow road, the encroaching hedgerows.

'Look, I've got to get over the border. It'll be dark soon.'

'What's the hurry? The border stays open all night.'

'I'm being serious. If you want to meet and ask some questions, we can do so in Enniskillen or Omagh in a few days' time.'

'You're pale, Alan. You've been through a lot, today. There's a cup of tea waiting for you at the station. We can talk whenever you're ready.'

'What are you doing playing the investigating detective with me,' asked Pearson. 'Stopping me like a common suspect from going about my business.'

'I'm not really, Alan, and you're not a suspect. But Maguire is dead, isn't he? And questions have to be asked.'

'True. We all have questions about what happened this morning.'

But there were no answers to the questions, at least not right now. No answers to the questions that still puzzled Pearson about his culpability in Maguire's murder. The truth lay just beyond his reach, on the other side of the border, and he knew that he would have to pursue it. The recklessness that he felt rise inside him was a new phenomenon, something he must have picked off Maguire. It was the stone-cold recklessness of a conscience that had come to waylay his career, perhaps even destroy it.

'Get out of my way, Jack.'

He crouched behind the steering wheel, staring at the Garda checkpoint and beyond it the border. He knew that he possessed secrets that his colleagues and Shaw had no inkling of, and at the same time, he possessed nothing at all. He had been pursuing these shadows ever since he'd met Maguire along the Lagan towpath, without knowing he had been pursuing them, and now the pursuit had turned into something deeper and more deadly.

'I can't do that, Alan,' said Shaw.

The gleam of metal further up the road caught Pearson's eye. Peering through the drizzle, he saw the military checkpoint he had left behind an hour earlier, half-submerged amid the low hills and thick hedges. But that was impossible, even in this labyrinth of wriggling roads. He had been travelling north for more than an hour. He turned to stare up at Shaw, his stomach heaving with the sense of dislocation. It wasn't physical nausea. It was the strain of locating himself repeatedly in this spiderweb of roads, jarred by the memory of Maguire's body and the secrets he might be carrying inside. He looked in the rear-view mirror and saw another Garda car pull in behind him, preventing him from reversing to freedom.

'Have you been following me?' asked Pearson.

'We had to keep an eye on you, Alan. Make sure you were safe.'

'Safe?'

'Yes, safe.'

'Just let me drive on. As an officer of the law I demand that you clear the road.'

'If it was down to me, I'd let you keep driving. But I'm just one man and even I can't change the investigative procedures of this country. A man was murdered on my turf today, and you were the last to speak to him...'

'You have three seconds to tell your officers to clear the road.'

'Wait, Alan, think of what you're doing.'

'I have my foot on the accelerator.'

'Then press it. Drive through my officers. That's the only way you're getting over the border tonight.'

Pearson pressed his foot on the accelerator and gunned the vehicle towards home.

Acknowledgements

With grateful thanks to Andrew Pepper, my wife Clare, and my mother Marie and sister Charlotte for guiding me along the prayer paths of Station Island.

NO EXIT PRESS

More than just the usual suspects

'A very smart, independent publisher delivering the finest literary crime fiction' – *Big Issue*

MEET NO EXIT PRESS, the independent publisher bringing you the best in crime and noir fiction. From classic detective novels, to page-turning spy thrillers and singular writing that just grabs the attention. Our books are carefully crafted by some of the world's finest writers and delivered to you by a small, but mighty, team.

In our 30 years of business, we have published award-winning fiction and non-fiction including the work of a Pulitzer Prize winner, the British Crime Book of the Year, numerous CWA Dagger Awards, a British million copy bestselling author, the winner of the Canadian Governor General's Award for Fiction and the Scotiabank Giller Prize, to name but a few. We are the home of many crime and noir legends from the USA whose work includes iconic film adaptations and TV sensations. We pride ourselves in uncovering the most exciting new or undiscovered talents. New and not so new – you know who you are!!

We are a proactive team committed to delivering the very best, both for our authors and our readers.

Want to join the conversation and find out more about what we do?

Catch us on social media or sign up to our newsletter for all the latest news from No Exit Press HQ.

f fb.me/noexitpress 🐦 @noexitpress
noexit.co.uk/newsletter